GRACE FOR TOMORROW

Eva Schmidt

WestBow
PRESS®
A DIVISION OF THOMAS NELSON
& ZONDERVAN

Copyright © 2016 Eva Schmidt.

All rights reserved. No part of this book may be used or reproduced by any means, graphic, electronic, or mechanical, including photocopying, recording, taping or by any information storage retrieval system without the written permission of the author except in the case of brief quotations embodied in critical articles and reviews.

Scripture taken from the King James Version of the Bible.

WestBow Press books may be ordered through booksellers or by contacting:

WestBow Press
A Division of Thomas Nelson & Zondervan
1663 Liberty Drive
Bloomington, IN 47403
www.westbowpress.com
1 (866) 928-1240

Because of the dynamic nature of the Internet, any web addresses or links contained in this book may have changed since publication and may no longer be valid. The views expressed in this work are solely those of the author and do not necessarily reflect the views of the publisher, and the publisher hereby disclaims any responsibility for them.

Any people depicted in stock imagery provided by Thinkstock are models, and such images are being used for illustrative purposes only. Certain stock imagery © Thinkstock.

ISBN: 978-1-5127-5016-4 (sc)
ISBN: 978-1-5127-5017-1 (hc)
ISBN: 978-1-5127-5015-7 (e)

Library of Congress Control Number: 2016911596

Print information available on the last page.

WestBow Press rev. date: 08/18/2016

That as sin hath reigned unto death,
even so might grace reign through
righteousness unto eternal life by Jesus Christ our Lord.

—Romans 5:21

DEDICATION

I dedicate this book to my husband,
to my children, and to my grandchildren.
You have taught me what unconditional love means.

CHAPTER 1

Splat. A snowball hit her square in the back.

"David!"

Mary scooped up a fistful of snow and formed it into a ball as she spun around to chase her brother. She fired the snowball at his head. He ducked, and it missed. Laughing, he threw another one at her. Mary sidestepped that one in full stride as she raced after David, rolling another scoop of snow between her hands. David ducked behind a haystack. Veering off her path, she snuck up on him from the other side, taking care not to startle the pigs that had burrowed into the haystack for warmth. She peered around the corner. He had his back turned. Her right arm came up. *Smack.* The snowball hit him squarely between his shoulders. She turned and sprinted in the opposite direction before he even had a chance to turn around.

She could hear David's footsteps behind her. She waited until he had almost caught up, and then she stopped short and bent forward, sending David somersaulting over her back and into the soft snow. Mary tumbled into the snow after him, laughing so hard her side ached.

"Hey," David said with a laugh, rolling over in the snow, "you're in for it now."

He grabbed for her, but Mary quickly rolled out of his reach.

"David and Mary!" Papa called from where he was feeding the

cattle. "I think you both have work to do. You'd better get it done before it gets dark."

"Jo, Papa," they replied in unison as they picked themselves up.

"Oh, I got you real good." Mary couldn't stop laughing as she dusted the snow off her heavy winter parka. "You should have seen yourself fly into that snow."

"I'm going to get you back," David promised, giving Mary a brotherly shove before jogging over to the barn to finish his chores.

Mary chuckled as she tightened her bright red scarf around her face to protect against the cold winter wind. She jogged back to where she had been gathering snow. She scooped up a pail of the sparkling white powder and dumped it into the large galvanized tub perched on the wooden toboggan. When the tub was full, Mary grabbed the weathered rope and pulled the rickety toboggan to the small white farmhouse where she had lived all her life. She scooped up a pail of snow from the tub and carried it into the house. Warm air enveloped her as she opened the door and dumped the snow into a forty-gallon barrel inside the porch.

"That looks like enough snow for today, Mary," said Mama, coming through the door. Her arms were piled high with frozen laundry.

Mary could not understand why Mama insisted on hanging the clothes outside to freeze-dry in the cold winter air. Mama said it made the laundry smell fresh and clean. Mary thought it made the laundry smell like their dog, Skipper, when he came into the house after spending time in the cold and the wind. *Ugh.*

Mama's fingers were red from the cold. She laid the clothes over a couple of wooden kitchen chairs and rubbed her hands together. The stiff pant legs stuck straight out. It took a couple of minutes for them to thaw enough to be hung over the wash lines strung across the kitchen and living room.

Mary continued transferring the snow into the barrel. When she was finished, she leaned the toboggan up against the side of the house before going inside.

Mama was stoking the fire in the cast-iron cook stove when Mary entered the kitchen. Potatoes were already boiling on the back of the stove, and the house was filled with the delicious aroma of chicken roasting in the oven.

Mary took the kettle of hot water from the stove and poured it over the snow in the barrel. Melted snow was their only water supply during the winter, when the creek froze up. She refilled the kettle with snow and put it back on the stove to melt. Then she emptied the washbasin into a five-gallon slop pail and refilled it with warm water from the stove's water reservoir. The tepid water and soap felt good on her cold hands. She let her hands rest on the bottom of the basin for a while, relishing the warmth before she dried them with a fresh-smelling towel.

A blast of cold air hit her as David came in from milking the cows.

"It sure is cold today," David observed, kicking the door closed behind him before setting two galvanized pails brimming with milk on the floor next to the cream separator. "Maybe there won't be any school tomorrow."

"Ha, you wish!" Mary exclaimed. "You just don't want to go to school," she said as she poured the warm, frothy milk through the strainer sitting on top of the galvanized cream separator. She turned the crank, slowly at first and then faster until reaching a steady rhythm. The separator hummed as the milk and cream poured out of two separate spouts into waiting buckets.

Mary jumped as David poked her in the ribs. She spun around and cuffed his ear with one hand while still turning the crank with the other.

"Don't do that, David," she warned, giving him what she hoped was a mean look.

David laughed, and the twinkle in his warm hazel eyes indicated he was in his usual teasing mood.

"Oh yeah?" He laughed while jabbing playfully with his fists and dancing lightly back and forth on his toes. He gave her a gentle jab on her shoulder. "I owe you, remember?"

Mary laughed again at the memory of David flying into the snowbank.

"David, quit bothering your sister. Mary, please set the table when you're finished," Mama said as the cream separator started winding down. "David, you go wash up for supper. It will be ready in a couple of minutes."

Mary set the buckets of milk and cream in the pantry to cool and then returned to the kitchen just as four-year-old Benny came running into the room, barreling into David's legs at full speed. Mary laughed as David was caught by surprise and almost fell over. Then the wrestling match was on. At fifteen, David pretended to struggle hard, but he always let Benny wrestle him to the floor. Benny sat on David's stomach, hands up high in victory. David grabbed Benny and tickled him until he was giggling and gasping for breath.

"*Junges! Junges!*" Mama exclaimed in Plautdietsch, a German dialect they spoke. "Now go wash up. Papa will be in any minute." Mama removed the gravy from the stove and drained the water from the potatoes. Another cold blast of air announced Papa's arrival just as Mary finished setting the table.

"Sure is cold today!" Papa exclaimed while removing his heavy winter boots and parka. "David, did you give the cows extra hay?"

"Yes, I did." David's voice was muffled by a towel as he dried his face. "Maybe there won't be any school tomorrow if it's this cold."

"*Na*, it wasn't cold enough to stop you and Mary from horsing around." Although Papa tried to sound annoyed, there was a sparkle in his dark brown eyes.

Papa poured fresh water into the washbasin and took his turn washing up. Mama finished placing the remainder of the food on the table, and they all took their places. Then they bowed their heads. In the custom of Mennonite homes, Benny prayed out loud since he was still in the process of memorizing the prayer, while the rest of the family prayed silently.

"Did you get Bessy checked today?" Mama asked as she passed the potatoes to Papa. Papa was always the first to dish up.

"Fritz Regier came and had a look. He gave me some salve to try on her." Papa passed the potatoes back to Mama and proceeded to dish up some chicken. Bessy was their best milk cow. She had cut her upper hind leg on the barbed-wire fence.

"How long does he think it will take to heal?" Mama asked as she spooned food onto Benny's plate and set it in front of him.

"Should be noticeably better in a couple of days," Papa said. Then he looked at David. "We'll keep her in the barn for a couple of days to make sure she doesn't get an infection."

"Okay," David answered around a mouthful of food.

Mary glanced across the table at David. She had never thought of him as good looking; he was just her brother. But during lunch at school today, she had overheard some girls gushing over his looks.

I suppose he can hold his own in the looks department, she thought, studying the way his unruly cinnamon-brown curls fell down over his forehead. *I suppose that dimple in his left cheek might seem endearing to the right girl.*

She noticed Benny carefully avoiding the peas on his plate. He disliked vegetables.

"Benny, eat your peas." Mama had noticed as well.

Mary grinned. Benny never got away with it, but he always tried.

"*Ach*, Mama, I don't like peas," Benny complained.

"You have to eat them. They're good for you."

"But, Mama," he whined.

"Mind your mama, Benny," Papa said in his no-nonsense tone of voice. Benny looked at his plate dolefully and picked two peas up on his fork.

"David, do you have homework?" Mama asked, pouring milk into Benny's glass.

"No, Mama," David answered. "I got it all done in school."

David rarely had homework. He disliked school and wouldn't spend extra time at home with his nose stuck in a book. If he didn't get the work done in school, then it just wouldn't get done.

"Maybe your grades would be better if you had homework once in a while," she said. "Benny, be careful. Don't spill your milk." She reached over and pushed his glass farther onto the table.

"*Ach*, Mama, I'm passing," David protested.

"You're a smart boy. You could do a lot better than just passing." Anna Hildebrandt wished David had a greater interest in school. She wanted him to graduate, but she was afraid he might drop out.

"School is getting to be more important in our changing world, David," Papa said. "When I was a young boy, all a person really needed to know was how to read and write and do arithmetic. But with all the changes I see happening, I don't think that will be enough for you children."

Anna could see her son wasn't enjoying the conversation, and she wanted mealtime to remain pleasant, so she turned her attention to her daughter. "Mary, have you finished the story you were writing for your language arts class?" *I don't need to worry about Mary's homework—she enjoys it.* Anna gave her head a shake. *How can two children be so different?*

"Yes, I did. I handed it in today," Mary responded. "I just have some reading to do for social studies."

After the dishes were done and the freeze-dried laundry hung to dry, Mary retreated to her room, while Mama retired to her rocking chair in the living room. David was whittling away at some project, while Benny made a tower with the unused blocks of wood.

Humming a tune, Anna slipped one of her husband's gray wool socks over a glass quart jar and deftly started darning the hole in the heel. Her lips turned up into a tender smile as she glanced at her husband, who was reading the newspaper in his easy chair. She wondered how long it would be until he dozed off.

She sighed contentedly as she worked. *Thank you, Lord, for my husband and children.* Anna had never thought herself poor because she lacked the amenities of the modern world. Theirs was a sheltered world, isolated from the city by many miles of ill-kept gravel roads.

Mary lit the oil lamp in her bedroom, curled up in her bed, and settled down to read. She pulled a colorful patchwork quilt over her legs to take off the chill. She opened her social studies textbook and spent some time reading her assignment before doing what she enjoyed most: reading her library book.

CHAPTER 2

Francis placed her hand on her swollen belly as she climbed the grimy stairs to their third-story apartment. It wouldn't be long now until the baby made an appearance.

Slightly out of breath, she pushed at the grubby brown door on the third level and walked down the dimly lit hallway with worn orange carpet and scuffed yellow walls. The smell of vegetable soup greeted her as she pushed open the door to her apartment.

"Mommy!" Two-year-old Brad sprang up from where he was playing on the floor and ran to greet her. Francis stooped down to pick him up.

"How's Mommy's big boy?" she asked, hugging him and nuzzling her face into his soft neck.

"Come see." Brad squirmed to be put down. She set him on the floor and followed him.

"Brad make road." He pointed to his Matchbox cars and trucks scattered all over the floor amid pens, pencils, and crayons lined up on the faded brown and yellow linoleum.

"Wow!" Francis exclaimed. "That's pretty nice."

"Daddy help Brad," he explained, glancing up at Mike, who appeared from the kitchen.

"That's right," Mike said, wiping his hands on a towel, his sky-blue eyes twinkling. "Daddy and Brad made a road for Brad's cars and trucks."

Brad went back to playing with his toys, and Francis followed her husband into the kitchen.

"Smells like vegetable soup." She smiled as Mike kissed her cheek.

"So it should." Mike pulled out a kitchen chair and motioned for her to sit. "Sit down, and put your feet up. Lunch is pretty much ready."

Francis sighed gratefully as she lowered herself onto the chair. It was getting more difficult to wait tables as she grew bigger. It didn't help that she had to get up at four thirty in the morning to be at work by five thirty. Luckily, her shift ended at one, so she could spend her afternoons at home.

"Busy day?" Mike asked, setting the hot pot of soup on the table.

"Not really." Francis poured a ladle of soup into Brad's bowl to cool. "I just tire easily."

"I wish you didn't have to work." Frown lines creased Mike's forehead. He grabbed the plate of sandwiches and set it on the table.

"I know you do," Francis said, crumbling soda crackers into Brad's soup, "but we need the money."

"Brad, come eat!" Mike called to their son, and then he turned back to Francis. "I wish there was some other way. Maybe I could get a second job."

Brad climbed up onto his chair, and Mike set the bowl of cooled soup in front of him.

"Good soup," Francis said as she sipped from her spoon, savoring the taste on her tongue. She bit into a sandwich. "I'll be fine," Francis said, referring to Mike's comment. "I just need to rest when I get home. I won't be able to work for a while after the baby arrives, and that will already set us back."

"You shouldn't have to work. I hate it."

Francis heard the frustration in her husband's voice and laid a hand on his arm. "Honey, I know you hate it. Don't worry," she said. "I'll be fine. We'll be fine."

The baby moved, making Francis's abdomen lopsided. Francis and Mike laughed as they both put their hands on her tummy.

"You're right." Mike smiled, holding her gaze. "We'll be fine. We'll figure it out." He bent over and kissed her lips. "I love you, baby."

"I love you too," she whispered, her bluish-gray eyes moist.

After lunch, Mike left for his two-to-ten shift at the service station, and Francis cleaned up the kitchen, grateful that Mike always made lunch so they could eat together before he left. Their consecutive shifts didn't leave much time for each other, but at least they didn't need to pay a babysitter.

"Brad, come sit with Mommy." Francis sat down on the flowery brown secondhand couch they had bought at the thrift store, holding up his favorite children's storybook about the little red fire engine.

Brad left his cars and trucks scattered on the floor and crawled up into her lap. Francis read to him until his eyes started drooping, and then she carried him to his bed and tucked him in. She straightened up, arching her back to relieve the tension. "I can't wait for this baby to arrive," she muttered to herself as she sought the comfort of her own bed.

Sinking into the bed, she grabbed Mike's pillow, stuffed it behind her back, and then placed another pillow between her knees. A tired sigh escaped her partially open lips as she relaxed and closed her eyes. However, sleep did not come. Mike's worried face popped into her mind. If only she could do something to ease their financial situation. Ever since she'd told Mike she was pregnant with their second child, he had started stressing about their finances.

Her mind wandered back to when she first met him. As a senior in high school, she worked part-time as a carhop at the local A&W drive-in, much to the chagrin of her mother, who could not believe her daughter would stoop to such a menial task, but Francis enjoyed the wide variety of people she met.

She saw the headlights of the black sedan turn on and walked out of the A&W to take the order. She walked up to the driver's open window and looked down into the bluest eyes she had ever seen. His work coveralls hinted at a muscular body, and the cutest blond curls stuck out from beneath his Blue Jays baseball cap. An electric current coursed through her body as their eyes locked for a moment.

"Groovy!" he exclaimed, letting his gaze run over her appreciatively.

Francis felt the heat rising up from her neck, suddenly feeling self-conscious in her brown-and-orange carhop outfit.

"Mike, cut it out," an older guy said from the passenger seat. "Don't pay him any attention, miss."

Francis's fingers trembled slightly as she took their order: two Papa burgers with fries, lots of ketchup, and two large root beers.

"You busy tonight?" Mike asked when she came back and hung the tray over his window. "We could catch a movie."

"I don't go out with guys I don't know," Francis said, turning to go. Lots of guys tried flirting with her. She didn't take them seriously.

All afternoon, she couldn't get his sky-blue eyes and blond curls out of her mind. Twice, she overturned a glass of root beer.

"Great. I didn't even bring an umbrella," Francis mumbled to herself later that afternoon as she opened the door and stepped into the cold, misty rain, heading down the sidewalk.

"Hey, sugar."

She hadn't noticed the black sedan. Glancing up, she saw Mike beckoning her. "Since it's raining, I thought I'd give you a ride home. Jump in," he said.

After the slightest hesitation, Francis threw caution to the wind and agreed. Mike leaned over and opened the passenger door, and

Francis slipped in. A woodsy scent assailed her nostrils, and she noticed the air freshener hanging from the rearview mirror.

"It's pretty miserable out there." Mike smiled as she settled into the passenger seat. "I took a chance that you didn't bring a car. Am I right?"

"No, I didn't," Francis replied. "Since the sun was shining this morning, I didn't even bring an umbrella. I should know by now how quickly the weather can change."

Mike laughed. "I've only been here a couple of weeks, and I'm just finding out how true that is."

"Where are you from?" Francis asked as Mike put the car in gear and reversed out of the parking stall. He looked good in his tight jeans and Beatles T-shirt.

"Medicine Hat," Mike replied, and then with a quick glance in her direction, he asked, "What's your address?"

Francis rattled off her street address and sat back as Mike concentrated on merging the car into traffic.

"So you still in school?" Mike asked once the car was in the flow of traffic.

"Yes, senior year," Francis answered. "What do you do? What brings you to Calgary?"

"I work on road construction, so I move around a lot." Mike glanced at her as they stopped at a red light. "I'm an only child. My parents are divorced and busy with their own lives. I thought it would be better for all of us if I cut out on my own, so when I turned sixteen, I dropped out of school and joined the road construction crew. Been with the same crew these last four years."

Francis quickly did the math. That made him three years older than she was.

When they turned onto her street, she asked him to drop her off a couple of doors down from her house.

"My mom would have a fit if she knew I had caught a ride with a stranger," she said.

"I agree." Mike's eyes twinkled. "You shouldn't accept rides from strangers. But since we're not strangers anymore, can I see you again?"

Francis felt a little flutter in her heart. "I would have to meet you somewhere so Mother doesn't find out."

They arranged to meet at the mall for a movie the following week. Francis stepped from the car and walked down the street toward her house without looking back.

The bed groaned as Francis eased herself onto her other side. She placed the pillow back between her knees, and her gaze fell on their wedding picture.

They were together as much as their jobs and school would allow during that winter and into spring. Her mother was appalled when she found out her daughter was dating a high school dropout—a construction laborer at that. She alternately threatened and cajoled Francis but to no avail.

When Francis announced that Mike would escort her to her high school graduation, her mother threatened that she would not attend. However, as graduation drew closer and Francis did not capitulate, her mother relented.

Francis's lips curled into a nostalgic smile as she reminisced.

Mike looked dashing in his rented tux that night. After the graduation ceremony, they stayed for the dance in the school gymnasium. The entire place was decorated in a medieval theme. Her soft pink gown was patterned after that era, and she felt as if she were Juliet and Mike were Romeo. Dance after dance, they swayed to the music, sometimes in a slow dance and sometimes to upbeat music that left them both in need of a cool glass of punch. They left the dance early and drove out to a viewpoint overlooking the lush green Bow River valley. The western sky was painted in a spectacular array of pink and orange as the sun sank behind the white peaks of the distant mountains. Arms entwined, they stood there, marveling at the magnificent sunset.

Francis turned to speak to Mike, when she realized he had

gone down on one knee and was holding up a small open box displaying a single solitary diamond ring.

She gasped as the ring twinkled merrily up at her.

"Francis, I love you with all my heart." His blue eyes were misty as they looked up into hers. "Will you marry me?"

She knelt down beside him on the soft green grass and hugged him. "Yes! Yes! A thousand times yes!"

"Really? You'll marry me?"

"I love you, Mike!" she exclaimed. "I would like nothing better in the world."

Mike slipped the ring onto her finger, tenderly took her face between both of his hands, and kissed her.

With her head resting on his shoulder, they lost all sense of time as they sat on the spongy spring grass, making plans for their future together. At first one at a time and then in multitude, the stars came out of hiding and twinkled their blessing on them.

Francis shuddered involuntarily as her mind conjured up the memory of the following morning, when Mother noticed the ring on her finger.

"What is that?" she demanded, pointing at Francis's hand.

"Mike asked me to marry him." Francis's eyes sparkled at the memory.

"What?" Mother exclaimed. "Are you out of your mind? You are not marrying that boy. I forbid it!" Mother's voice rose as she continued. "Gary, you tell her she can't marry that boy."

"Caroline, don't get yourself so worked up." Father folded his newspaper. "You're going to give yourself a heart attack."

"She cannot marry that gold digger. He's just after our money. Gary, what would our friends say?"

"Honey, they won't get married right away." Father spoke quietly, trying to calm Mother down.

"This whole thing must be called off," Mother said determinedly. "I knew we should not have allowed him to be her escort. Right away, he took advantage. Francis, you must give that ring back."

"I will not." Francis's voice shook with emotion. "I love Mike, and I want to marry him." She appealed to her father. "Mike loves me. It has nothing to do with money."

"It's still a long time before any wedding is happening," Father said. "You still have four years of college. There's no rush to make any decisions yet."

"I'm not going to college." Francis twisted the ring on her finger as she dropped another bombshell. "Mike and I want to get married by fall."

"No way!" Mother shrieked. "I absolutely forbid you to see that boy again! No daughter of mine will marry a construction worker. You are going to college. End of discussion."

Francis turned and ran from the room and up the stairs. She slammed her bedroom door and threw herself across her bed.

Mother is totally unreasonable, she fumed to herself. She punched her pillow as tears of frustration ran down her cheeks. *Mother will not stop us.*

That July, a week after her eighteenth birthday, Francis and Mike were quietly married by a justice of the peace with only a few of Mike's friends to witness the nuptials. They moved into Mike's tiny one-bedroom apartment. It was a big adjustment for Francis, and she soon realized how quickly the money they earned disappeared each month. However, their love for each other compensated for their meager lifestyle.

Francis knew Mother was disappointed that she couldn't plan a big, lavish wedding and invite all her friends and Father's business associates, but she thought once they were married, Mother would come around. It turned out she was wrong. Mother forbade Francis to bring Mike home, and Francis refused to go without him. They were at a stalemate that continued for the ensuing years.

Her sister, Monica, and brothers, Ted and Jim, came to see her and Mike occasionally, and Father stopped by once in a while. But Mother never came.

Brad was born the following spring. Francis called home, but Mother refused to speak to her, and Father was away on a business trip. She spoke with Monica, and later that day, Monica and her brothers came to see her at the hospital. When Father returned from his business trip, he dropped in to meet his tiny grandson. Mother didn't even call.

Shortly after Brad was born, the three of them moved with the construction crew north to Edmonton. They found a small two-bedroom apartment that wasn't too expensive. Mike worked with the crew all summer, but when winter came, he got laid off. He got a job working the late shift at the service station a couple of blocks from their apartment, but it didn't pay as well as construction. To make ends meet, Francis took a waitressing job at a local restaurant.

Father stopped by a couple of times when he was in town on business, but Mother still wouldn't talk to her. Ted, Jim, and Monica came to see them the summer before Ted went to university, intending to become a medical doctor. Jim and Monica were still in grade school. Francis clutched at her chest as the familiar sting of rejection pierced her heart. If only Mother would have a change of heart, she would be able to see all of her family more often.

Mike's parents seemed relieved that he was on his own and no longer their responsibility. Mike and Francis didn't see them often, but Mike would talk on the phone with them occasionally.

Francis touched her cheek and realized it was wet. Angrily, she wiped at her eyes and gave her head a shake. *Shouldn't waste my time thinking about things I can't change,* she thought, scolding herself. *I have Mike and Brad, and pretty soon I'll have another little one. That's all the family I need. If Mother wants to stay away, then so be it.*

She was not going to wallow in self-pity. She turned over in bed, readjusted the pillows, and forced the memories from her mind.

"Mary!" called Mama later that evening as she put more wood in the stove. "It's time for devotions."

Mary finished reading the page she was on and then exchanged her library book for her Bible, blew out the flicker of light in the oil lamp, and joined the rest of the family at the kitchen table for their nightly family Bible reading. Benny brought his favorite Bible storybook.

"Let's turn to the first chapter of John," Papa said when they were all seated around the table. Mama helped Benny find the right Bible story so he could look at the pictures while the rest of them read.

"David, would you start us off?" Papa asked.

David slowly read the unfamiliar German words. Since the government made the Mennonites give up their private German schools in the early part of the twentieth century and send their children to English-speaking public schools, people like Mama and Papa were adamant their children learn their ancestral language at home. It was the language their church used.

Mary continued reading where David left off, slowly wrapping her tongue around each syllable.

"In verse one, who is the Word?" Papa asked in their familiar Plautdietsch after they finished reading the chapter.

Mary reread the first verse. "God?" she asked hesitantly.

"Verse two says that the Word was with God," Papa pointed out. He then directed them to reread verse fourteen.

"Jesus?" David asked.

"That's right," Papa said. "Now look at verse three."

"Jesus made the world?" David asked. "I thought God made the world!"

"Remember, Jesus is God," Papa said. "There's God the Father, God the Son, and God the Holy Spirit, and these three are one. They worked together to create the world. Now let's look at verses four to eleven, and tell me—who is the Light?"

Mary reread the passage. "Jesus?" she asked.

"Yes," Papa said. "Now look at verses twelve and thirteen." Papa reread the verses for them. "This clearly states that if we receive Jesus and believe in him, then we have the power to become the sons of God."

"But Jesus is the Son of God!" Mary exclaimed.

"Yes, he is," Papa said, "and if we believe in Jesus, then we become the sons of God as well."

Mary had difficulty grasping that concept. How could a person like herself be considered a child of God?

"Let's pray," Papa said, closing his Bible.

They all bowed their heads and, in unison, repeated the German version of the Lord's Prayer.

"I'll get the song books," Mama volunteered as she got up from her chair and left the room. Papa followed her, and they soon returned, with Mama carrying a couple of hymnals and Papa his accordion.

As Mary sang along to the sweet chords of the accordion, her heart filled with peace. She had no doubt that God was real. She believed that Jesus was alive and that he was God's son. She did her best to be good and hoped that someday she would live in heaven with Jesus. However, the thought of dying frightened her, so she tried not to think about that part. She was young and had lots of time.

After the family worship, Mary helped Mama prepare a snack of cream cookies, chocolate cake, and peaches they'd canned last summer.

"Benny!" Mama exclaimed, barely keeping the cookies from flying off the dish in her hand as Benny ran right in front of her.

Grace for Tomorrow

"How often do I have to tell you not to run in the kitchen? We nearly had to eat these cookies off the floor."

"Yes, Mama," he said, and before he could resume his pretend flying, David caught him, and they wrestled. Benny squealed and wiggled when David pinned him to the floor and tickled him.

After the snack, Mama helped Benny put on his pajamas and then tucked him into bed with his heavy wool blanket and teddy bear.

Mary slipped into her parka to pay a visit to the outhouse. As she stepped through the door, the cold stung her face and bit her nose. A million tiny stars winked at her from the dark November sky as the dazzling northern lights danced in pale shades of green and silver. A huge full moon lit her path, twinkling its reflection off the blanket of snow.

God created everything so beautifully, she mused.

Inside the outhouse, she rested her thighs on her hands to avoid the cold sting of the wooden bench. The frigid temperatures made it hard to respond to the call of nature. Mary quickly closed the outhouse door with the swivel lock and ran all the way back to the house.

A little out of breath, Mary removed her parka and hung it up on a wooden peg in the porch. She poured fresh water into the washbasin and washed her hands and face. Mama was tidying up in the kitchen, while Papa and David were sitting at the table, discussing the amount of feed and hay to give to the animals during this cold spell. They needed extra of both to keep them warm.

Mary entered her small, cozy, bedroom and lit her oil lamp. She laid out the clothes she would wear tomorrow, slipped her flowery flannel nightgown over her head, and knelt on the throw rug by her bed to pray before blowing out the lamp and climbing into bed.

Mary shivered as she slipped beneath the covers. The sheets and comforter felt cold. She curled up tightly, wrapping the wool comforter firmly around herself to trap in the warmth emanating from her body. As she started warming up, she straightened out her legs a little at a time, warming the rest of the bed. The moon cast a silver glow into her room, outlining the sparse furnishings: a dark brown dresser with a cracked mirror, a small clothes closet, and a rickety night table. As she warmed up, drowsiness took over, and she drifted off to sleep.

CHAPTER 3

Francis woke up to a severe tightening sensation around her middle. Her gaze fell on her bedside clock: 2:45 a.m. She tried to relax as the pain increased. *Breathe,* she told herself. She put her hands on her abdomen and closed her eyes, breathing in and out until she felt the pain decreasing. She lay wide awake in bed, even though she had only gone to sleep at midnight. She looked at Mike's sleeping face beside her. He looked peaceful. She would let him sleep for a while yet.

Her mind mulled over the things she had to do. She had to call Mrs. Cox, who lived down the hall. The dear lady had promised to come stay with Brad when the time came. Hopefully, they could wait till morning before going to the hospital. Francis hated to wake her up in the middle of the night. Her bag was packed and ready to go. *Thank goodness I just did the laundry, so Mike and Brad should have enough clean clothes to last them a few days,* she told herself as another pain started in the front of her abdomen and worked its way around the back, tightening at a steady, relentless pace. She breathed through it, and when the pain subsided, she looked at the clock: 3:05. Twenty minutes had passed.

Slowly, she swung her legs over the side of the bed, pushing herself up into a sitting position. Her lower back ached. She rubbed it for a while before putting her feet into her fuzzy blue bathroom slippers and pulling her housecoat on over her nightgown. She needed to use the bathroom.

By six o'clock in the morning, Francis decided to wake Mike up. She sat down on the bed and touched his shoulder. He didn't move. She shook him gently.

"Mike, wake up."

Mike opened his eyes. "What?" He noticed Francis was fully dressed and sat up abruptly.

"I think it's time," she said softly. Mike threw the covers off and jumped out of bed. He grabbed his clothes and hurried into the bathroom.

"When did it start? Why didn't you wake me sooner? Did you call Mrs. Cox?"

The questions came so fast she couldn't answer them. It didn't matter. She was in another world—a world of pain and breathing, absorbed in another contraction. When the pain subsided, she heard a light knock on the door. Mrs. Cox had arrived.

Mike helped Francis down the two flights of stairs and out to their car. He opened the passenger door and helped her get in. Francis smiled slightly as she watched him dash around the front of the car and swing himself into the driver's seat. He started the engine, and they sped off.

Two hours later, Francis heard the high-pitched squeal of her newborn baby as she sank back into the pillows.

"It's a girl!" the doctor announced.

"Hear that, honey?" Mike beamed down at her. "We have a girl!"

"Chantel Yvonne Webber." Francis let the name roll over her tongue as the nurse placed the tiny infant in her arms. "Oh, Mike, isn't she beautiful?" Tenderly, she touched the soft baby cheek.

"Adorable!" Mike breathed. He bent down and kissed Francis and then took the little bundle into his arms.

Mary woke to the sound of Papa stoking the fire in the wood stove. She lay in bed, loath to face the chill of the morning. She could feel the cold air on her face.

"Mary!" Mama called. "It's time to get up."

"*Na jo*, Mama." Mary yawned. She wrapped the wool comforter tightly around her as she leaned over to grab the clothes she had laid out last night. She pulled the clothes under the covers with her to warm them up. She hated to get out of bed on cold winter mornings.

"Mary!" Mama called again, more urgently this time. "Are you getting up?"

"Yes, Mama," Mary answered. With the comforter wrapped loosely around her, she sat up in bed and pulled her nightgown up over her head. She shivered as she quickly put on her red wool sweater. She huddled beneath the comforter awhile longer and then swung her bare legs over the edge of the bed and pulled her navy under-the-knee-length skirt on. After she put on her heavy navy tights and a pair of slippers, she felt warmer, but she still hurried into the kitchen, where the welcome warmth of the wood stove enveloped her. She warmed herself at the stove for a while before donning her parka and boots to pay a visit to the outside toilet. It was still dark outside. The full moon of last night was covered with clouds, so she switched on the flashlight she'd brought.

By the time Mary had finished washing up, Mama and Papa were already seated at the table, and David came stumbling into the kitchen. Mama never planned breakfast to be rushed, but it usually was since both Mary and David had an aversion to getting out of bed in the morning. Benny was the only one to sleep in. When they were finally all seated at the table, they bowed their heads for silent prayer.

"I thought there wouldn't be any school today," David grumbled around a mouthful of porridge. "I can't believe the buses are running on such a cold day."

"It's not as cold as it was last night," said Papa. "It warmed up some during the night. Looks like it clouded over. I have to make more feed for the pigs today, so I'm hoping it will warm up some more."

"You two will have to hurry up," Mama said. "The school bus will be here in ten minutes."

Mary finished her bowl of porridge, bowed her head for a quick thank-you prayer, and hurried into her bedroom to comb her hair. She pulled her fine light brown hair back into a ponytail, grabbed her books, and hurried into the porch to don her parka and boots.

"The bus is coming!" Mama called from the window where she was watching for the headlights. "See you later, and be careful!" she called after the children as they hurried through the door into the cold, dark winter morning. It was so dark they had to concentrate on following the narrow tracks down the driveway.

The yellow school bus was already waiting for them at the end of their driveway. Mary and David hurried onto the bus. "Good morning," Mary said to her friend Lena as she slid into the seat next to her. They were in the same grade and had been best friends for years. Lena wore her volume of auburn curls pulled back in a ponytail.

"Good morning," said Lena, closing a book. "Did you finish your reading assignment?"

"Yes, I did," Mary answered. "You?"

"Just now," Lena responded, her blue eyes sparkling as Mary shook her head in exasperation.

Schoolwork wasn't easy for Lena. She had difficulty learning new concepts, but she was always cheerful.

"David didn't think there would be school today," Mary said.

"I hoped there wouldn't be." Lena sighed. "Mama is going to start sewing Christmas dresses for the girls, and I was hoping I could stay at home and help." She loved helping her mother around the house and would much rather stay home and help take care of her eight younger siblings. She enjoyed sewing, knitting, and crafts.

"What kind of dresses are they getting?" Mary asked. She hoped she'd get a new dress for Christmas. She would have to ask Mama.

"Oh"—Lena's eyes sparkled excitedly—"Mama bought this very nice fabric; it's a deep pink with white flowers. The girls are going to be so pretty in those dresses."

"Are you getting a new dress as well?" Mary asked.

"Yes, mine is burgundy, and Mama bought some silky material for a sash. You should get your mama to buy the same material, and then we could wear identical dresses!" exclaimed Lena.

"What a wonderful idea. I'll ask Mama tonight," Mary responded excitedly, and then she blurted out, "Papa is planning a hayride for Christmas Eve."

"A hayride!" exclaimed Lena. "That is so exciting!"

"Yeah, Papa said we can each invite three friends over, and he will take us on a hayride. He says it will do the horses good to get some exercise. When we get back to the house, we'll have hot chocolate and Christmas baking. Can you come?"

"I'll ask Mama tonight," Lena responded. "That will be so much fun. Who else are you inviting?"

"Martha and Sarah, and David is inviting John, Mark, and Henry."

The girls chatted about the upcoming hayride until they got to school. Inside the school, they stopped at their lockers to exchange their parkas for books and then walked down the hall to their homeroom class. They passed David's friend John in the hall. He smiled at them, and Mary felt a warmness rise up from her neck as she smiled back.

"He likes you," Lena whispered with a giggle, a knowing sparkle in her eyes.

"He just thinks of me as David's little sister." Mary sighed. She had told Lena about her secret crush on John.

"I don't know," Lena responded thoughtfully. "I've been watching him, and he always smiles at you. Notice how he was looking at you?"

"You're imagining things," Mary said, brushing her off.

John and David spent a lot of time together, and Mary loved it when they allowed her to hang out with them. Lena was the only person she had ever told about her crush on John. It had happened last summer, when the two boys had built a log cabin in the bush on Papa's land, about a quarter mile from her house. John had come over whenever he could to work on the cabin, and Mary had always come up with some excuse to spend some time with them.

As the girls entered their classroom, they were joined by more of their friends. Everyone was excited about the upcoming Christmas holidays and the school Christmas program.

"Good morning," Mr. Scratch said as he entered the classroom.

"Good morning," the students echoed as they scurried to their desks and slid into their seats.

Mr. Scratch took a Bible from his desk and read a portion of it. Then they all stood at attention beside their desks and recited the Lord's Prayer and sang "O Canada."

"Mama, Lena is getting a burgundy dress for Christmas with a silk sash. Could I have a dress like that too?" Mary asked after school. "We want to have identical dresses for the Christmas concert."

"Well." Mama looked up from her ironing. "I want to sew you a new dress for Christmas, and I haven't bought the fabric yet. Papa and I are going to town tomorrow, so I'll see if I can get the same fabric Lena has."

"Oh, Mama, thank you!" exclaimed Mary before biting into a freshly baked chocolate chip cookie. "I can't wait to wear it."

"Don't get too excited yet, Mary," warned Mama, setting the propane iron aside and readjusting the shirt on the ironing board.

"We don't know if they still have the same fabric at the store. Now, you change out of your school clothes, and get your chores done. David, how many cookies have you had already? You'd better stop eating, or you'll spoil your appetite for supper."

Mary swallowed the last of her cookie and milk and headed for her bedroom to change. She always changed into her at-home clothes after school. She hung her school clothes over the back of a chair and put on a blue wool skirt and heavy pullover.

"Mary, are you coming?" David called from the kitchen.

"I'll be right there," Mary answered as she fixed her ponytail. Pulling a sweater over her head always messed up her hair.

"David never understands why changing takes me so long," Mary muttered under her breath. "He has short hair and doesn't need to worry about messing it up. Even when it does get messed up, he just runs his fingers through it, and it looks presentable again. And he doesn't wear tights." She pulled and wiggled into her tights. Tights were the most awful thing to wear; they always twisted and turned, and after she put them on, they were either too short at the waist or so long that they sagged between her legs. Both were uncomfortable. She always wore her worst ones at home and saved the better ones for school and Sundays.

David had already pulled the toboggan over to the wood pile and was splitting wood when Mary joined him.

"Finally! Sure takes you a long time to change your clothes," David muttered. "Sure glad I'm not a girl."

"So am I," Mary said as she started stacking the split wood onto the toboggan, careful to keep a watchful eye on the wood David was splitting.

Mary stuck out her tongue to catch the softly falling snowflakes. "I love the snow."

"I hope we get snowed in so we can't go to school tomorrow." David heaved the ax over his head and brought it down on another block of wood.

"It will have to start snowing a lot more for that to happen."

When the toboggan was stacked high with wood, David pulled it to the door while Mary pushed from behind. At the door, they piled as much wood onto their arms as they could and carried it into the porch, where they deposited it into a large blue wood box. They had to get a couple of loads to fill up the wood box. Then Mary took the toboggan and the large galvanized tub to haul snow to replenish their water supply, while David went to milk the cows.

Since it was Wednesday, the family piled into their '57 pickup truck after the supper dishes were done and headed off to church for hymn singing. A few vehicles were already in the parking lot when they pulled up to the small white church surrounded by a stand of pine trees.

Lena was waiting just inside the church door. "I was starting to think you weren't coming," she said in way of greeting as Mary came through the door.

"*Ach*, we're not that late!" Mary exclaimed. Lena's family was always early. Mary didn't know how they managed it with all those children. She took Lena's hand, and together they walked into the sanctuary.

The church was sparsely furnished, with a brown wooden pulpit front and center at the end of the aisle. Two benches stretched the length of the wall on either side of the pulpit. Preachers sat on one side, and song leaders sat on the other side. The pews stretching to the back of the sanctuary were constructed of wooden slats painted gray. The men and boys sat on one side of the church, while the women and girls sat on the other side. Mary and Lena sat down beside Sarah and chattered quietly as they waited for the hymn sing to begin.

CHAPTER 4

"Mommy, one more." Brad held out his hand. Francis picked up another ornament for him to hang on their small store-bought Christmas tree. She would have to rearrange the ornaments later when Brad wasn't looking, but for now, he was enjoying decorating the tree.

"That's all there is, honey." Francis showed him the empty box. "All we have left is the star that goes on top."

"Let me! Let me!" Brad begged as she took the silver star out of the box.

"You can't reach, honey. The star goes way up on the top of the tree."

"Hold me, Mommy." Brad held out his pudgy little arms.

Francis laughed as she picked him up. "All right, Mommy will hold you." She gave the star to Brad and held him up so he could put it on the tree. It took awhile, and it looked quite lopsided, but after a few attempts, the star was on the tree. Francis quickly set Brad down and fixed the star so it wouldn't fall off. Then she switched the tree lights on and the house lights off.

Brad jumped up and down excitedly. "Mommy, look. Pretty tree!"

"Yes, the tree is pretty. Brad did a good job decorating it." Francis turned the house lights back on. Chantel started fussing, so Francis went into the children's bedroom. She changed Chantel's diaper before picking her up.

"Are you hungry, little one?" Francis asked, kissing her month-old infant on her cheek.

"Brad want cookie." Brad ran ahead into the kitchen.

"Okay, Brad, you go sit at the table, and Mommy will give you a cookie."

Brad climbed up on a chair at the table. "Brad sit in Daddy's spot," he announced proudly.

"All right, you sit in Daddy's spot." Francis placed a cookie and milk in front of Brad, fixed Chantel a bottle of milk, and sat down on the couch with her. After Brad finished his snack he went back to playing on the floor with his cars. Chantel started nodding off and by the time she finished her bottle she was asleep. Francis held her for a while longer, lightly running her finger over the infant's soft cheeks, relishing the feel of the baby in her arms. Chantel's tiny pink lips tugged upward into an involuntary smile.

"Read story, Mommy." Brad held out his favorite fire engine storybook.

"Okay," Francis said. "Mommy will put Chantel in her crib first."

She lay Chantel down in her white crib and tucked her soft pink blanket gently around her. Then Francis snuggled on the couch with Brad in her lap and read the book to him.

After she put Brad down for a nap, Francis rearranged the tree ornaments. She didn't think Brad would notice. When she was sure Brad was sleeping, she brought out the few gifts she and Mike had purchased for the children. She tenderly wrapped a bright red fire engine complete with lights and sirens. Brad was sure to love it. She wrapped a teddy bear storybook and a coloring book with pictures of cars for Brad. Then she wrapped a soft doll and a teddy bear for Chantel.

Francis wrapped the gold watch she'd gotten for Mike. She had been lucky to get it on such a good sale. All summer, she had put a little money aside from each of her paychecks so she could get Mike something nice. *He deserves it,* she mused. *He's been so stressed out lately.*

She had just cleaned up from wrapping the gifts, when Mike came home from work. He took off his shoes and jacket at the door and came over and gave her a hug.

"Why don't you fix us some hot chocolate while I go shower?" he asked, giving her a kiss on the cheek.

"All right," Francis said, hugging him back. "I'll do that."

She fixed them each a cup of hot chocolate and took the cups into the living room. When Mike came out of the shower he sat down on the couch and pulled Francis down beside him.

"Scrawny-looking tree," he mused, watching the flickering lights. "I wanted to do better by you, Fran. I didn't want us to be living like this, barely scraping by."

"All I need is you and the kids," Francis replied, putting her hand on his arm. She knew he felt bad for not being able to provide the lifestyle she had grown up with. "High society is not my cup of tea, Mike. You know that."

"But it's not fair to you," he muttered. "Things would be so much better for you if I had never appeared on the scene. Your mother's right; I'm not good enough for you."

"Don't say that." Francis held her fingers over his lips. "I love you. That's all that matters."

"I love you too." Mike took her hand and kissed her fingers.

He downed the last of his hot chocolate and stood up, pulling her up with him. "Come on. It's bedtime. You have to get up early to go to work." With the tip of his finger, he gently brushed a lock of hair from her face. "Are you sure you can handle being back at work already?"

"Don't worry about me," Francis responded. Going back to work with a month-old baby was difficult, to say the least, but they would manage. "I don't think I get as tired working now as I did before she was born. I wish I didn't have to work on Christmas Eve, but at least I have Christmas Day and Boxing Day off."

"Well, I don't have to work Christmas Eve, so I'll fix us a nice supper, and then we'll take the kids for a tour around town to see the Christmas lights. What do you think?"

"That would be nice. Brad will love that." She loved the feel of Mike's arm around her as they walked to their bedroom. She had Mike and the kids. That was all she needed.

The school buzzed with excitement as students prepared for the Christmas concert that afternoon. Their classroom Christmas parties would follow tomorrow morning, and then school would be out for the two-week Christmas vacation. Mary had picked Sarah's name in their class gift exchange. They would open the gifts at their party. She was sure Sarah would love the light pink stationery set with a flowery border that was waiting for her under the classroom Christmas tree. Sarah loved writing. It was the perfect gift for her.

"Mary," Sarah said, breaking into Mary's thoughts, "you look so pretty in your new dress. I love that sash." Sarah had such a bubbly personality that she always sounded excited, and today was no exception.

"Thank you," said Mary. "You look beautiful in that dress. That shade of pink makes your hair look even blacker. It suits you very well."

"Thank you. I'm so nervous." She giggled. "I don't know if I'll be able to sing. Have you seen how the gym is filling up?"

"I know," Mary responded. "I'm nervous too. I saw Mama, Papa, and Benny come in. Is your family here? What if I mess up completely? I'll never be able to face anyone again."

"There's Lena and Martha." Sarah waved at them, and the girls rushed over.

"Mrs. Warkentin wants us to line up backstage," Lena said, her face slightly flushed from all the excitement. The girls rushed to the music room, where the choir was already lining up to go onstage for the opening number. They were all fidgety and giggly from the excitement and nervousness of performing in front of a large group of parents, siblings, and relatives.

As the choir filed onto the stage, Mary felt butterflies in her stomach. Mrs. Warkentin played the opening bars on the piano, and as soon as they started singing the familiar Christmas carols, Mary's nervousness left her. As she sang, she let her eyes search the crowded gym for her parents and Benny. She spotted John sitting with David and some other boys. He was looking straight at her, and Mary quickly looked away. She spotted Benny waving at her from his seat a couple of rows from the front. He was sitting on his knees on a chair between Mama and Papa. Mary smiled at him as she sang.

The choir filed off the stage and took the seats reserved for them in the gym. The grade-one class did a recital on the meaning of Christmas. The grade-two students were dressed up as shepherds as they sang "Away in a Manger." The grade-three class did a skit portraying the shepherds coming to see Mary, Joseph, and the baby Jesus in the stable. Two little boys covered with a brown sheet were the donkey. They had trouble synchronizing their steps, so sometimes the donkey was long, and sometimes it was short. The audience chuckled quietly, but all enjoyed the skit.

Soon it was time for the choir to quietly exit the gym and line up to go onstage. Mary, Lena, and Sarah stood side by side in the center of the front line. The choir sang two songs, and then the three girls took a couple of steps forward toward the microphones. Mrs. Warkentin played the introduction of "O Holy Night" on the piano. At their cue, the girls' clear, strong voices lifted in song and resonated off the walls and ceiling. Mary was filled with a sense of awe at the meaning of the words, and without realizing it, she closed her eyes as she sang, lifting her heart to honor the One whose birth they were celebrating. They sang the harmony with their souls, effortlessly reaching the high notes. When the last chords of the song died away, there was a slight pause, and then thunderous applause broke out as the curtains closed.

"Good job, everyone," Mrs. Warkentin said, congratulating them after they had filed off of the stage and gathered in the music room again. "You all sang very well." She turned to the three girls. "You did a wonderful job with that song. I knew you would do well, but you exceeded my expectations."

"Yeah, you girls were great," Martha agreed. "I saw some of the women dab at their eyes when you were done."

Mary felt that familiar warm feeling spread from her neck into her cheeks as the other choir members agreed.

"I'm going to see if I can find Mama and Papa before they leave. Maybe I can catch a ride home with them." Mary started toward the door. "Merry Christmas, everyone!" she called over her shoulder.

"Merry Christmas!" the others responded as she closed the door behind her.

Benny saw her before she saw him, and he darted between people as he ran toward her.

"Mary, I saw you!" he exclaimed as Mary scooped him up into her arms. "I waved to you. Did you see me?"

"Yes," Mary answered, giving him a hug, "I saw you."

"Why didn't you wave to me, Mary?" he asked, leaning back against her arms so he could peer into her face.

"If I had waved at you, everyone else would have thought I was waving at them," Mary responded, making her way through the crowd to her parents. "There were a lot of people there."

"Yes," Benny agreed. "I sat on my knees so I could see you better."

"May I go home with you?" Mary asked as she reached her parents. "It's almost home-time already."

"Yes, you may," Mama said. "Would you please find David so he can come with us as well? Be sure to tell your teacher you are leaving with us."

"Can I come too?" Benny asked, anticipation dancing in his green eyes—cat eyes, David called them.

"Yes," Mary said, setting him on the floor and taking his hand, "but you have to walk, because you're getting too heavy for me to carry." They started off down the hall toward the lockers. As soon as Benny spotted David, he pulled free from Mary, ran to David, and threw his arms around David's legs.

"What are you doing here?" David ruffled Benny's blond curls.

"I came with Mary to find you. Do you want to come home with us?" Benny asked.

"I sure do," David answered. "You can come with me, and we'll go get my jacket."

"Mary." John quietly stepped beside her as David and Benny left. "I loved your singing."

"Thank you," Mary responded, suddenly feeling shy.

"Here." John reached into his pocket. "I got this for you." He handed her an envelope. "Merry Christmas."

"Thank you," Mary said, taking the envelope. "Merry Christmas to you too."

Just then, David and Benny came around the corner, and John turned away from her. Mary gazed at her name scrawled across the envelope in her hand. Catching herself, she crushed it against her chest, covering it with her arms, as she rushed off to get her jacket. She hid the envelope in her books. She would look at it later in private.

As soon as they got home, Mary hurried into her bedroom and sat down on her bed, her heart pounding. She removed the envelope from her book. Her fingers trembled as she removed a card depicting Mary, Joseph, and baby Jesus in a stable with a bright star shining down on them. *John gave me a Christmas card. That must mean he likes me!* Inside was a verse wishing her a merry Christmas and a happy new year, but her eyes turned to what he had written: "Mary, I want you to know that I like you a lot. I hope you feel the same way about me. Merry Christmas." He had signed it simply "John."

Mary hugged the card to herself. "John likes me," she whispered to herself. "John likes me for me, not just as David's little sister." This was the best Christmas gift she could have received. She closed her eyes, savoring the moment, and conjured up a picture of John, with his curly black hair, chocolate-brown eyes, and lopsided grin.

"Mary, we're waiting for you!" called her mother. Mary quickly hid the card in her dresser, changed into her at-home clothes, and joined her family at the table for their after-school snack.

CHAPTER 5

Francis pulled her coat tightly around herself as she stepped out into the cold wind on the morning of Christmas Eve. At five thirty, it would still be dark for hours. She bowed her hooded head into the wind as she hurried down the sidewalk to the diner. She was apprehensive when walking alone in the dark, especially on early mornings when the streets were still deserted. The streetlights cast eerie shadows on the freshly fallen snow, and she tried not to think of the potential evil that lurked in the back alleys or around the next corner.

Her ears were tuned to hear any noise that was out of the ordinary. She could hear the sound of police sirens in the distance, reminding her that crime was on the rise in the city. The diner was just up ahead, and she quickened her pace. Almost in panic mode, she rushed through the door and pushed it shut behind her. She stood leaning against the door for a couple of seconds, catching her breath. "That's silly to get so worked up over nothing," she muttered to herself. Willing her pulse to slow down, she removed her scarf, coat, and boots and went into the kitchen, where Maggie had already turned on the grill in preparation for the breakfast crowd.

"Good morning, Maggie," Francis said to the middle-aged cook. "It's really cold out there this morning."

"Good morning, Francis," Maggie said cheerfully. "The coffee is already made, so why don't you grab a cup before the breakfast crowd arrives? You look frozen."

"I could sure stand some." Francis shivered. "Are you going to join me?"

"Yes, I will," Maggie replied.

Francis removed two coffee mugs from the shelf, and Maggie filled them with the steaming dark liquid.

"What are your plans for Christmas?" Maggie asked as she slid into the nearest booth.

"Mike is making supper tonight, and then we're taking the kids to see the lights." Francis took her place across from Maggie and wrapped her cold fingers around her cup. "That's about it. What about you?"

"Dale and I are going to the Christmas Eve service at our church tonight. You're welcome to join us," Maggie said. She continued as an uncomfortable look passed over Francis's features. "Viona and Jim are coming for Christmas dinner tomorrow. Patrick couldn't make it home for Christmas this year."

"How's Viona doing?" Although Francis had never met Maggie's daughter, she felt a kinship with her since Viona was expecting her first baby in spring.

"She's doing very well." Maggie sipped her coffee.

"Merry Christmas, ladies," Pauline sang out as she danced into the room with reindeer antlers on her head.

"Merry Christmas!" The women laughed at her. Pauline was the clown of the staff, always keeping the mood light and cheery.

In unison, Maggie and Francis took their empty cups to the kitchen, and then Francis unlocked the front door and switched on the Open sign. The breakfast crowd started arriving, and the place was soon buzzing with voices.

Lord, Francis needs you, Maggie prayed silently as she cooked. *Draw her to you. It's Christmas, and the poor girl can't even go home to her family.* Maggie had a habit of praying for the people she worked with, but she felt a special concern for Francis, especially since she'd come back to work just one short month after giving birth. *Lord, that must mean they are struggling financially. Please take care of her and her little family.* She set the full plates on the counter for the waitress and started on the next order.

Francis was exhausted by the time she donned her jacket and boots just after one o'clock. As she stepped out of the diner, she felt momentarily blinded by the bright sunshine. The sun reflected off the snow like a million tiny stars, causing her to blink a few times before her eyes got used to the brightness. She pulled her scarf around her face and trudged the few blocks back to her apartment. The sidewalks were busy with people scurrying around, doing last-minute shopping. Cars sped past her on the street in either direction. She tried to stay as far away from them as possible so she wouldn't get splashed with the brown snow and salt slush.

As Francis climbed the stairs to her apartment, she could hear Chantel crying. She hurried her steps, hoping that Mike wouldn't be too annoyed with the crying baby. As she stepped into her apartment, Brad came barreling into her, wrapping his little arms around her legs. She stooped down and gave him a hug.

"How's my little man?" she asked, lifting him up. She kissed his chubby cheek.

"Brad see lights," Brad informed her excitedly. "Daddy and Brad see lights!"

"We have to wait until it gets dark to see the lights, honey," Francis responded, giving him an extra hug before setting him down on the floor. "We'll all go see the lights after supper."

Brad turned and raced down the hall, revving his pretend car engine. Francis hung up her coat just as Mike came out of the kids' bedroom, carrying a crying Chantel.

"What's wrong with Chantel?" Francis asked. She could see Mike hadn't started making lunch.

"I don't know," Mike said. "She's been like this all morning; she just keeps crying. I gave her a bottle, but she doesn't want it, and I changed her diaper."

"Brad hungry," Brad interrupted.

"Here. You take the baby, and I'll make some lunch." He handed Chantel to Francis.

"Does she have gas?" Francis followed Mike into the kitchen.

"Maybe. I don't know." He started opening cupboard doors.

Francis cuddled the crying baby to her shoulder, rubbing her back gently as she retrieved the baby bottle from the bedroom. She squirted a few drops of gripe water into the baby's cheek, taking care that Chantel would not gag on it. Then she swaddled Chantel in her blanket and settled down on the couch, gently rocking her as she gave her the bottle. When the bottle was nearly empty, Chantel drifted off to sleep, and Francis was able to lay her down in her crib.

Brad was already sitting at the table when Francis entered the kitchen. Mike set a pot of tomato soup and a plate of grilled cheese sandwiches on the table.

"Boy, she was really miserable all morning," Mike said as he sat down. "How was your morning?"

"Very busy," Francis responded. "Seemed like nobody wanted to eat at home today."

"Maybe you should take a nap as well," Mike said. "I'll clean up the place while you and the kids have a nap."

"Thank you, Mike." Francis smiled at him. "I really appreciate that."

"Brad and Daddy see lights," Brad said from his chair.

"Yes, little man," said Mike, ruffling Brad's hair, "but first you have a nap. We will go see the lights after you've had a nap."

Later, Francis stretched as she woke up from her nap. As she got out of bed, she could hear Chantel fussing again. She peeked into the children's bedroom, where Brad was still fast asleep, before she went into the kitchen to find Mike fixing a bottle for Chantel. She took Chantel from Mike's arm and cuddled the baby.

"Did you sleep well?" Mike asked as he gave her a quick hug.

"Yes, I did," Francis replied. "What about the kids?"

"As you can see, Brad is still sleeping," Mike said. "Chantel didn't sleep very long, though."

"I wonder what's wrong with her." Francis cuddled Chantel closely, gently patting her back.

She went into the small living room and sat down on the couch. Mike brought her the baby bottle, sat down next to her, and flicked on the TV. Francis brushed Chantel's soft hair back from her face as she was feeding. Soon the baby's eyelids drooped, and she fell asleep. Francis held her for a while, relishing the feel of the sleeping infant. *What a miracle she is,* Francis thought to herself, her heart swelling with love. *Such a small, perfect person.*

Brad came into the room, dragging his blanket and holding his teddy bear, his pudgy little fist rubbing at his eyes.

"Come here, little man." Mike held his arms out to Brad, who willingly climbed up to cuddle with Daddy.

Mary removed a pan of buns from the oven and slid another pan in. This morning, Mama had washed the floors while Mary wiped down the furniture, which had left time in the afternoon for baking. The house smelled of freshly baked buns, apple pie, and cream cookies. Mary could hardly contain her excitement as she hurried to do her chores.

Tonight was their hayride. She wondered if John would pay her any special attention. Her face flushed with excitement at the thought. His card was safely hidden away in her sock drawer. David would tease her unmercifully if he knew. Mama and Papa might be concerned if they suspected she was getting that kind of attention from a boy.

"I'll be thirteen next month," Mary told the reflection in her dresser mirror. "I'm almost a teenager." She put down the cloth in her hands, removed the rubber band from her hair, and twisted it up into a French roll. *That makes me look like I'm sixteen,* she told herself.

Sighing audibly, she dropped her hair down and tied it back into a ponytail. *Sixteen is so far away!* Papa had strict rules about dating.

Papa and David were busy outside, shoveling manure out of the barns, feeding the animals, bringing in firewood, and melting snow that would last them through the holidays. Since Mary was busy helping Mama in the house, she didn't have to bring in the snow today. Benny, all bundled up in his warmest winter clothes, had gone outside to help. Mary could see him through the window, petting the horses as they munched on the oats he fed them from a bucket. A trickle of fear ran down her spine, and she hoped he would be careful not to get too close to their hooves.

The gifts waiting to be opened Christmas morning were all hidden away, and even though Mary had dusted in every room of the house this morning, she hadn't come across any. Mary was excited about the gifts she would give her family. She had embroidered a set of pillowcases for Mama and sewn and stuffed a teddy bear for Benny. Not able to think of anything useful she could make for Papa and David, she had bought them each a jackknife.

CHAPTER 6

"Daddy, look!" Brad exclaimed excitedly later that evening as they drove up and down the city streets, looking at the variety of Christmas decorations. "Santa! Horsey!"

Mike chuckled. "Those are reindeer, Brad. They're pulling Santa's sleigh."

The elaborate life-size display of reindeer, a sleigh, and Santa lit up the entire front yard of an especially large house completely outlined with red, green, and blue twinkling lights.

Brad pushed his little nose up against the car window. "Santa come to Brad's house now?"

"Honey, Santa only comes after you go to sleep." Francis smiled, enjoying her young son's obvious pleasure. Even Chantel had stopped fussing. She lay sleeping on Francis's lap. Slowly, they drove down one street after another while Brad alternately jumped up and down on the backseat in his excitement or craned his neck to get a better view of the elaborate displays of Santas, snowmen, candy canes, elves, and manger scenes.

When Brad looked like he was getting tired, they stopped at a restaurant for hot chocolate.

"Santa!" Brad exclaimed excitedly, pulling at Mike's arm as soon as they entered the restaurant.

Francis followed Brad's gaze, and there in the far corner, Santa was posing for pictures with kids on his lap. He handed the children candy canes before sending them back to their parents.

"Santa bring Brad presents." Brad nodded knowingly, his eyes sparkling.

"That's right, little man." Mike chuckled, ruffling his son's hair. "Santa will bring you presents."

While they waited for the hot chocolate, Mike took the children to sit on Santa's lap and have their picture taken.

"Ho, ho, ho," Santa said as Mike placed Brad and Chantel on his lap. "Who do we have here?"

Brad stared up into Santa's face, a bit shy now that he was up close to the jolly bearded man. The photographer snapped a picture just before Chantel started crying. Quickly, Mike took Chantel in his arms while Santa gave Brad a candy cane and set him down on the floor.

"Mommy, look!" Candy cane held high, Brad ran back to his mother, who was watching from their booth.

"Wow! Aren't you a lucky boy?" Francis pulled Brad up onto the seat beside her.

Mike paid the photographer for the Polaroid picture and then joined them at the table, handing Chantel to Francis. The waitress brought their hot chocolate while Mike peeled the plastic off of Brad's candy cane.

When they returned to the car, Francis laid the sleeping baby in her basket on the backseat. Brad yawned and curled up on the backseat as well. With both children asleep, Mike pulled the car off the street and stopped at a viewpoint overlooking the North Saskatchewan River.

He pushed the gearshift into park, reached across the seat, and pulled Francis into his arms. "Ah, this is more like it." He sighed as Francis snuggled up against him, her soft hair brushing his chin.

"That is beautiful." Francis swept her hand to encompass the scene before them. The silvery light of the full moon danced across the frozen river, bringing sparkling life to the pristine snow. Overhead, stars twinkled their approval as the northern lights swirled across their elaborate stage. An outline of tall, dark pine trees on the opposite bank provided a perfect backdrop for the scene.

"You are beautiful," Mike murmured as he kissed the top of her head.

Francis sighed, allowing her exhaustion to melt away as she rested her head on his shoulder. "This reminds me of the night we got engaged," she murmured dreamily. "Just you and me." She laughed softly and added, "And now the kids, of course."

"This is what life should be like," he said. "Just you and me and the kids." His arm tightened around her possessively. *Free from the constant worry of trying to make ends meet,* he added to himself bitterly. The endless list of bills they had fallen behind on weighed heavily on his mind. Even though Francis had only taken a month off of work, the lost money for that month had an impact, and now they faced the extra cost of formula and other baby supplies. *I can't even provide for my own family properly,* he fumed silently. *Stuck in this dead-end job.*

"Honey, relax." Francis poked him in the ribs, peering up into his troubled face. "Why are you so tense?"

Good job, buddy, he thought, admonishing himself. *You sure know how to spoil the moment.* He took a deep breath and released it slowly.

"That's better." Francis smiled up at him.

"I was thinking about work," he admitted sheepishly.

"Hey, you're on days off, and it's Christmas, so let's enjoy it," Francis said, and then she added sternly as she poked his ribs with each word, "No more thinking about work."

"You're right." Mike laughed as he hugged her to himself. "Now, where were we?"

Chantel started fussing, so Francis pulled herself out of Mike's arms and leaned over the backseat to put the errant soother back in the baby's mouth.

Mike sighed as he shifted in his seat, put the car in gear, and headed back home.

Mary opened the door before Lena could knock.

"Hi, Lena," she bubbled. "Come in."

"Am I the first one here?" Lena asked, entering the warm house.

"Yes, you are. I'm sure the others will be here soon," Mary answered, taking a quick look out the window. "Oh, I see more headlights." She turned back to Lena. "Papa and David are hitching up the horses, so they should be ready soon. Oh, I'm so excited!" she exclaimed, putting on her heavy winter parka, scarf, and mittens.

"Me too," Lena said. "It's going to be so much fun."

The girls went outside just as David and Papa pulled up with the horses and sleigh. Sarah and Martha were getting out of Sarah's father's car.

"Hi!" Mary and Lena called in unison.

"Let's get up on the sleigh," Mary said when the girls joined them.

The girls ran over and climbed up on the sleigh as another two cars drove up, and David's friends tumbled out. They all scrambled into the back of the sleigh, with David bringing up the rear, and sat down in a circle on the hay. Mark had brought his cousin Deon, who was visiting from the city, so it was a bit more crowded than Papa had expected. Mama and Benny rode up front with Papa.

Mary wondered if it had just ended up that way or if John had purposefully chosen to sit next to her. Either way, she wasn't complaining, especially when he edged closer to her as the horses started trotting down the driveway. The bells David had put on the sleigh tinkled merrily as they rode along.

Once Papa had the horses trotting on the road, he started singing "Joy to the World," and they all joined in. When the song was finished, David started singing "Hark! The Herald Angels Sing," and then Lena started another carol. They kept on singing one carol after another as the sleigh slid smoothly over the crunchy snow. The golden moon smiled down on them with a million soft beams while the northern lights danced and rolled in their soft shades of silver and green across the star-studded night sky.

Mary's joyful heart beat a little faster as she sat snuggled between John and Lena, singing and laughing. The pungent odor of spruce and hay filled her nostrils as Papa guided the horses through a stand of trees proudly showing off their green needles, which refused to succumb to the cold. They were intermixed with straight, stark poplar trees that reached their sparkling hoar-covered branches up to the sky.

"Oh, look—a falling star!" exclaimed Sarah, pointing to a streak of light falling across the night sky.

"We have to make a wish," said Martha. They all laughed at that, but Mary secretly made a wish that this magical evening would never end. She felt John's mittened hand cover hers as it lay between them on the hay, and her heart fluttered in her chest.

"I wonder which star was the one that guided the wise men," Henry mused.

"It was probably the brightest star that's in the sky," David said.

They all gazed up at the stars, trying to pick out the brightest.

"It would be in the east," Mark said.

"I don't think so," John said. "The wise men came from the east, so the star would have been in the west."

"You're right!" David exclaimed. "I never thought of it that way. I always thought the star was in the east."

"Me too," all four girls said in unison.

The horses turned into their driveway, and even though Mary was cold, she felt a pang of regret that the hayride was almost over. They all jumped off of the sleigh as Papa brought the horses to a halt in front of the house. The boys helped Papa unhitch the sleigh at the barn and take care of the horses, while the girls helped Mama in the kitchen. By the time they brought the food out, the orange flames of a bonfire crackled merrily. They arranged the food, cups, and hot chocolate on the makeshift table the boys had made by placing a sheet of plywood on two wooden sawhorses.

"Here are the sticks," John announced, setting a handful of sturdy twigs down at the end of the table.

"Let's get to it." David grabbed a stick and jammed a wiener through the pointy end. "I don't know about you, but I'm hungry."

"Me too." Henry chuckled, grabbing another stick, and the others followed suit.

"You guys should have gotten longer sticks!" Mary exclaimed. "The fire is hot on my face."

"You sure it's the fire that's heating your face?" David teased, and then he quickly added, "If they were longer, they would curve too much, and the wieners would fall off."

"You're probably right, David," John said, wiping his brow, "but I have to agree with Mary. This fire sure is hot."

"Yeah, David, maybe you shouldn't have made the fire so hot." Mark laughed, rotating his hot dog.

"I could always douse it with snow." David grinned, grabbing a handful of snow.

"Don't you dare!" they all yelled in unison.

David laughed as he let the snow fall back to the ground.

Amid the joking and laughter, the wieners got roasted, and they all sat on wood stumps around the blazing fire, eating hot dogs and drinking hot chocolate.

"I thought we might tell the Christmas story in our own words," Papa suggested when he finished eating. "I'll start, and we'll continue around the circle, each person contributing the next part of the story."

They all agreed, so Papa started. "Mary and Joseph were

betrothed to be married, which is like modern-day engagement," he said in way of explanation. "Mary was going about her daily chores, when a man appeared in her room. Mary was startled and probably frightened as well, but the man said, 'Don't be afraid. I am Gabriel, an angel sent by God.'" Papa paused as he looked to Mama sitting beside him. "Your turn."

"The angel told Mary that she would have a baby. Mary was surprised and asked how this could be, because she wasn't even married. Gabriel told her that her baby would be the Son of God and that he would redeem his people from their sin. Of course, being a Jew, Mary knew all about the Messiah that everybody was waiting for. She must have been very excited that she would be the Messiah's mother." Mama looked at Benny, who was sitting beside her. "Benny, can you tell us about the shepherds and angels?"

"It was very dark, and the shepherds were watching their sheep." Benny emphasized the word *very*. "Then, suddenly, it got very bright because lots and lots of angels came." He extended his arms emphatically. "They said Jesus was born and the shepherds should go see him."

Mary heard muffled chuckles as everybody tried hard not to laugh at Benny's animation.

"Very good, Benny." Mama smiled at him. "Now Lena will tell us what came next."

When it was Deon's turn, he said he wasn't very familiar with the Christmas story, so Papa said that was okay and just to continue on to the next person.

Mary had never heard of anyone who didn't know the Christmas story. She wondered what it would feel like to celebrate Christmas without understanding what the occasion for celebration was. She sneaked a peek at Deon. He didn't look that different from the other boys. His hair was a bit longer and stuck out from beneath his tuque, and his pants were tighter. Come to think of it, she didn't think he had been singing any of the carols either. She would have to ask Papa about that later.

When the flames reduced to embers, Papa asked everyone to help clean up. The girls helped Mama clean up the food, while the boys cleaned up the wood stools and makeshift table. They were almost done, when the first set of headlights came down the road.

"That's my papa," Sarah said, turning to Mary's parents. "Thank you very much for the sleigh ride and the food. I had a great time."

"Yes, thank you very much," Martha echoed.

"You're welcome," Mama said. "We were glad you could come."

"Thanks for coming, Sarah and Martha," Mary added. "See you in church tomorrow. Merry Christmas!"

After saying, "Merry Christmas," Sarah and Martha left just as another car pulled up. Soon their friends had all gone home. Papa dumped a shovelful of snow onto the glowing embers, and the snow sizzled and melted. He dumped another shovelful of snow on to make sure the fire was out, and then they all headed inside.

The evening of fresh air had made Benny so tired he lay down on the couch without removing his jacket. Mary cleaned up the kitchen while Mama undressed Benny and put his pajamas on. Papa stoked the fire in the wood stove, causing the sparks to shoot up toward the ceiling.

"I get the biggest bowl!" David exclaimed, heading toward the pantry.

"No!" Benny responded. Finding new energy, he slipped out of Mama's grasp and dashed past David, leaving Mama holding his pajama pants. "I get the biggest bowl."

It was an old Mennonite custom for the children to set out bowls on Christmas Eve in anticipation of the gifts they would find in them the next morning.

"I'm bigger than you," David teased, "so I get the biggest bowl."

"No," Benny said, "I want the biggest presents."

David laughed as he handed Benny the biggest bowl. Mary got a bowl as well, and they all set them on the kitchen table. Then

Mama picked Benny up, put his pajama pants on him, and tucked him into bed.

"Tonight was lots of fun," David said, plopping down on the couch.

"Yes, it was," Papa agreed, sitting in his favorite easy chair.

"Papa," Mary said, joining David on the couch, "why didn't Deon know the Christmas story? I don't think he sang the Christmas carols either. The only time he sang along was when we sang 'We Wish You a Merry Christmas.'"

Papa looked thoughtful as he turned to his soon-to-be-teenage daughter. How he longed for his children to not only know the Christmas story but also experience the true joy of it deep down in their hearts. He wanted them to know the joy of knowing Jesus as their own personal Savior. "*Ach*, Mary, not everyone teaches their children the true meaning of Christmas," Papa explained. "There are too many people in this world who teach their children about Santa Claus and omit the real reason for celebrating Christmas."

"But isn't Deon's mama Mr. Friesen's sister?" David asked. "The Friesens teach their kids about Jesus."

"Yes, but just because they are brother and sister doesn't mean that they both believe the same thing," Papa said.

"Didn't their parents teach them both about the Bible?" Mary asked, her curiosity piqued.

"I'm sure they did," Papa responded, rubbing his chin thoughtfully, "but knowing what's in the Bible and understanding it are two separate things. The Bible says that without the Holy Spirit in us, we cannot truly understand it. The Holy Spirit reveals the truth to us. We only have the Holy Spirit living in us when we accept Jesus as our Savior. If Deon's mama and papa have never committed their lives to Christ, they can't fully understand the Bible, so it is easy to fill their lives with other things."

"Well, I'm glad we know about Jesus." Mary yawned. "Christmas just wouldn't be the same if we didn't."

"That's right." David stood up. "I'm going to bed."

"Me too," Mary said, stifling another yawn.

CHAPTER 7

The moon was shining its soft beams onto Mary's bed when she awoke. She peeked at the illuminated hands on her alarm clock. It was five o'clock in the morning. She wasn't allowed to get up before six o'clock on Christmas morning. Mama and Papa were strict about that. Mary turned over and shut her eyes, but sleep escaped her, as her mind was captivated with anticipation. She loved Christmas. It was her favorite time of year: presents, food, family, friends, concerts, and the wonderful story of Jesus.

Her thoughts reverted to Deon. How did his family celebrate Christmas? Did he really believe the Santa Claus story? What would it be like to celebrate Christmas without Jesus? It had never crossed her mind that people celebrated Christmas in different ways.

Mary fluffed up her pillow and turned over onto her other side. What would it be like to live in the city? Did no one there know the true meaning of Christmas? *How sad.* She felt a tug at her heart. Someone needed to tell them.

Mary peeked at the clock again: 5:45. She turned off the alarm. Reaching out with one arm, she pulled her clothes under the comforter with her to warm them up. She shivered. Keeping herself covered as much as possible, she started dressing.

Mama stoked the fire in the cook stove as Mary stepped out of her bedroom. David came out of his bedroom, and Papa entered the kitchen with Benny on his arm. When Benny saw gifts in his bowl, he wiggled out of Papa's arms, dashed to the table, scrambled up onto a chair, and started pulling things out.

"An airplane!" he squealed with delight as he picked up the toy and held it up for all to see. He jumped off the chair. Holding the airplane above his head, he ran in circles around the room.

Papa chuckled. "Benny, are you going to see what else is in your bowl?"

"Oh, *jo!*" Benny flew the airplane back to his bowl. After setting it down on the table, he dug in again. This time, he came up with a wooden barn complete with farm animals carved out of wood.

Mama laughed as he jumped up and down in unabashed excitement, his soft blond curls bouncing on his head.

"Oh my, this is pretty!" Mary exclaimed, holding up a pink dress with stylish three-quarter-length sleeves. She held it up in front of herself and twirled around the room, making the full skirt billow out.

"This is better." David laughed, holding up a new silver watch.

"Nice," Mary agreed, and then she dug back into her bowl and pulled out a book written by her favorite author, a paint-by-number set of Jesus feeding the five thousand, a set of liquid embroidery paints, and a pair of pillowcases with a design that she could paint. "I'm going to have lots to do this winter."

David unearthed a slingshot, a paint-by-number set of Jesus walking on the sea, and a new winter parka.

"Mama, can I eat the candy now?" Benny had found the gifts of candy, peanuts, and oranges that were in the bottom of their bowls.

"You can have one candy now," Mama told him. "Then you have to have breakfast."

Papa donned his parka and went outside. He came back with a beautifully carved coffee table varnished in a deep walnut color, which he presented to Mama.

"*Ach*, Jacob, you shouldn't have." Mama was deeply touched, her eyes misty, as she admired her husband's handiwork. "When did you build this? I had no idea."

"Let's just say I wasn't always working with the cattle when I said I was." Papa chuckled. "I trust you will forgive me for that."

"This is beautiful!" Mama exclaimed. *"Dankeshoen."*

Mama asked David to bring out Papa's gift. David went to his bedroom and came back with a new red toolbox for Papa.

"I can sure use this!" Papa exclaimed, opening the various compartments. "It will help me be more organized. *Dankeshoen.*"

David presented Mama with a pair of oven mitts and Papa with a new carving tool. He gave Mary a five-year diary complete with lock and key.

"Thank you, David." She smiled up at her brother. "I love this."

"I thought you might want to write all about your boyfriends," David teased, his hazel eyes sparkling.

"I don't have boyfriends." Mary cuffed him.

"Really?" David raised his eyebrows. "I thought—"

"David, stop teasing," Mama said.

Feeling the familiar heat rising from her neck into her face, Mary escaped to her bedroom to get the gifts she had for her family.

After all the gifts were exchanged, Papa and David went outside to do the chores while Mary helped Mama prepare a breakfast of hot porridge, and Benny played noisily with his new toys.

Francis felt herself waking up slowly. She stretched her legs and looked at the clock on her bedside table: 7:15 a.m. It was Christmas morning. Mike snored softly beside her.

Listening to the early morning sounds of traffic on the street below, she let her mind wander back to Christmases past. They always had been packed with expensive gifts and parties. Though she didn't miss the hoopla of social gatherings, she did miss her family. Francis wondered if they were opening gifts already. Did Mother miss not shopping for her? Did she ever think of her? Did she ever wonder what her grandchildren were like?

Maybe Mother will call today. She didn't often look into the void in her heart where her mother's love was supposed to be. She wiped at a tear that trickled out of the corner of her eye.

Throwing her legs over the side of the bed, she sat up. *It is Christmas, after all,* she thought, scolding herself, *and I have a loving husband and kids to share it with. Why am I dwelling on the past?*

Francis grabbed her robe and hurried into the bathroom. She would shower before the children woke up. She was just making coffee, when Chantel started crying. She dashed into the children's bedroom, hoping to pick Chantel up before she woke Brad, but Brad was already sitting up in bed, rubbing his eyes.

"Chantel wake me up." He yawned.

"I'll take Chantel. You lie down and sleep some more," Francis responded.

"No." He started crawling out of bed. "Brad get up too."

Francis picked up both children, and as she carried them to the kitchen, she heard Mike turn on the shower. She set Brad down on a chair. Still cradling the baby in one arm, she took a bottle of milk from the fridge and stuck it into a pot of hot water to take the chill off. She got a bowl of cereal for Brad and poured herself a cup of coffee before sitting down at the table to feed the baby.

"Merry Christmas." Mike ruffled Brad's hair before stooping to give Francis a peck on the cheek. He smelled of soap and aftershave.

"Merry Christmas." Francis smiled up at him.

Mike grabbed a mug from the mug tree.

"Presents!" exclaimed Brad excitedly, pushing away his cereal.

"You eat your breakfast first, little man." Mike poured himself a mug of coffee. "Then we'll open presents. Come here. Daddy will help you with your cereal."

As soon as Brad finished his breakfast, he slid off of his chair and scampered into the living room. Laughing at his eagerness, Mike and Francis followed.

"Just a minute, little man." Mike chuckled as Brad picked up a brightly wrapped present. "I'll give you your presents. They're not all for you, Brad; some are for your sister."

Mike handed one of the presents to Brad, who immediately tore the wrapping off and held up a bright red fire engine.

"Fire truck!" he exclaimed excitedly, pressing buttons that made the lights flash and the siren blast.

"There goes any semblance of peace and quiet." Mike grinned at his wife.

"Brad, do you want to help Chantel open her presents?" Francis asked when Brad finished unwrapping his gifts.

"Yes." Brad jumped up from the floor, eager to help. "Chantel too little."

"That's right," Mike agreed. "You be a good big brother and give her a hand."

Brad tore at the paper of Chantel's presents while his sister rested contentedly in her mother's arms, oblivious to all the commotion. Her fretfulness of yesterday had disappeared. Brad picked up a doll from the wrapping and tried to give it to Chantel. Francis quickly took his little hand so he didn't dump it on her face.

"Look, Chantel, a doll," Brad said.

Chantel looked up into her brother's face, oblivious to the gift he was trying to get her to look at.

"Chantel will play with it when she's a bit older," Francis explained. "She's too little to play yet."

Losing interest in his sister's gifts, Brad dropped the doll on the floor and went back to his fire engine. Francis laid the baby on the couch, retrieved Mike's gift from under the tree, and handed it to him. Mike looked at the wrapped gift in his hand. He turned it over and over.

"Well, open it," Francis urged.

Slowly, Mike unwrapped the gift and picked up the gold watch that was inside.

"You shouldn't have gotten me something this expensive," he said, looking at Francis. "Where did you get the money for this?"

"I saved a little bit from each check," Francis responded. "It was on sale, and you need a watch. Don't you like it?"

"Yes, thank you," Mike said, giving Francis a quick hug before slipping the gold band over his left hand. "It's very handsome."

He struck a pose, and Francis laughed.

"You would look good on the catwalk," she teased.

Mike made an exaggerated theatrical exit from the room, twirling his left hand up in the air, making Francis laugh even harder. He came back in a couple of minutes with a newly finished wooden rocking chair. Francis's eyebrows flew up in surprise.

"Merry Christmas," he said as he deposited the chair in front of Francis.

"Wow! Mike, thank you." She threw her arms around him before sitting down on the chair.

"It's not new," Mike admitted sheepishly. "I bought it at the secondhand store. I just gave it a new coat of paint."

"It's exactly what I need to rock my babies," Francis said, rocking back and forth.

At church that morning, Mary sat with Lena, Martha, and Sara. Excitedly, they told each other about the gifts they had received. The song leader led them in a couple of songs from their German song book. The church grew quiet as the pastor took the pulpit and expounded on the details surrounding the first Christmas. Mary tried to concentrate on the German message. She could understand most of it if she concentrated hard enough, but today was difficult, as she was so excited for the rest of the day.

After church, Mary and her family went to the home of her maternal grandma and grandpa for Christmas dinner.

"Come in," Grandpa said, greeting everyone at the door. "Hurry up and close the door; don't let the cold in," he said each time the door opened again to let more people in. All the aunts, uncles, and cousins came for Christmas dinner.

Grandma bustled about in her kitchen, directing her daughters and daughters-in-law as they helped put the final touches on the meal of turkey, mashed potatoes, and salads. When the food was all on the table, Grandpa and the uncles came out of the living room and took their places around the table, opposite their wives. The children waited until the adults were finished eating, because there was not enough room at the table for all of them.

When the dinner dishes were done and the kitchen restored to some semblance of order, the entire family gathered in the living room to sing Christmas carols and open gifts. The younger children recited Bible verses and poems or sang songs they had memorized for the occasion. Grandma and Grandpa rewarded each grandchild with a brown paper bag filled with peanuts, candy, an orange, and a small gift. Amid much chatter and laughter, gifts were exchanged among adults and children alike while they indulged in the candy, peanuts, and oranges that Grandma had set out.

"Let's play Clue," Cousin Anita suggested after the gifts were opened and the adults had settled down to visit.

Mary and her cousins went in search of the board game and set it up on the kitchen table.

CHAPTER 8

Francis pulled her coat tighter around her as she closed the restaurant door. According to the calendar, spring had arrived, but the wind still cut through her coat. The once-beautiful snowbanks had shrunk in the springtime sun, leaving them gray and moldy.

Her stomach growled. She hoped Mike had fixed lunch.

When did he start changing? she asked herself, dodging puddles and people on the sidewalk. Her mind retraced the months once again, as it often did lately, and as with every other time, she came to the same conclusion: *When Chantel was born. Actually, probably even before that. When we found out I was pregnant.* That was when he'd first started stressing about their finances. However, it was after the baby was born that he'd really started changing. At first, she'd thought it was because Chantel was a fussy baby.

He used to be ambitious and optimistic, a fun person. Now he's sullen and depressed, his time at home spent mostly staring at the TV screen. Francis's heart ached, and she bit her lower lip as last night came to mind.

Mike had come home from work late. She'd been worried sick that something had happened to him. When he'd come in an hour late, he'd mumbled something about going out with the guys before he sat down on the couch and flicked on the TV. Francis had made them each a cup of hot chocolate. She had been determined to talk to him. Setting the steaming cups on the coffee table, she'd sat down beside him on the couch. She'd waited for a commercial to come on.

"Mike, I've been wondering what's bothering you." She'd touched his forearm as she gently broached the subject.

"What do you mean?"

She should have backed off at the harshness in his voice. She should have heeded that warning.

"You're not happy anymore," she'd said, pressing on. "When you're at home, all you do is sit in front of the TV. You don't talk to me; you don't play with the kids. Are you having trouble at work?"

Mike had stood up and walked over to the window. When he'd turned around to face her, she had seen rage smoldering in his eyes. "How dare you," he'd said, scowling. "I work my butt off for you and the kids."

"I know you do," she'd said, trying to reassure him.

He'd closed the space between them and towered over her, his fists clenched at his sides. A muscle had twitched in his jaw.

"Mike, you're scaring me." She had been able to smell alcohol on his breath. "I'm sorry."

"You're sorry?" His laugh had sounded evil. "Sorry for what? That you married me? Admit it." His voice had risen. "I'm not good enough anymore, am I?"

"Mike, the children are sleeping," she had said, not wanting him to wake the kids.

He'd punched her hard. Pain had coursed through her left shoulder. A startled look had passed over his eyes. He'd turned abruptly and left the room.

Now her fingers gingerly brushed the bruise on her shoulder. This wasn't the first time he had hit her, but this time had been more vicious than the other times.

Sighing, she pushed open her apartment door. The pungent odor of onions assailed her nostrils. Brad came running and threw his arms around her legs. She gave him a quick hug before removing her coat and boots. Then she scooped him up into her arms for a real hug and planted a kiss on his pudgy cheek.

"Hi, honey." Mike smiled as he placed burgers and fries on the table. "How was work?"

"Busy." Francis set Brad down on a chair, throwing a wary glance in Mike's direction. "Thanks for making lunch. I got off a bit late. Is Chantel sleeping?"

"Yeah." Mike came up behind her and folded his arms around her. "She was a little fussy, so I gave her a bottle and laid her down." Francis winced as Mike's arms tightened around her.

"Here—let me see." Mike pulled her sweater down over her shoulder, revealing the angry bruise. "Oh, baby, I'm so sorry," he said, stooping down to kiss the bruise. "I didn't mean to hurt you. I love you. I promise it won't happen again."

Francis turned in his embrace to search his sky-blue eyes. "I love you too. I'm sorry I made you angry."

"Look," Mike said, "we'll just make sure it doesn't happen again, okay?"

She nodded as he kissed her lips. With her head resting against his shoulder, she told herself they would be fine. Every marriage had difficulties. Mike had not meant to harm her. She'd seen the startled look in his eyes, as if he hadn't realized the force behind the punch. She would just be more careful not to make him angry.

They sat down for lunch. Francis fixed a plate for Brad and then for herself.

"The burgers are delicious." Francis was always careful to compliment Mike's cooking. "I am so hungry I could eat a horse."

"Mommy eat a horse?" Brad stared at his mother with wide eyes.

Francis laughed. "No, honey, I don't really want to eat a horse. That's just a saying."

Brad gave her a funny look but resumed eating.

"By the way," Mike said on his way out the door after lunch,

"Jason invited us to his wife's birthday party this Saturday. You'll need to get a sitter for the kids."

He pulled the door shut after him, leaving Francis gaping at the closed door. They never went to parties. She had no desire to attend a party with his coworkers. From the little she had seen and heard about them, she didn't think they were the type of people she wanted to associate with.

Then again, maybe it will do us good to go out, she argued to herself, trying to suppress the anxiety mounting in the pit of her stomach. *Maybe an evening of fun without the kids is just what we need to get back on track.*

Saturday evening, Francis pulled her best dress from the recesses of her closet. The deep royal blue brought out the blue in her eyes. The little cap sleeves complemented her long arms. The neckline was high enough to be modest, and a knee-length full skirt flowed down from an empire waist. She carefully put on her makeup and the pearl earrings Mike had given her for her birthday when they were first married. She clasped the matching string of pearls around her neck for the final touch.

The doorbell rang. Francis hurried to open the door for the babysitter. Sally was a teenager from the same apartment block who was happy to earn a bit of extra money.

"The children are both sleeping and will probably not wake up. Here's the phone number where you can reach us if you need to." Francis showed Sally the paper she had carefully laid on the counter for easy access. "We'll be home around midnight."

"Are you ready to go?" Mike asked, standing in the doorway, holding her coat.

When they got in the car, Mike pulled her close. "You look like a million bucks," he said softly. Francis smelled alcohol on his breath.

"Have you been drinking?" she asked, turning her face up to look at him.

"It's okay, Francis. I only had one little drink to loosen up. Don't worry," he responded, starting the car.

"I must admit I'm a bit nervous about meeting a bunch of new people," Francis said. "It's been a long time since we've gone to a party."

"It's not a big deal," Mike replied, keeping his eye on the traffic. "It's mostly going to be people from work."

"But I don't know the people you work with," she pointed out.

Minutes later, they pulled up to the Doyle residence, and Mike shut the engine off. He took her face in his hands and kissed the tip of her nose. "I love you."

"I love you too," Francis said, finding strength in those words.

The night was a disaster from the time they stepped through the door and were greeted by a tall, slim man dressed in bell-bottom pants and a leather-fringed vest over a Beatles T-shirt. His jet-black hair hung down to his shoulders, and his bearded face was accentuated by a pair of eyes that were equally as dark as his hair. Francis noticed that the smile curving his thin lips didn't reach his eyes.

"Hi, Jason," Mike said. "This is my wife, Francis."

Jason took both of Francis's hands in his as he let his gaze sweep over her, making her feel uncomfortable.

Francis turned to Mike but saw he was already talking with a tall blonde woman in a flowery shift dress accentuated by a heavy gold chain hanging loosely around her hips. Beaded jewelry hung from her ears and neck, and her long blonde tresses cascaded down her back past her waistline.

"This is my wife, Cheryl." Jason put his arm around Cheryl's waist as he introduced the two women.

"Happy birthday," Francis told Cheryl.

"Glad you came." Cheryl smiled at Francis. "Make yourself comfortable." She waved her hand toward the main living area, where a number of people were sitting either on the floor or on flowery couches.

There's a lot of people here that Mike doesn't work with, Francis realized as she quickly scanned the room. Cigarette smoke hung in the air along with another more pungent odor that Francis could not pinpoint. Heavy metal music blasted from an elaborate cabinet-style record player.

Mike walked over to a group of guys playing games at a card table and pulled out a chair, leaving Francis standing in the middle of the room. She took in her surroundings. The roomy entrance gave way to a large sitting area. An earth-tone Bohemian tree of life wall hanging covered a fair amount of the far wall. Peace symbols, rock band posters, and lava lamps caught her eye.

"Hi. I'm Diane," a soft voice said beside her. "I work in the office. You must be Francis."

"Yes, I am." Francis shook the proffered hand. Diane was of medium build, and her well-groomed auburn hair curled around her ears, providing a perfect frame for her cheerful face. She wore a pink circle skirt with a white blouse.

"I saw you come in with Mike," she explained. "Let's grab those empty seats over there." Diane led the way to a couple of seats by the window. Francis found herself relaxing as Diane pointed out Mike's coworkers from the safety of their chairs. Conversation flowed easily, and Francis soon found out that Diane had been a stay-at-home mom until her husband died of a heart attack two years ago, leaving her with twin sixteen-year-old boys.

"I had to go to work," she said. "Besides needing the money, I had to get out of the house. Work forced me to focus on something other than my grief. I was lucky to get the office job at the service station. It doesn't pay much, but it puts food on the table."

"Are your sons still in school?" Francis asked.

"They graduated last spring and are both in college now but still live at home."

After Diane excused herself, Francis stayed where she was,

trying to be as inconspicuous as possible. She watched the interactions of the people around her but was careful not to make eye contact with anyone. Her head had begun to pound in rhythm with the beat blasting from the speakers. She was aware that alcohol was flowing freely, and more than once, she noticed Mike refilling his glass. She wished she could attract his attention to signal that she wanted to go home.

It was nearing midnight when she finally found the courage to interrupt the group at the game table.

"Mike?" She touched his arm. "We need to go home."

"Why?" he asked a little too loudly.

"Please, Mike," she said in a quiet voice, hoping he would follow suit. "We need to go."

"We can't go home now. The fun has just begun." Mike looked a bit unsteady as he got to his feet. She didn't want to make a scene, but she wanted to get out of this situation.

"We need to go home. I told the babysitter we would be home by midnight." She laid a hand on Mike's arm to steady him.

"You can't split already," Cheryl protested, coming up behind Francis.

"We need to go home to our children," Francis explained. "We left them with a babysitter."

"Why don't you run along to your kids, and Jason can drop Mike off later? Mike's right; the evening's still young." Cheryl smiled sweetly.

"Yeah," Mike agreed, nodding emphatically. "Yeah, you could do that. Wait." He dug around in his pocket. "Here are the keys." He held the keys toward her, but they fell out of his hand.

Cheryl giggled as she bent over to pick them up and then deposited them into Francis's hand. "Problem solved." Cheryl smiled broadly as she wiggled her fingers in a little wave.

Francis felt her face heat up as she turned and headed toward the door. Jason was there to help her with her coat.

"Too bad you're ditching the scene already. I'll pop by with Mike later."

Francis opened the door and darted out. The cold air hit her hot face. As the door swung closed behind her, she brought her hands up to her cheeks. *What just happened in there? How could Mike want to stay?* She hated to leave him there, but she couldn't think of any other option. She could not stay there a minute longer herself.

We should never have gone, she fumed to herself as she slipped into the driver's seat. She turned the key in the ignition, and the motor purred to life. She took a deep breath before pulling out into the street.

Francis let herself into her apartment and woke Sally, who was sleeping on the couch. After she paid Sally and let her out of the apartment, she tiptoed into the kids' bedroom to check on them. Brad was sleeping spread eagle without a blanket, so she tucked his blanket around him. She kissed his rosy cheek, and he turned in his sleep. Then she softly stepped up to Chantel's crib. Chantel looked flushed, and Francis caressed the baby's cheek. She felt warm to the touch. Francis loosened the blanket around the baby and then stole quietly out of the room.

Francis wandered into the kitchen, poured water into the kettle, and set it on the stove to heat. She took a mug off the tree, dropped in a chamomile tea bag and a spoonful of honey. When the kettle started whistling, she added hot water to the mug and let it steep. Then, tea in hand, she went into the living room and curled up on the couch with a blanket.

Her stomach churned as her mind replayed the events of the evening. She clutched the blanket to her chin, repressing the threatening tears.

Crying won't help. I'll talk to Mike tomorrow, she told herself.

She turned on the TV, but the solitary channel showed a war movie, so she flicked it off. She got up and paced to the window. Pulling back the curtain, she peered down at the deserted street below, her fingers curling around her mug. A singular car made its way down the lonely street. Francis watched it expectantly, but it drove right by her apartment. She let the curtain fall back into place.

Chantel whimpered. Francis set down her mug, and went to pick up her baby before she woke Brad. Chantel still felt warm to the touch, so Francis gave her some baby aspirin. She prepared a bottle of milk and sat in her rocking chair. The baby had trouble breathing while she was feeding. Every few seconds, she turned her head to catch her breath. *She's probably coming down with a cold.* Francis softly sang lullabies, and eventually, Chantel drifted off to sleep. For some time, Francis continued rocking her baby, drawing comfort from the feel of the child in her arms.

"Hope you get better soon," Francis whispered, stroking the soft baby hair back from Chantel's forehead. She hated it when the children were ill. When Chantel started fidgeting in her sleep, Francis gently laid her back in her crib.

Francis went into the bathroom to remove her makeup and change into her pajamas before returning to the living room. She curled up on the couch, pulling the blanket up under her chin. *I wish Mike would come home.* She couldn't get rid of the uneasiness she felt.

The sound of a key in the door startled Francis from her sleep. Why was someone at the door? Why was she sleeping on the couch? In a flash, it all came back to her as Mike opened the door and stumbled in. He didn't even stop to take off his shoes but came right at Francis. His eyes narrowed menacingly. He grabbed the front of her pajamas and pulled her up off the couch.

"How dare you leave me!" he growled.

Francis swallowed past the fear rising in her throat. "I had to come home to the kids, Mike."

"The kids, eh? Always the kids. What about me, huh? You embarrassed me in front of my friends." The first punch landed hard in her stomach. As Francis doubled over, the second punch caught her shoulder, sending her crashing to the floor.

"Don't ever embarrass me like that again!" he shouted as he kicked her in the side. She stifled a scream as pain seared through her body. She covered her face with her hands as he towered over her menacingly. For a moment, his bloodshot eyes blazed down at her. He clenched his fists in front of him. Then he sank onto the couch, his energy spent.

Brad cried. She needed to go to him, but she was afraid to move. She watched as Mike slouched against the back of the sofa. Only after she heard him snore did she move from her crouched position on the floor.

"Mommy!" Brad cried insistently. "Mommy!"

Francis picked herself up off the floor. Her body ached. Her head spun, and she grabbed the rocking chair, willing the dizziness to go away.

"Mommy!"

Francis stepped around Mike's legs and gingerly made her way to the children's bedroom. Brad sat up in bed, rubbing his eyes.

"Mommy, I'm scared."

Francis sat down on the edge of Brad's bed and pulled the little boy into her arms.

"Shhh, baby," she crooned, smoothing the hair back from his face. "Mommy's right here. Everything will be all right." She softly rocked Brad back and forth, ignoring the pain that pulsated through her body.

When Brad settled down, she laid him back on his pillow and lay down beside him until he slept. Quietly, she hobbled out of the children's bedroom and went back into the living room. Mike was still sleeping in a slouched position, his head back against the couch and his mouth wide open. She grabbed a throw cushion and pulled Mike's head and shoulders down onto it. After removing his shoes, she pulled his legs up onto the couch and covered him with the blanket she had been using. She shuffled to the door, locked the deadbolt, turned out the lights, and went to bed. Only then did she release the pent-up emotions and let the tears flow freely into her pillow.

CHAPTER 9

Mary relished the warm rays of sunshine as she helped Mama plant the garden. She loved the long days of spring, when she could finally escape the confines of their little house without the constriction of coats and boots. The birds chirped in the trees, and Benny tried to keep track of a squirrel he had seen among the leaves. The furry brown animal barely showed itself before skittering away among the green foliage, only to show itself in another place a few moments later. Mama sang as she planted, and Mary joined in, carefully placing the tiny seeds into the warm, fertile earth. It was hard to believe that these tiny seeds would grow up into luscious plants that would produce delicious vegetables, which they would preserve in preparation for the long winter months.

"That's all there is," Mama said as she finally straightened up, placed her hands on her hips, and stretched her back. "That's all we can do. The rest is up to God."

Mary knew what Mama meant. They could plant the seeds, but only God could make the sun shine and the rain come at the right times to make their garden fruitful. She picked up the garden tools and put them in the shed while Mama went inside to start supper. There was always an abundance of work on the farm, but Mary didn't mind. She enjoyed working alongside Mama.

Mary heard a scream and turned around to see Benny lying

in a mud puddle, crying. She ran over and took his arm, pulling him up.

"Benny, what happened?" she asked, wiping at Benny's tears.

"I wanted to catch the squirrel," he sputtered.

"Here—let's go inside and get you cleaned up." Mary led him to the house and helped him remove his muddy clothes.

"*Oba*, Benny!" Mama exclaimed. "What happened to you?"

"I wanted to catch the squirrel," Benny said, pouting, his tears drying up. "Then I slipped and fell, and the squirrel got away."

"*Oba, oba!*" Mama exclaimed. "Come with me, and I will get some clean clothes on you," she said, taking hold of Benny's arm. "You must be careful where you walk, even when you are trying to catch a squirrel."

Later, during supper, Benny told Papa and David how he'd almost caught the squirrel.

"You and I should make a slingshot, and then I'll teach you how to shoot squirrels." David reached over and tousled Benny's hair.

"Oh yes!" exclaimed Benny excitedly, laying his fork down. "Let's go now."

"Eat your supper first," Papa said, pointing at Benny's plate.

After the supper dishes were done, Mary took her homework outside and sat on the grass. She drew her sweater around her. Evenings were still a bit chilly, but she loved the freedom of being outside after the long winter months cooped up in the house.

Opening her social studies textbook, she leaned back against a tree to read the assigned chapter. Instead of focusing on the page in front of her, her mind wandered ahead to the coming Sunday afternoon, when she and David were planning to go down to the river with their friends. They would have a wiener roast and play beach volleyball. She could hardly wait.

I need to focus, she told herself, her eyes going back to the top of the page. She didn't remember a word she had read. She started again.

"In ancient India, people were divided into castes," she read.

She especially looked forward to spending time with John. At thirteen, she wasn't allowed to date, but that didn't stop her from daydreaming. She dreamed of the day she would marry John. Since he was a few years older, she worried he might find someone else.

If only time would go by faster. She sighed. Again, she pulled her eyes to the top of the page. She'd have to reread again.

"Hey." David plopped down on the grass beside her. "You're always doing homework. I say that if I can't get it done in school, it's not gonna get done, 'cause I'm sure not going to give up my free time to do homework."

"Yeah, well, I like to learn," Mary responded, "but to tell you the truth, I was thinking of our plans for Sunday."

"Can't wait to see John, eh?" David laughed, pulling at a blade of grass.

Mary felt the heat rising into her cheeks as she cuffed him. "I didn't say that."

"But you thought it, didn't you?" David teased, wiggling his eyebrows at her. Then he continued before she could answer. "Well, you're too young to think of guys." He lay back on the lawn, chewing on the blade of grass. "I don't want to get involved with girls, at least not for the next ten years or so. I want to do something useful with my life. I just don't know what yet."

"You can always go into farming with Papa. Isn't that what you want to do?" Mary asked. She had always assumed David would take over the family farm someday.

"No, I don't think so." He had a faraway look in his eyes. "Farming's okay, I guess, but it's not for me. I want adventure; I want to see the world. I want to make a difference, you know, like helping people in Africa or India. Something like that."

"Well, you'll need money for that," Mary pointed out, "and how are you going to get enough money without getting a good education? And to get a good education, you have to study."

"Hey, I'm still in school, and I have passing grades. What more do I need?" David stood up. "I'm going to see how Benny's making out with his slingshot." He chuckled as he turned and sauntered across the lawn. Mary turned her mind back to her studies.

Sunday after lunch, Mary packed a picnic basket of food for their wiener roast. Now that David had his driver's license, Papa allowed him to drive their old Ford pickup. That made socializing easier for Mary as well, since David could drive her to her friends' houses or, like today, take her and her friends to the river.

"Mary," David said, poking his head in the door, "if you're not ready soon, I'm leaving without you."

"No, you're not." Mary laughed. "'Cause I'm getting the food, and I know you wouldn't go without that." She closed the picnic basket and headed for the door.

David grabbed the basket and put it in the truck bed. Mary jumped into the passenger seat while David slid behind the wheel. As they headed down the road, Mary turned up the radio, and they sang along with popular country songs. Along the way, they picked up Lena and Sarah. Mary scooted over next to David to make room for the girls.

It wasn't long before David turned the truck off the road and onto the narrow, winding trail down to the river. Lush green trees created a canopy overhead.

"We're the first ones here," Lena observed when they broke through the trees and saw the sandy beach spread out ahead of them.

"You're going to get stuck," Mary warned as David drove the truck onto the sand.

"I hope not." David chuckled, driving a little farther before parking the truck.

They all spilled out of the truck and chose a soft, sandy spot to set up the volleyball net. David got the poles and net off the back of the truck, and the girls helped him set it up as others started arriving.

"David, I think your truck is stuck," Henry said, coming to join them. He'd parked on solid ground at the edge of the sand.

"Hope not." David sounded unconcerned. "I didn't want to carry all this stuff that far. If I am stuck, then you guys are going to have to push me out."

"You wish!" John threw the ball at David. David caught it and threw it back.

They picked teams and started their game among a lot of shouting and laughing. It was hard to run in the shifting sand.

"Mine!" yelled Martha, lunging for the ball coming at her. She underestimated and missed the ball as she landed full length in the sand. The others laughed as she got up, shaking sand from her hair. It didn't take long until Martha was the one laughing, as they all got their turn slipping in the sand. They served, bumped, spiked, and blocked until they were hot and tired.

When they finally decided they were hungry, the boys built a fire, set up their fishing poles, and slung fishing lines into the river. Then they gathered green willow branches and whittled them down for roasting sticks while the girls got the food out and arranged it on the end gate of Papa's truck. They roasted wieners and marshmallows over the fire, keeping an eye on the fishing lines.

As the afternoon turned to evening, they built a huge campfire. John got his guitar out, and they all sat around the campfire, singing and telling stories. Mary loved the long summer evenings when the sun didn't set till around eleven o'clock. Even after the sun set, the sky didn't get totally dark unless it was cloudy. She had heard that on a clear evening, one could read a newspaper outside all night without a light. She'd never tried it, but she didn't doubt it was true.

All too soon, the shadows lengthened, and it was time to pour water on the still-crackling embers. Amid shouting good-byes to each other, they all piled into their vehicles and headed home.

Francis hurried from one table to the next, taking orders and serving coffee. The little restaurant was much busier these days. She was glad that her shift ended right after lunch, allowing her to escape the restaurant during the heat of the hot summer afternoons. It was already quite warm by the time she left.

"Francis, have coffee with me," Maggie said as Francis entered the kitchen. "I think you could stand a break, and I'm sure Mandy will be happy to fill in for you for a while." She turned to Mandy, who was washing dishes. "Mandy, would you be so kind as to work the floor so Francis and I can take a break?"

"Of course," Mandy, the bubbly teenager, said. "I'd be glad to."

Maggie filled two cups with coffee and set them on the table reserved for staff. Francis sat down across from her and eased her feet out of her shoes as she sipped at her coffee.

"This place is really buzzing these days," Maggie said with a sweeping gaze over the restaurant. "Never seen it so busy." Then she turned to Francis. "So how are your little ones these days?"

"Brad is such a little helper." Francis smiled over her coffee cup. "He's so good with Chantel. Chantel is coughing again. That girl always seems to have a cold." She absently massaged her shoulder.

"Are you hurting again?" Maggie's eyes filled with concern.

Francis brought her hand down and stared into her coffee. "Just a bit of an ache in my shoulder," she muttered.

"Look, Francis, I don't want to interfere, but I want you to know that I'm here for you whenever you need me. You don't have to live with abuse." Maggie had a way of discerning the situation. Although Francis had never told anyone, Maggie had picked up on it.

"It's not that bad," Francis replied, swirling the coffee around in her cup. "I just need to be more understanding. Mike is a good person; he just has a temper when he drinks."

"Which is happening a lot lately, isn't it?" Maggie prompted her gently, her soft gray eyes filled with compassion.

Francis thought back over the last seven months. Mike had made a habit of meeting with his buddies from work at least once a week. More times than not, he would come home irritated about something or other and take it out on her. Yes, it was happening more frequently, and she was at a loss as to how to stop it. The kids were always asleep when Mike came home, so they were not affected. Mike was good with the kids. She just needed to find a way to help him relax. They should never have attended Cheryl's birthday party. Neither she nor Mike ever mentioned that night, but after that, she'd started noticing lipstick on his shirts when he came home. She never confronted him about it, but she guessed he was more than just friends with Cheryl. Instinctively, her hand went back to the tender spot on her shoulder, and she rubbed it gingerly. She looked up and saw Maggie watching her with concern written all over her face.

"He's good with the kids," she responded feebly.

"I'm just a phone call away," Maggie replied before changing the subject to talk about her new granddaughter and her volunteer work at the seniors' home.

It broke Maggie's heart to see Francis like this. *Francis needs to admit her abusive situation and seek help. I wonder what kind of bruises the poor girl is hiding beneath her clothes.* Maggie could only imagine. *Poor girl—disowned by her mother and far away from her family. I'll do what I can for her,* she resolved silently. She thought of her own daughter and what she would do to protect her if her husband were abusive. She had half a mind to call Francis's parents and tell them what was going on, but she didn't, for fear of making the situation worse.

The midday sun beat down on Francis as she trudged home, exhausted. If only she could magically change Mike back to the person she had fallen in love with. She couldn't get her mind off of the lipstick stains on Mike's shirts, and mental images of him with Cheryl tortured her. She didn't dare confront him, and she certainly didn't dare talk to him about marriage counseling, for fear that would spark another rage.

I will just have to try harder to be a good wife, she resolved, thankful that he didn't touch the kids. Of course, they were asleep by the time he came home, and by the time they woke up in the morning, he was sober again. He didn't abuse her when he was sober, either.

He's basically a good man. He just needs to keep away from the booze, she told herself for the hundredth time.

"I'm home!" Francis called as she slipped through the door.

"Mommy!" Brad ran to her, and she scooped him up for a hug. Chantel sat on the floor with arms outstretched. Francis set Brad down and picked Chantel up for a hug.

"Daddy has a headache," Brad said. Mike was lying down on the couch, watching TV. "So we have to be quiet."

"I see," Francis responded as she put Chantel down beside her toys. She washed her hands and started preparing lunch. *No wonder Mike has a headache,* she thought. *After staying out extra late last night, he was wasted. It's a miracle he could even get out of bed this morning.* She swallowed her growing bitterness. It wouldn't help for her to turn bitter.

"Can I help?" Brad asked. He had turned three last spring, and he loved to help her.

"Wash your hands, and you can set the table," Francis responded, emptying a can of mushroom soup into a pot. Mike didn't start lunch after a night at the bar, and she didn't dare mention it.

Brad returned from washing his hands, and Francis gave him a couple of bowls to set on the table.

"Go tell Daddy lunch is ready," Francis told him. Brad ran off to get his dad while Francis lifted Chantel into the high chair.

"Hi." Mike looked disheveled as he dragged himself into the kitchen. "How was work?"

"Busy," she responded, scooping soup into the children's bowls.

"Don't know if I can go to work today. I've got a bad headache."

Francis blew on the soup for Brad and then placed the bowl in front of him. She started feeding Chantel. They couldn't afford for Mike to stay home from work because of his drinking, which was already taking a large chunk out of their meager budget.

"I see," she responded when she saw the irritable look in Mike's eyes.

"I could use a little bit of understanding here," Mike said. Francis absently touched her sore shoulder. Mike glowered at her, and she dropped her hand. He had stopped apologizing for his abusive behavior.

"You don't have it so bad," he growled. "I'm a good provider for you and the kids. Don't you have a roof over your heads and food on the table?"

"Mike, please," Francis implored, glancing at Brad, who was busy eating his soup. "If you have to stay home because you're sick, then so be it. Have you taken some aspirin yet?"

"No, I don't like taking pills," he responded sullenly.

"Let me get you some." Francis got up from the table. "You'll probably feel much better soon."

To her surprise, Mike took the pills and went to work. After cleaning up from lunch, she put the kids down for a nap and went to lie down on her bed. She was exhausted. She couldn't sleep when Mike was out, and last night, he finally had gotten home at two o'clock in the morning. He had been in a foul mood and hit her again. At four thirty in the morning, she had been barely able to drag herself out of bed. She couldn't afford to stay home from work. As it was, she had a hard time scraping up enough money for her family's basic needs.

Francis woke up to a knocking sound. She sat up and shook

her head. Where was she? Hearing another knock, Francis realized someone was at the door. She got out of bed and quickly walked down the hall. *I hope this doesn't wake up the kids!* She opened the door and was immediately engulfed in her father's arms. Emotions welled up in Francis's chest and spilled over as tears onto her father's immaculate blue shirt.

"Francis, what's wrong?" her father asked, patting her back as he held her close.

"Nothing." Francis pulled back, wiping at her eyes. "I was just sleeping, and this is such a surprise." She pulled him in and shut the door. "I'm so happy you came. It's been a long time since I've heard from anyone back home." Her tone was wistful.

"I'm in town on business and just finished my last meeting, so I have the rest of the day to spend with you." He smiled as she invited him into the living room. He sat down on the couch and looked around. "Where are the babies?" he asked.

"They're still sleeping. Can I get you a cup of coffee or tea? Or do you prefer iced tea?"

"I'll have a glass of iced tea, please."

Francis poured two tall glasses of iced tea, added ice cubes from the freezer, and joined Father in the living room.

"So how is everyone?" Francis asked.

"Mother is as busy as always with her social functions. Ted got honors in med school last semester. He is currently on tour in Europe. Jim is thinking of going to law school after he graduates," Father said, filling her in.

"But he still has a couple of years in high school, right?"

"Yes, he has another two years. For now, he is running around with his friends, going to parties, and golfing. Monica is away at summer basketball camp."

Francis noticed Father spoke with a lot of pride. "It's good to catch up on family, even though it makes me miss them more," Francis admitted, sipping the icy liquid. *Wow,* she thought to herself. *A trip to Europe, while I'm struggling just to survive.*

"You should bring the children and come visit," Father said.

"Really?" Francis said. "Would Mother allow Mike in the house?"

"I'm working on her." Father's eyes looked a bit sad, and Francis's face fell. For a moment, she'd thought maybe Mother had had a change of heart. "You and the kids could come," he said.

Brad came into the room, rubbing his eyes as he climbed onto Francis's lap. She bit her lip and told herself to enjoy this time with Father and not waste time wishing for things that weren't meant to be.

"Did you have a good nap?" Francis asked as she cuddled Brad close to her.

"Hey, buddy." Father dug into his pocket and came up with a roll of fruit-flavored Life Savers candy. "Come sit with Grandpa, and let's see what's in here."

Brad looked at the candy and then back at Grandpa.

Father held the roll out to him and smiled. "Come here, Brad, and let's see what Grandpa has for you."

Brad hesitated for a bit, but it didn't take long until the candy won him over.

"You are getting to be such a big boy!" Father exclaimed, lifting him up onto his lap. "How old are you, Brad?"

Brad held up three pudgy fingers.

"Three already!" Father exclaimed. He took a piece of candy from the wrapper and handed it to Brad. Chantel started fussing, so Francis went to the children's bedroom and picked her up. On her way back, she stopped in the kitchen to fix a bottle.

When she came back into the living room, Father and Brad were sitting on the floor, playing with Brad's fire truck. She sat down on her rocking chair and watched them play while she fed Chantel her bottle.

"What time does Mike get off work?" Father asked, getting up from the floor. "I want to take you all out for supper."

"He gets off of work at ten," Francis answered. "He starts at two in the afternoon."

"Then I guess it's just the four of us." Father sat down on the couch.

"We're going to a restaurant?" Brad stood up, his toys forgotten. "Can I have ice cream?"

Father laughed as he tousled Brad's hair. "If you want ice cream, you can have ice cream."

"Only if you eat your supper," Francis said, "but first, we have to get you cleaned up."

Francis washed the children and dressed them in clean clothes. She took great care in dressing herself so Father wouldn't see the bruises and put on a little makeup so she'd look less tired. She had to be careful how she dressed these days, which was a pain since the weather was hot.

Father took them to an upscale family restaurant on the other side of town. Francis allowed herself to relax in the pleasant surroundings and enjoy the excellent food and service. Brad and Chantel behaved surprisingly well. Brad kept busy with the pictures and crayons the waitress brought for him.

After they finished their meal, they took the children to the park. Brad showed no fear as he tried everything the playground had to offer, while Chantel enjoyed swinging in the child safety swing.

When they got home, Francis bathed the children and put them to bed. They were tired from their exciting evening out. When the children were settled, Francis fixed two tall glasses of iced tea, handed one to Father, and sat down in her rocking chair across from where Father sat on the couch.

"Now that I've told you everything that's happening back home, tell me about yourself," Father said, sipping his iced tea. "How are you doing? Can I help you out with anything?"

"We're doing just fine," Francis lied, keeping her eyes on the glass of iced tea in her hands. "I still have my waitress job in the mornings, and Mike works evenings. It works well for us."

"You look exhausted," Father said. "You're not sick, are you?"

"No, not at all," Francis replied, looking up and meeting his gaze. "The kids are growing so fast I can hardly keep up with them."

Father relaxed back into the couch and told her what wonderful kids she had. They talked for a while longer before Father said he had to leave.

"I have an uneasy feeling that something is amiss here," he said as he reached for the doorknob. "Are you sure everything's fine?"

"Oh yes, absolutely," Francis assured him with what she hoped was a convincing smile. "Thank you so much for stopping in today. It was so good to see you again." She gave him a hug and winced when he hugged her back.

"I had a very good time with you and the children." He studied her face. "Tell Mike I'm sorry I missed him, and you take care."

After Father left, Francis sat in her rocking chair for a long time, thinking of her childhood, her family, and the life she had left for Mike. She wondered what Father and the rest of her family would do if they knew about the abuse. They would drag Mike through the courts and destroy their marriage. She couldn't let that happen.

Did my family see something in Mike that my love for him made me too blind to see? The thought flitted through Francis's mind.

CHAPTER 10

The heat of summer turned into cooler days and the glorious array of red, yellow, and orange colors of fall. The days were shorter, and the nights were nippy. Long hours spent canning fruits and vegetables were over; the shelves in their cold storage were lined with jars of canned preserves. Papa and David had finished combining and working the fields in preparation for winter.

On an exceptionally warm day, when autumn defiantly challenged the onslaught of winter, Mary took her homework outside to her favorite spot on the green grass. Her concentration was soon broken when David plopped down beside her.

"What's up?" Mary asked. David had been unusually quiet lately.

David selected a blade of grass and pulled it from the ground. "Nothing, really." He shrugged, smoothing out the blade between his fingers.

"You look like you have something on your mind," Mary said, noting the way he was studying the blade of grass as if it had the answers to all of life's questions.

"Well, the Grace Gospel Church is having revival meetings next weekend, and some of the guys are going. They asked John and me to go with them. I don't know. I've never been at one of their church services, just their youth group activities."

"Does John want to go?" Mary asked, putting down her books.

David raised an eyebrow as he grinned at Mary with a knowing twinkle in his eyes. "Interested in John, are we?" he teased, and then he added before she could rebut, "John would go if I go."

"Have you asked Papa if you can go?"

"No, I don't know if he would allow it."

"Well, you're obviously struggling with the decision, so why don't you ask Papa first? If he allows you to go, then go, and if he doesn't, then don't. Then you'll have your answer."

"That's a good idea," David said. "That's what I'll do. Why didn't I think of that?" He gave his head a shake as he pushed himself up onto his feet.

"Because you're not a girl," Mary said, laughing at him.

"Humph." David made a playful jab at her before jogging off to the barn to find Papa.

David and John had been attending youth group meetings and activities at the Grace Gospel Church for a while now. Although it was also a Mennonite denomination, the Grace Gospel Church was less traditional. They had Bible studies and fun events for teenagers. Even though most parents at Mary's church strictly forbade their children to attend other denominations, Mama and Papa allowed David to go. Mary often heard Papa speak to their pastors about instituting church activities for youth. She knew Papa was frustrated that outside of attending church services and Sunday school, there was no effort made to reach out to the younger generation.

Her studies forgotten, Mary gazed off into the distance as her mind pondered. In numerous Christian novels, she had read about people getting saved. It wasn't something that was spoken about freely in their church, so she wasn't sure what to think about it. She didn't feel she knew enough about it to make a decision. Since David had started attending the youth group, Papa had allowed them to subscribe to a Christian youth magazine. Mary found the stories interesting, and she always read the magazine from cover to cover. The stories were usually about people who didn't know there was a God and never went to church. When they heard about Jesus, they got saved. Mary believed in God and Jesus and attended church regularly, so she figured getting saved probably wasn't for her.

 Mary shivered as she broke out of her reverie. She gathered her books and went into the house to finish her homework.

Francis removed her sweater and slung it over her arm as she walked to the medical clinic after work. It had warmed up nicely since that morning. The leaves crunched under her feet as she took the shortcut across the park. She hardly heard the children laughing and calling to each other as their mothers pushed them on swings or caught them at the bottom of the slides.

 She was nervous. She hadn't told Mike about this appointment. She'd decided it was better to be sure first. She pushed open the glass door of the clinic, and the smell of antiseptic assailed her nostrils. The petite blonde receptionist smiled up at her.

 "Francis Webber," Francis announced quietly. "I have a one o'clock appointment to see Dr. Scott."

 The receptionist put a check mark beside Francis's name in the appointment book. "Have a seat in the waiting area," she said, smiling.

 Francis sat down to wait; she hoped it wouldn't take long. She had told Mike she had to work late today, so he wouldn't expect her home for another hour. She hoped he would make lunch for the children. She picked up a *Reader's Digest* and flipped through it absently.

 "Francis?" a nurse called. Francis stood up and followed her into a small laboratory.

 "I understand you're here for a pregnancy test." The nurse smiled at Francis.

 "Yes, that's right," Francis said nervously.

"We'll run some tests, and you'll know soon enough." She handed Francis a small plastic cup and showed her to the washroom. After the nurse measured her height and weighed her, she took Francis into a small examining room.

"Take a seat in here." The nurse smiled pleasantly. "Dr. Scott will just be a few minutes."

Francis let her eyes roam the room. An examining table stood against a wall that sported a chart showing the muscles within the human body. Another chart showed a fetus in its mother's womb. Francis put her hands protectively over her abdomen. Was there really a new life starting in there?

"Good afternoon." A middle-aged man with graying hair stepped into the room. He smiled kindly as he shook Francis's hand. "I haven't seen you here in a while. How are you?"

"I'm fine," Francis answered, nervously picking at her nails. "I think I might be pregnant," she blurted out.

"Well, I'm very happy to inform you that you are indeed pregnant." Dr. Scott smiled. "Congratulations! I took the liberty of checking your test results already."

"Thanks," Francis replied, her hands once more fluttering to her abdomen.

"Now, if you'll hop up onto the examining table, we'll get you checked out," Dr. Scott said.

Francis removed her shoes and climbed up onto the examining table. Dr. Scott checked her vital signs and then asked her to lie down so he could feel her tummy.

"It will be too soon to hear a heartbeat," he told her, "but we'll see if we can feel the little one in there. How many children do you have, Francis?"

"Two," Francis responded. "Brad is three, and Chantel is eleven months."

"Perfect." The doctor nodded as he gently probed her abdomen. "You have a bruise on your right side here. Can you tell me what happened?" he asked.

Francis closed her eyes. She had hoped he wouldn't notice. "I bumped into the corner of the table," she said.

The doctor raised his eyebrows. "Well, then you will have to be more careful. Everything seems to be normal." He held out a hand to help Francis sit up and then turned and sat down at his desk. "Start taking prenatal vitamins to keep your strength up, and be sure to make an appointment to come see me in a month," the doctor advised before she left.

Francis stepped into the bright sun, and a breeze made her skirt flutter. She was apprehensive about this pregnancy.

How will I tell Mike? she wondered. They had not planned on having another baby this soon.

She hurried along; she didn't want to be any later than she had to. No matter how hard she tried to be a good wife and mother, Mike always found fault, and she would find herself on the receiving end of his terrible temper. She climbed the stairs to their apartment and opened the door, a little out of breath.

"It's about time," Mike said, glowering at her.

"I told you yesterday that I had to work late today," Francis responded.

"Well, you know I can't be late for work," he rumbled, reaching for the car keys. He always took the car when he stayed out late.

"Mike, please come home after work," Francis pleaded. "We need to talk."

"Don't I always come home after work?" he asked, raising an eyebrow at her.

"You know what I mean," she replied as Mike went out, slamming the door behind him.

Francis picked Chantel up from where she was sitting on the floor. Soft blonde curls framed her cherubic face. Francis gave her a quick hug and set her on her high chair. She went to the cupboard and got a jar of baby food.

"Brad, honey, where are you?" she called.

"Mommy!" Brad cried as he came barreling into the kitchen

to give her a hug. "I was playing with my trucks. I didn't hear you come home."

"Did you finish your lunch?" she asked, hugging him back.

"Yeah, Daddy made pizza." His blue eyes sparkled.

"So I see," Francis said, picking up a piece. "It looks yummy."

"It is," Brad answered. "I ate two pieces. Daddy said if I eat that much, soon I'll be big like him." He puffed his little chest out.

"Whoa there," Francis replied, tousling his hair. "Don't grow up too fast."

She spent the day doing laundry and playing with the kids. She felt exhausted, so when Chantel took a nap, she found a kids' show for Brad and napped on the couch while he watched TV. When Chantel woke up, Francis took the children to the park. She swung Chantel in the baby swing while keeping an eye on Brad, who was playing on the slide. She wondered if the tiny life forming in her womb was a boy or a girl.

Francis noticed a young woman, probably her own age, watching the children play from one of the benches. She seemed sad, so while Brad and Chantel played in the sandbox, Francis went over and sat down beside her.

"Hi," she said. "I'm Francis. I haven't noticed you here before."

"Hi. I'm Gloria." The young lady smiled up at her. Her thick midnight-black hair hung in curls down past her shoulders. Her soft chocolate-brown eyes spoke of deep sadness.

"I usually don't come here, but I was passing by today and saw the children playing, so I stopped to watch them. I guess you could say I was having a pity party." She smiled again, and Francis noticed the red rims around her eyes.

"Anything you want to share?" Francis asked. "Sometimes talking to a stranger helps."

"I just came from the clinic, and the doctor confirmed what we've suspected for a long time." She dabbed at her eyes with a tissue. "I am unable to bear children." Her voice caught.

Grace for Tomorrow

"Oh, I'm so sorry." Francis took her hand, thinking of her own little one just starting to form in her womb.

"Richard and I have been married five years, and we wanted to start a family right away. When it didn't happen, we finally resorted to a bunch of tests. I just got the results from my doctor today." She bit her lip. "We will never have our own children."

"Maybe you should get a second opinion," Francis said, trying to hold out some hope.

"I don't think I want to go through all that again." Gloria gave a tired sigh and then added wistfully, "God must have other plans for us. I just wish I knew what they were."

Gloria took her leave, and Francis gathered up her own children to go home. Brad ran ahead, pointing out the birds in the trees, as Francis pushed Chantel along in her rickety stroller.

The thought of Gloria caused her to chide herself. *Here I've been anxious all day, wondering how we will support a third child on our meager finances, while Gloria will never know what it is like to hold her own flesh-and-blood child in her arms.*

Francis determined that she would take things as they came and count her blessings. Somehow, everything would work out.

"Mary, wait up!" Lena called at the end of gym class. Mary waited at the end of the soccer field for her friend to catch up.

"What's up?" Mary asked when her friend fell into step beside her.

"Have you heard about the revival meetings this weekend?" Lena was still a little out of breath.

"Yes, I have," Mary said. "Why do you ask?"

Lena glanced over her shoulder to make sure nobody was close enough to hear her. "Papa and Mama want to go." Her voice was just above a whisper.

"Really?" Mary stopped in her tracks. "Your parents?"

"I know!" Lena exclaimed. "Papa's sister attends that church, so she told Mama and Papa about it. Apparently, the speaker is a long-lost friend of theirs."

"Have you ever been there before?" Mary asked as she started walking again.

"No, I haven't," Lena said. "I'm a bit nervous because I don't know what to expect."

"David is going as well," Mary said. She pulled at the glass door and stepped back to allow Lena to enter ahead of her.

"Your parents allow that?" Lena asked as they entered the spacious foyer.

"Papa gave his permission. You know David's been attending some of their youth group functions."

"Oh yeah. I hadn't thought of that."

"Come on, girls—hustle!" Miss Payden called as they entered the gym.

Mary and Lena picked up the pace, joining their classmates in the gym's locker rooms.

CHAPTER 11

After the children were in bed for the night, Francis made a cup of tea and snuggled up on the couch with a blanket and a book, tuning out the hum of traffic on the street below. A steady rhythm of raindrops spat against the windowpane. Unable to concentrate on her book, she glanced at the wall clock again.

I hope Mike will come straight home from work tonight. She got up and walked over to the window. Pulling back the curtain, she gazed out onto the street. Streetlights reflected in the puddles and then disappeared momentarily as cars splashed through them. A lone pedestrian hurried through the drizzling rain. She would tell Mike about the baby when he got home. She took a deep breath, trying to calm the fluttering of apprehension in her chest.

Maybe the baby will bring him to his senses, and he'll be himself again, she told herself, trying to stay positive.

She let the curtain fall back into place. She walked down the hall, peeked in on her sleeping children, and then went into her bedroom to change into her nightgown. Wrapping a blanket around herself, she went back to the living room and picked up her book. She tried hard to concentrate on the story, but sometimes she found herself having to reread a page or two. As the clock ticked toward midnight, her apprehension grew into a tight knot in her stomach.

Just past midnight, keys turned the door lock, and Mike

stumbled in. Francis could tell he'd been drinking, and she swallowed the fear that welled up inside her.

He's often home later than this, she reminded herself, willing her racing heart to calm down. She waited until he had removed his shoes and jacket.

"Come sit with me," Francis said, laying her book aside. "We need to talk."

Giving her a quizzical look, he sat in the chair across from her. "What do you want?" he asked sullenly. "I'm tired, and I want to go to bed, so make it quick." Francis noticed the emptiness in Mike's eyes, as if his soul had left him.

"I went to see the doctor today," she blurted out, her fingers nervously picking at the blanket.

"What for?" he asked, his eyes narrowing.

"We're going to have a baby," she said softly. "I'm pregnant."

Shock registered in his eyes. "You can't be serious." A look of sheer panic crossed his face. "Francis, we can't afford another kid."

"I know it'll be tough, but we'll handle it. We'll make do."

"Make do nothing!" Mike exploded, moving to the edge of the chair. "What are you thinking? We already have two kids we can't afford!" His voice continued to rise as it increased in volume. "How do you think we'll support another one?"

"Mike, please, we can make it," she said, reaching out to touch his arm. "We always have. I'll work as long as I possibly can and go back as soon as possible after the baby's born." She didn't dare mention that it would help if he stopped drinking.

Mike shot out of his chair and grabbed the front of her nightgown, pulling her to her feet as the blanket dropped to the floor in a heap. "You are not going to ruin my life, sweetheart," he snarled, pulling her up against his chest. He smelled of alcohol and perfume. It made her sick to her stomach. "You want another baby? You take care of it!" he shouted in her face, grabbing her shoulders. "You're not going to trap me with your little schemes."

"Mike, stop—you're pulling my hair," she whimpered.

The punch to the side of her head sent her sprawling, and her head hit the rocking chair. She screamed as he landed a kick in her right side and another in her back. He yanked her up by her hair. Totally out of control, his eyes blazing, he punched her over and over, releasing his pent-up fury on her. Blackness engulfed her.

Francis slowly made her way out of the dark fog. She tried to open her eyes, but her eyelids felt thick and heavy. The bed was too hard. She rolled over to find a more comfortable position, and a sharp pain shot through her abdomen. Instinctively, she curled her legs up to her tummy. They felt wet and sticky. Her head throbbed, and her body ached. She forced her eyelids open and realized she was lying on the floor. *Mike.* Slowly, she turned her head and searched the room for him as memories flooded back. He wasn't there.

Where is he? she wondered. She pulled herself up into a sitting position but immediately doubled over and clutched her abdomen. She felt as if a vise clasped her midsection in its grip.

No! Oh God, no! Not my baby! A sob caught in her throat as she realized what was happening. She clutched her abdomen and doubled over with another searing contraction.

No! Francis cried silently. *Please, no!* Tears poured down her face. A sharp pain stabbed through her breaking heart. Her unborn baby had fallen victim to her daddy's rage. The tiny life had been snuffed out almost before it began.

How could Mike do this to me? To us? Sobs wracked her body as she half sat and half lay on the floor with her head propped up on the side of the couch.

Darkness enveloped her again. She didn't know how long she lay there. When she woke up, the awful pains had subsided. Another thought registered in her foggy brain: *I can't let the kids see me like this.* Slowly and painfully, she got up on her knees. Grasping the couch for support, she rose to her feet. She clutched the back of her rocking chair to wait out the momentary dizziness that swept over her.

Francis hobbled to the bathroom. Delicately, she removed her soiled clothes, stepped into the shower, and let the warm water wash over her aching body as her tears kept a steady stream down her face.

Taking care not to trip on the tub, she stepped out of the shower, wrapped herself in a big towel, and examined herself in the mirror. Her eyes were swollen, and she had bruises on her face and body, but as far as she could tell, she didn't have any broken bones.

She wrapped her bathrobe around herself and then gathered some rags and shuffled back to the living room to clean up the floor. After throwing the rags into the garbage, she hobbled into the children's bedroom. She pulled Brad's blanket up to his chin and then did the same for Chantel, softly brushing the hair back from their angelic faces.

They must never know, she vowed. *They must never know what their daddy is capable of.*

Tears fell onto Chantel's bed, and Francis quickly wiped them away. She turned, quietly slipped into her bedroom, and lay down on the bed. Mike wasn't there. She wondered where he was. She fell asleep only to wake up a few minutes later. She turned over onto her other side.

She was walking to work, when a dark figure jumped out of the back alley and ran toward her, wielding an ax over his head. She tried to run, but her feet wouldn't move. As the ax came down on her, she yelled and woke up with a start. Her heart was pounding, and her body was wet with perspiration. She was relieved that it was just a nightmare. As her memories came back to her, though, she wasn't sure if the nightmare in her sleep was worse than the one she was living. She untangled the bedsheets from her legs and lay back on her pillow.

When her alarm rang, she knew she couldn't go to work. She called in sick and slept some more.

"Daddy?" Francis woke up to Brad's call. Her bedroom door opened, and Brad came shuffling into the room, holding his teddy bear in one arm and dragging his blanket behind him.

"Mommy, is it Sunday?" he asked, confused at seeing her in bed.

"No, honey, it's not Sunday," she answered. "Mommy's not going to work today."

"Why do your eyes look all funny?" Brad asked, climbing into bed.

"I fell and hurt my eyes." Francis pulled him close, closing her eyes. Her head throbbed, and it was hard to keep her eyes open. Her whole body hurt, but the physical pain did not compare to the deep ache in her heart over the loss of her unborn child and the shambles of her marriage.

"Where's Daddy?" Brad asked, snuggling close.

"I don't know. Maybe he went to work early." She kissed his forehead. She had no idea where Mike was.

"I'm hungry," Brad said after a while.

"Well then, let's go make us some breakfast," Francis responded, wondering how she could do this. Brad slid out of Mike's side of the bed, and Francis sat up gingerly. As she stood, her head swam, and she grabbed on to the dresser.

Pull yourself together, she told herself. *You can't faint. You have to take care of the kids.*

When the dizziness passed, she put on her housecoat and shuffled to the bathroom. She was glad the flow had slowed down. She hobbled to the kitchen and got out some Corn Flakes and milk. She made a bowl for Brad and another one for herself. Her jaw ached. When Chantel woke up, Francis shuffled to her bedroom to get her. She gasped at the pain that shot through her body when she picked Chantel up.

Mind over matter, she told herself. *You can do this!*

She carefully made her way back to the kitchen and set Chantel on her high chair. After breakfast, the children played in their pajamas while she rested on the couch, watching them. She didn't have the energy to dress them. She dozed on and off throughout the morning.

"Mommy, I'm hungry." Brad looked up from the floor, where he was playing with Chantel.

Francis looked at the clock on the wall: 12:35.

"Okay, Brad, I'll get us something to eat." Francis gingerly got up from the couch, clutching the back of the chair until the dizziness subsided. Then she went into the kitchen and emptied a can of chicken noodle soup and water into a saucepan. They would have soup and crackers. She didn't have the energy for anything else.

I wonder where Mike went and when he'll be back.

It wasn't like him to be gone in the morning and not be home for lunch either.

When the children took their afternoon nap, Francis went to her bedroom to lie down. That was when she noticed that the closet door was open. Mike's clothes were gone.

Francis gaped at the empty closet. Waves of unbelief coursed through her. She checked his dresser drawers. They were empty. She lay down on her bed, curled up into the fetal position, and let the tears flow silently down her face.

Francis called in sick the next day as well. There was nothing else she could do. Her marriage was over, her body was sore, her heart was broken, and her emotions were raw.

She needed time to allow her body to heal itself, as it surely would. Her heart was another matter. She wasn't sure the painful void in her chest would ever go away. Her children were her only consolation. She had to stay strong for them. When Brad asked for his daddy, she told him he had gone away for a while. How could she take care of her children and work at the same time?

What will I do? She racked her brain, but in her weakened condition, she couldn't come up with a plausible answer.

That afternoon there was a knock on her door, and for a moment, Francis froze in fear.

Mike? she thought. Then she relaxed. *Mike wouldn't knock,* she told herself as she went to the door.

"Maggie!" Francis exclaimed when she saw her friend standing there.

"My dear girl!" Maggie gasped at the sight of Francis. Both eyes were swollen and turning a dark blue with some purple around the edges, her lip was cracked, and she had an ugly bruise on the side of her face.

Francis reached out and pulled Maggie in. She didn't want a scene in the hallway. She invited Maggie to sit at the kitchen table while she poured them each a cup of tea.

"What happened to you?" Maggie asked as she took a seat at the table.

"It's a long story." Francis sighed, setting two cups of tea on the table. It was good to see a friendly face. "I don't know what to do. How can I go to work when I have two small children to take care of?"

"Where are the children?" Maggie asked. Toys were scattered everywhere, but there were no children in sight. Dishes were piled up on the cupboard.

"They're taking a nap," Francis answered, gingerly lowering herself onto a chair.

Maggie reached out and took Francis's hand. "Francis, listen to me." She waited until Francis looked at her. "I'm here to help you. I know Mike has been abusing you, and it's obviously getting worse. I want you to pack up some clothes for yourself and the kids, and I will take you home with me. You cannot continue to stay here under these conditions. You have to be out of here by the time Mike comes home from work."

"Mike left," Francis mumbled, still finding it hard to believe their marriage had come to this. "He got angry with me a couple of days ago, and he took all his clothes and left." Tears started trickling down her cheeks.

Maggie put her arms around Francis and let her cry. Francis wept long and hard. She wept for the baby she would never meet. She wept for her two children, who deserved a better life. She wept for her broken marriage.

Maggie grabbed a box of tissues off the counter and handed some to Francis.

"I want you to tell me everything," she said. "I want you to stop making excuses and tell me the truth. I'm serious. I want to help you, and I can't help you unless you tell me what's really going on."

Francis felt the weight on her shoulders lift a tiny bit. How long had it been since anyone helped her? It seemed she always had to be the strong one. Maybe Maggie would be able to help her figure out how to go back to work and still care for her children. Her world was spinning, and she couldn't make decisions.

Little by little, Francis told Maggie about the staying out late, the alcohol, the perfume, the lipstick stains, and the months of escalating abuse. At times, she cried for a while before she went on. Maggie listened in stunned silence as the story unfolded to the point where her stomach threatened to be physically sick. She tried hard not to let it show. It was important to let Francis talk about it. Then Francis delivered the ultimate bombshell: Mike had beaten her and left her the night she told him they were expecting their third child.

"You're pregnant?" Maggie gasped.

Francis dropped her face into her hands and sobbed as she shook her head. It was awhile before she was able to wrench the words out of her heart and let them spill over her lips. "Not anymore," she cried brokenly.

Maggie gathered the sobbing woman in her arms as the tears ran down her own face. Her heart broke for her young friend. She had suspected abuse, but this was beyond any of her fearful imaginations. By the time the sobbing subsided, Maggie had reached a decision.

"The morning after he beat me, I didn't know where Mike was, but then I saw he had taken all his clothes." Francis dabbed at her swollen eyes with a tissue. "I haven't heard from him since."

Maggie breathed a silent prayer for wisdom and then took control of the situation.

"When the children wake up, you are coming home with me," Maggie told Francis gently but with authority. "You have to get out of here in case Mike returns; plus, you can't properly take care of the kids right now. You need someone to take care of you."

"Maybe that would be best," Francis conceded, wringing the soggy tissue in her hands. "I'm having a hard time coping right now."

Maggie helped Francis pack clothes for herself and the children. She felt a sense of urgency to get Francis and the children to a safe place. She tried hard not to think of what would happen if Mike came back before they were gone. Once they were safe, they could figure out what to do from there. First of all, Francis needed to see a doctor.

The louse! Maggie stormed inwardly. *I can't believe a husband can do this to his wife!*

Maggie called her husband, Dale. Briefly, she told him what had happened and asked him to come pick them up as soon as the children finished their naps. Next, she called the medical clinic and made an appointment for Francis to see Dr. Scott later that afternoon.

Francis went along with Maggie's suggestions. Hurt, confused, and unable to think straight, she allowed Maggie to take over. However, she balked at going to the doctor.

"I don't need to see the doctor," she told Maggie. "I don't have any broken bones, and my bruises will heal on their own."

"You need to go for your children's sake," Maggie insisted.

"You need to get well as quickly as possible so you can take care of their needs."

Francis capitulated. "It's going to be really awkward, though."

"He's a doctor. He's probably seen worse," Maggie said, although she couldn't really think of anything worse herself.

When the children woke up, Francis explained to them that they were going to go to Auntie Maggie's house while Maggie called for Dale to come pick them up.

Dale was sympathetic and kind, a jovial man with a round face and graying hair. He had a heart condition that didn't allow him to work, so he was at home all day while Maggie worked her shift at the restaurant. Brad and Chantel took to him right away.

Maggie showed her to the room that used to be her daughter's. The children would share her son's room. Patrick was a truck driver in the oil fields up north and wasn't home much. Dale brought out some toys left behind by their two grown children and volunteered to stay with the children while Maggie took Francis to the doctor's clinic. When they left, Dale was already sitting on the floor, playing cars and trucks with Brad while holding Chantel.

Dr. Scott was professional while he examined Francis extensively.

"You've lost a lot of blood," the doctor told Francis, "and you may have internal injuries as well. It's hard to tell. I'd like to keep you in the hospital a couple of days for observation."

"I can't stay in the hospital," Francis objected. "I have to stay with my kids. I'm all they've got. Maggie and Dale are strangers to them. I don't want to make this anymore traumatic for them than it already is."

"You have a point," the doctor said. "Will you promise to stay off your feet for a couple of days then?"

"I'll do my best," Francis said. "I hate to be a burden on the Pitmans, though."

"If you have any unusual symptoms, I want you to come to emergency immediately." He wrote a prescription and told her what to watch for. "The other thing to discuss is notifying the police." Dr. Scott looked at Francis seriously. "I advise you to press charges against Mike. I can testify to your miscarriage and injuries."

"I don't want to do that." Francis shook her head.

"At the very least, you should get a restraining order against him," the doctor said. "What he did to you is a crime. I don't want him to have the chance for a repeat performance. Next time, it might be the kids."

Francis shook her head. "Mike loves the kids. He'd never hurt them."

Didn't Mike love you too? She pushed back the thought that sprang into her mind. It was too painful to contemplate.

"Francis, he caused your miscarriage."

She winced inwardly at the doctor's solemn reminder. "I'll think about it," she promised.

"Take these pills." Dr. Scott handed her the prescription. "And I want to see you again in a week."

Francis thanked him and went to find Maggie, who was waiting for her in the lobby.

That evening, after Maggie had bathed the children, Brad came running into Francis's room with a children's storybook in his hands. Chantel came crawling behind him. Brad climbed into her bed, and Francis reached down and lifted Chantel up into her bed as well. She cuddled both her children close as she read to them.

The story was about a boy with five loaves and two fish, which he gave to Jesus's disciples, and in some miraculous way, Jesus fed a whole bunch of people. Francis found the story interesting.

As a child, she had attended a large, beautiful, elegant church with her parents and siblings. But that was as far as her religious training went. She couldn't remember the Bible ever being read at their house. Attending church was more or less a requirement to ensure their good reputation.

Francis slipped out of bed long enough to tuck Brad and Chantel into their beds.

By the following Sunday, Francis was well on the road to recovery, so she and the children attended church with Dale and Maggie. It was a simple church, not fancy like her childhood church, but the people were friendly without being nosy. They assumed Francis and the children were relatives or friends who'd come to visit. Nobody set them straight. They sat together in the pew, and Francis enjoyed the beautiful hymns. The pastor had a message about birds—something about God not letting a sparrow fall without him knowing about it and about God loving people more than birds. He also said that God knew the number of hairs on every person's head. Francis found comfort in the message. There was something nice about a God who took care of sparrows and knew her intimately enough to know how many hairs she had on her head. There was more singing, and then the service was over. The pastor and his wife shook her hand after the service, welcoming her to their church and talking to her children.

During the week, Dale heard from a lady at church about a three-bedroom apartment available for rent in her apartment complex, which was just down the street from the Pitmans'. It was in a good neighborhood, had a park close by, and was within walking distance of the diner. Dale and Maggie sat down with Francis and talked to her about moving. They were reluctant for Francis to stay in her old apartment, in case Mike came back. At first, Francis was hesitant, but she agreed to go see the apartment with Dale, while Maggie stayed home with the children.

From the time they entered the building and went up the single flight of stairs to the second-story apartment, Francis fell in love with the place. It was newer than her current apartment, and the halls and stairwells were wider and brighter. The complex owner opened a door and waved her and Dale through. The entrance was small but bright and had a roomy closet. The dark mahogany kitchen cupboards were offset perfectly by bright yellow walls. Both the dining and living areas had large windows overlooking a spacious parking lot toward the rear of the building. The bedrooms and single bathroom were small but also had ample windows that brightened the rooms.

Francis asked the owner about rent and was surprised when he quoted her a price that was similar to what she paid for her current apartment. She told him she'd think about it.

"So what did you think of the apartment?" Dale asked as they walked back to the Pitmans' house.

"I like it," Francis admitted. "It's newer and brighter than my apartment. I just don't know how I would move all my stuff."

"I'm pretty sure if I asked some of our church friends, they would be happy to move your things for you," Dale said.

"I couldn't impose on your friends," Francis said. "You've already done so much for me and the kids."

"Think about it," Dale said as they walked into the house. "If you want to move, there will be a way to do it."

That evening, Dale, Maggie, and Francis sat down and discussed the pros and cons of the move. Francis felt excited about the possibility. She was a bit nervous about going back to live in her apartment. What if Mike came back?

The following day, Francis called her current landlord, gave notice of her intent to move, called the new landlord, and signed a lease agreement. When Francis and the Pitmans were confident that she was well enough to take care of the children on her own, Dale announced the date of her impending move in church, and on that day, a handful of men showed up with pickup trucks to move her furniture and the boxes Francis and Maggie had packed.

Gladys Kent, the lady who'd told Dale and Maggie about the available apartment, offered to babysit Brad and Chantel while Francis was at work. Gladys was a cheerful middle-aged widow with graying brunette hair that she kept swept up in a bun at the back of her head. She was willing to alternate her time with the children between the two apartments. While the children slept, she would stay with them, but when they were awake, she would take them to her own apartment so she could get her work done.

Francis contacted her boss at the restaurant and was able to change her shift from the early shift to the 11:00 a.m. to 6:00 p.m. shift. This would give her time with her children in the morning and again in the evening.

"Mommy, come here!" Brad called excitedly from his bedroom after the moving crew had left.

"I'll be there in a minute." Francis was tired, and her back ached. It had been a long day. She finished transferring dishes from boxes into her cupboard and then went to Brad's room.

"Wow!" she exclaimed. "You did a good job, Brad. Your room looks very nice."

Brad beamed at her, proud of how he had organized his room. His teddy bears were all neatly lined up on a shelf, except for the one he always slept with. That one was lying on his bed. Francis made a mental note to make the beds. His cars and trucks were lined up on the floor in the far corner of his room.

"Mommy, can you tell Chantel to stay out of my room?" Brad looked up at her pleadingly. "She'll mess up all my toys."

Francis smiled and ruffled his hair. "Yes, she probably would," she said. Since Chantel had learned to crawl, Brad's toys were never safe. "You can close your door, and then Chantel won't be able to come in."

"Okay." Brad smiled. "She has her own room to play in now."

Francis went back to the boxes to find the bedding. She would make the beds before she started supper. It had been a long day, and she hoped to put the children to bed early.

Later that evening, Francis sat on her rocking chair, holding both Chantel and Brad on her lap. She read them one of their favorite storybooks.

"Mommy?" Brad's eyes were serious as he looked up into Francis's face. "Will Daddy come home now that we have a new apartment? Does Daddy know that we moved?"

Francis hugged both her children close as a fierce pain shot through her heart. She took a deep breath and swallowed the lump that rose in her throat.

"I know you both miss Daddy," she told her children softly. "No, Daddy doesn't know that we moved into this apartment, but when he phones, I'll tell him we moved. How's that?"

"Will he phone soon?" Brad asked.

"I don't know, Brad," she replied honestly, not knowing how much to tell her little boy. "We'll have to wait and see. Now"—she did her best to sound cheerful—"you go jump into your bed, or I'll come tickle you."

Brad slid off of her lap and started running while Francis, with Chantel on her arm, followed him to his bedroom.

After the children were in bed, Francis made herself a cup of tea and sat down at her kitchen table, laying out all her bills in front of her. She took a sheet of paper and began to prepare a budget for herself. With only one income, it would be a tight budget, but she hoped she'd be able to get by.

CHAPTER 12

"Mama, I'm going for a walk," Mary told her mother as she reached for her jacket on a Saturday afternoon. The weather was unseasonably warm for late October, and Mary felt a need to get out of the house and enjoy the weather. Soon enough, it would start to snow, and then the cold would force her to spend most of her time indoors. Already, most of the leaves had fallen off the trees, and they crunched beneath her shoes as she walked down the path past the barn and out to the barren fields. The naked poplar branches reached toward the sky, bracing for the cold weather that would surely come.

Mary ambled along the side of the tree line, stooping occasionally to pick up a pinecone or an exceptionally colored leaf from the ground. She would use them to make crafts during the long winter months.

As she came closer to David and John's log cabin tucked away in a cluster of tall green spruce trees, she noticed smoke rising from the chimney. Wondering who was at the cabin, she decided to check it out.

After tapping lightly on the door, she didn't wait for a response before lifting the latch and opening the door. Warm air enveloped her.

David looked up from the book that lay open on the table. "What are you doing here?"

"I went for a walk and noticed smoke coming out of the

chimney, so I thought I'd check it out," Mary explained. Sweeping her arm to include the book on the table, she asked, "What are you doing?"

David tipped his chair back, put his hands behind his head, and grinned. "I just needed a quiet place to study."

"Oh, well, then I'm sorry I disturbed you." Mary turned to go and then spun around as his words sank in. "Study?" she asked, surprised. "You?"

David chuckled. "Yes, me."

Mary stepped closer to the table and saw that the book open in front of David was a Bible. She raised her eyebrows as she looked quizzically at her brother. She had noticed a change in him lately that she couldn't figure out, but reading the Bible in his cabin? This was not like David.

"What's up?" she asked, curious.

"You might as well sit down." David sighed, waving his arm toward the only other chair in the room. "But before you do, would you please throw another chunk of wood in the heater?"

Mary took a piece of wood from the pile stacked haphazardly beside the door and threw it into the airtight heater in the middle of the room. Sparks shot up, and she quickly closed the lid. Then she pulled the wooden chair up to the table and sat down.

"You know those revival meetings I went to?" David asked.

"*Jo*, I remember."

"They made me think. I mean, Mama and Papa have taught us about God and how Jesus came to Earth, died on the cross, was buried, and then rose and ascended into heaven."

"*Jo*, I can't remember a time I didn't know that," Mary said.

"Me neither," David said. "I always thought I was doing all right. I tried to be good. I don't steal or swear. I try to get along with everyone. I've never killed anyone, or at least that's what I thought."

"You did what?"

"No, no." David laughed at Mary's incredulous expression. "I didn't physically kill anyone. But the speaker said that if we have anger in our heart toward someone—to God, that is the same as if we had killed that person. He said that everyone is born with a sinful nature and needs to ask God for forgiveness. He said that just believing that there is a God isn't enough. Satan also believes in God and trembles. God can't look at sin and therefore can't look at us—because we sin.

"That's why Jesus came to die for us. Jesus took all the sin of everyone in the whole world upon himself when he went to the cross. Therefore, when Jesus was nailed to the cross, all our sins were nailed to the cross with him. Remember when Jesus was on the cross and cried out, 'My God, my God, why hast thou forsaken me'? God could not look on Jesus, because although Jesus had never sinned himself, he was filled with sin at that point—my sin and your sin and everyone else's sin. God can't look on sin because he is holy. Jesus shed his blood for our sin, and that is the sacrifice that God requires. God requires each one of us to accept Jesus's sacrifice for ourselves, or we cannot be saved. When we ask God to forgive us for our sins and accept that Jesus paid for our sins by shedding his blood for them, then God forgives us, and we become his children."

"Wow!" Mary exclaimed. "I never thought of it that way."

"Neither did I," David said. "It just made so much sense when he explained it like that. The pastor quoted the Bible a lot, so now I'm looking some of the verses up myself." He shuffled through the pages of his Bible and put his finger on a verse. "Look at this, Mary. Here in Isaiah, I found a verse he quoted: 'But we are all as an unclean thing, and all our righteousnesses are as filthy rags.' That tells me that I can't get to heaven by just being good."

Mary leaned forward and read the verse for herself. "I thought God wants us to be good. If we can't be good enough, then how can we ever get to heaven?"

"That's exactly what one of the disciples asked Jesus. Here—I'll show you a verse in John." David leafed forward, searched for a while, and then pushed the book toward Mary again, his finger on a verse. "Read this."

Mary leaned over and read the verse: "Jesus saith unto him, I am the way, the truth, and the life: no man cometh unto the Father, but by me."

"Remember John 3:16: 'For God so loved the world, that he gave his only begotten son, that whosoever believeth in him should not perish, but have everlasting life'?" David quoted from memory.

"Yes, I remember that verse," Mary said. She had learned it in Sunday school.

David flipped a couple of pages back and said, "The verse after that continues, 'For God sent not his Son into the world to condemn the world; but that the world through him might be saved.'" David sat back in his chair. "God wants us to be good and obey him, but without Jesus, all our goodness is worth nothing. We cannot pay for our sins ourselves, because we are sinners. We have to start by accepting that Jesus paid for our sin with his blood. Jesus was the only one who could pay for our sins, because he's the only one who was perfect."

"Have you talked to Mama and Papa about this?" Mary asked.

"Jo," David answered. "Papa confirmed that it is all true and told me to read the Bible and study it so I would know for myself. He said that sometimes we cannot understand the Bible because we are not ready to understand, but when God opens our understanding, then it all makes sense."

"I guess I should start reading my Bible more," Mary said. "I didn't realize it was that interesting."

"Another thing," David said. "The pastor gave altar calls, and one evening, John and I both responded."

"Really?" Mary exclaimed. David was full of surprises today. "What happened?"

"I felt such a heavy burden in my heart that I needed to ask God to forgive my sins and to totally start trusting him for everything. John felt the same way, so we went to the front. There were counselors there who took us into the basement and talked with us individually and prayed with us. I accepted Jesus as my Savior."

Mary saw the sparkle in David's eyes. "I can tell that makes you very happy," she said.

"Yes, it does," David responded, smiling. "I feel joy and peace in my heart. I can't explain it." David closed his Bible and stood up. "Looks like the sun is going down. We should probably head home."

"Oh my!" Mary exclaimed. Standing up, she picked up the dried leaves and pinecones she had deposited on the table. "Guess I lost track of time. Mama will want me to help her make supper."

David checked to make sure the fire in the heater was out, and then he and Mary walked home together.

Chantel was crying again. Francis wearily opened her eyes and sat up in bed, swinging her legs over the edge. She groped around in the dark for her slippers and then made her way into Chantel's bedroom. This was the third time she had gotten up for Chantel tonight. She picked up the fussing baby from the crib and went into the kitchen to fix her a bottle. She was warm to the touch, so Francis gave her a baby aspirin as well.

Brad was never sick, even when he was teething, Francis thought to herself. *Chantel always seems to have either a cold or a fever or both.*

"I'll have to make an appointment to take you to the doctor," she told her baby as she sat down in the rocking chair to give her the bottle. Chantel only took a few sips and cried again, turning her head sideways.

"Don't you want your bottle?" Francis asked softly, repositioning Chantel and trying the bottle again. She drank some more but still fretted. Francis got up and paced the floor, humming a lullaby, and eventually, Chantel dozed off. Since Chantel was waking up so much, Francis took her to bed with her.

Maybe I'll be able to soothe her back to sleep when she whimpers, Francis thought. *I'm too exhausted to get up again tonight.*

The next morning, Francis called the clinic and then called Gladys.

"Good morning." Gladys's cheerful voice rang through the phone.

"Good morning, Gladys," Francis said. "I called to tell you that I'm taking Chantel to the doctor. She has a fever and didn't sleep well. Would you mind keeping Brad?"

"Oh, the poor thing," Gladys responded. "What time is your appointment?"

"It's at nine thirty," Francis answered.

"You pack up both of the children, and I'll give you a ride," Gladys said. "I'll meet you downstairs at nine fifteen."

"Oh, you don't need to do that," Francis said.

"How are you going to get to the clinic?" Gladys asked. "You can't carry Chantel that far."

"I thought of that," Francis admitted. "I could call a cab."

"Nonsense. I'll drive you," Gladys insisted. "What are neighbors for?"

Francis thanked Gladys, and they hung up. She sighed in relief as she set the receiver in its cradle. She didn't deserve a kind neighbor like Gladys, but she sure was thankful for her.

The doctor examined Chantel and determined she had bronchitis. He gave Francis a prescription, and Gladys drove them to the drugstore.

"I'll stay in the car with the children," she told Francis as they pulled up to the brick building.

"I'll be as quick as I can."

Francis hurried in to get the prescription filled. At the checkout counter, she counted her dollar bills. With tension mounting in her shoulders, she realized she didn't have enough. She was keenly aware that the man behind her was impatiently shifting from one foot to the other, and her face flushed with embarrassment as she emptied her change onto the counter. She carefully counted out the correct amount and handed it to the clerk, relieved that it covered the cost. The clerk offered a sympathetic smile as Francis grabbed her purchase and hurried out of the store, glad that Gladys hadn't witnessed her embarrassment.

Back at her apartment, Francis was surprised when Gladys followed her in.

"I'll stay here with the children today," Gladys said, addressing Francis's questioning look. "A sick child should be able to sleep in her own bed."

"Oh, you don't have to do that," Francis answered. "I'll stay home with the children today. I'll just call the restaurant and tell them I won't come in. I can't ask you to take care of a sick child."

"You didn't ask; I offered," Gladys said. "If you really want to stay home, that's up to you, but I really don't mind taking care of the children, even when they're sick."

"I don't know how to thank you." Francis hugged Gladys. "You do so much for me and the children. I really can't afford to miss work if I don't have to, but I hate leaving Chantel when she's sick."

"I understand that." Gladys smiled. "But I know you need to work, and I'll gladly take care of the children."

We are so fortunate to have Dale, Maggie, and Gladys in our lives, Francis thought for the hundredth time as she made her trek to the restaurant. *What would I do without them?*

That evening, after the children were in bed, Francis laid all her bills out on the kitchen table. She had used the last of her money to pay for Chantel's prescription, and payday was still a week away. All day at work, she had mulled over what to do. She needed to buy groceries, at least the basics. She added up all the bills.

Maybe if I don't pay the phone bill this month, she thought. *Then I'd have a little more for groceries.* She did some calculating.

It wouldn't be enough. *Maybe the electric bill,* she thought, recalculating. *That would give me enough money for groceries, but do I dare? It's getting colder. What if my electricity gets cut off? Chantel's first birthday is coming up as well. I need to get her a gift.*

In an uncharacteristic surge of frustration and anger, Francis threw the pen across the room. "How could you do this to us?" she exploded angrily at an invisible Mike. Her own voice startled her, and she lowered her voice as she continued. "We loved each other. You loved the children. What happened to you? Where are you? Why did you do this to us? Why? Why?"

The silence taunted her.

I loved you. The kids loved you. Why couldn't that be enough for you? Why did you have to take up drinking and cheating? she continued silently, not wanting to wake the kids.

She pushed back her chair and went into her bedroom. As she threw herself across the bed, her tortured mind once again relived those months of escalating abuse and rejection. She wept until she fell into an exhausted sleep.

The first snowstorm of the winter whipped at her as Francis stepped out of the restaurant the following day. It was fitting that the elements were screaming at her, whipping her in shame and humiliation as she made the long trek to the food bank. She didn't know what else to do. The money she was making at the restaurant was not enough for her and the children to live on. Today she had asked her boss to give her weekend shifts as well. Maybe then she would earn enough to get by. But right now, she had no money and no milk in the house.

Francis kept her scarf wrapped around her head and partially covered her face as she stepped into the food bank. She kept her eyes averted as she voiced her needs to the friendly lady who greeted her. She just needed a quart of milk and a few essential groceries. She caught sight of a cardboard box that contained a few teddy bears some generous soul had donated.

"Do you think I could have one of those stuffed animals as well?" she asked tentatively. "My baby's first birthday is coming up. She's been sick, so I've had to spend my money on medication."

"By all means," the friendly lady said. "Which one would you like?"

Francis picked out a soft pink teddy bear and thanked the lady.

Stepping out into the cold, swirling snow, Francis kept her head down. As she walked home, she was consumed by shame.

What would Mother say if she could see me now? she wondered miserably. *Well, Mother, maybe you were right after all.*

Francis dropped the groceries off at her apartment before going to pick up the kids.

"Come in," Gladys called in response to Francis's knock.

The apartment smelled of gingerbread, and Brad was quick to show her the gingerbread house they had made.

"I don't know how you do it," Francis said. Stooping down, she gave Brad a hug before taking the baby from Gladys. "Chantel is sick, and you still have time to build a gingerbread house."

"Chantel is much better today," Gladys said. "The medication really seems to be helping."

"Oh, I'm so glad to hear that." Francis hugged Chantel, and the little girl grabbed at her hair. "Brad, please clean up the toys now."

"Brad tells me that Chantel's birthday is coming soon," Gladys said. "It's the day after tomorrow, right? Do you have plans for her birthday?"

"No, I haven't made any plans yet." Francis avoided making eye contact with Gladys. She was too ashamed to tell her that she could not afford to have people over.

"Would you mind if I baked her a birthday cake?" Gladys asked. "I would love to, and Brad would love to help me. That way, you wouldn't have to do it after you come home from work."

Francis looked up in surprise and relief. "Oh, that's not fair to you."

"Nonsense," Gladys said, brushing a stray strand of hair behind her ear. "It would be my pleasure. I thought that if you didn't have any plans already, we could ask Maggie and Dale over for cake and coffee. But I leave that up to you. I don't want to interfere."

"You're not interfering," Francis said. "That's a good idea. We'll have a little party."

"We'll have a party!" Brad squealed, jumping up and down and running circles in the kitchen. Both women laughed.

"Gladys, I know you're already doing so much for me," Francis said, "and I don't know how to ask you, but I talked to my boss about working some weekend shifts. Would you mind looking after the kids every other Saturday as well?"

"I don't mind at all," Gladys said. She had suspected that Francis was experiencing financial difficulties, and it broke her heart. She didn't imagine a waitressing job paid well. "Do you know what your hours would be?"

"I would work every other Saturday from eleven o'clock in the morning to eight o'clock at night," Francis said. "They're longer hours than my regular shift, but I would get the supper tips, which would help."

Francis returned to her apartment feeling a little better. Chantel would have a birthday celebration after all, and the extra shifts would help out financially.

CHAPTER 13

Winter came with a vengeance. Mary tugged her woolen tuque down over her forehead, put on her parka, and pulled the hood on over her tuque. She wrapped a scarf around her neck, making sure it covered her chin, mouth, and nose. She pulled on her snow boots and mittens before opening the front door. The frigid air bit at her exposed skin. She quickly grabbed the toboggan and headed to the woodpile, where David was already busy splitting wood. Although the temperature had warmed up a few degrees from the minus-forty-five degrees Celsius that morning, it was still dangerously cold. David and Mary worked quickly to keep warm. The chores still needed to be done.

It was only a few days before Christmas, and school had already been closed for a couple of days due to the cold weather. The annual school Christmas concert had been postponed until after the Christmas holidays. Mary was disappointed, but David loved it. It gave them a longer Christmas break.

The only consolation to the frigid temperatures was the beauty of the brilliant sunshine sparkling like diamonds on the pristine snow and the thick hoar frost covering the trees. Mary loved this display of God's magnificent artistry.

Mama filled her days with an extra amount of Christmas baking and got everyone involved with icing cookies.

"Mama," David said on one of these occasions as he carefully iced a cream cookie, "what do you think heaven is like?"

"Well, the Bible doesn't say a lot about what heaven is like." Mama took another sheet of cookies from the oven. "But it does describe it as very beautiful, with a lot of very precious gems and streets of gold. Why do you ask?"

"Jesus left heaven when he was born in a stable, and I was just wondering what it was like—what he left," David answered.

"I have often thought about that myself," Mama said. "Jesus left all the glory of heaven to come down to a wicked world where he was born in a stable because nobody had room for him. He didn't have an easy life—that's for sure."

"I wonder how Mary felt when the angel told her she would have a baby," Mary said.

"Not to mention how Joseph felt when he found out Mary was expecting a baby," David said.

"We will never know exactly how they felt," Mama said, "but if you want to know more about what heaven looks like, you can study the last few chapters in Revelation. I think the Bible doesn't go into great detail about heaven because our brains are unable to comprehend it."

"We'll have to go there to really know, you mean," David said, finishing off icing the last cookie and setting down both cookie and knife.

"I suppose so," Mama replied.

Francis couldn't help but be anxious as Christmas drew closer. The cold December temperatures meant her electric bill would be higher than usual. She didn't dare buy any extras for Christmas, and she racked her brain regarding how she could get the children at least one toy each. Her budget only allowed her to make simple meals for the children. On days when she worked, she didn't eat at home, limiting her food intake to the one meal she was allowed at the restaurant. She hated going to the food bank and did so only when she couldn't manage any other way.

She was losing weight, which wasn't lost on either Maggie or Gladys, but neither woman knew how to approach Francis on the subject. They knew Francis was too proud to accept handouts from them.

A week before Christmas, when it was obvious to Francis that she was unable to buy new Christmas gifts for her children, she went to the local thrift store to see if she could find something secondhand. To her surprise, they had a good selection of used toys that were still in decent shape. She picked out a few Matchbox cars and a Matchbox car garage for Brad and a doll with a little bassinet for Chantel. The total purchase was only a few dollars. She left the store with a lightness to her step that she hadn't had in a while.

I can't afford a Christmas turkey, but at least the children will have gifts. She smiled as she took the stairs up to her apartment, hid her purchases, and went to pick up the children from Gladys.

After work on Christmas Eve, Francis let Brad and Chantel help her hang ornaments on their little artificial tree. Brad was doing a good job, but Francis found it difficult to keep Chantel from removing the ornaments from the lower branches.

"Brad, do you want to put the star on top?" Francis asked after she hung the final ornament.

"Oh yes!" Brad exclaimed, jumping up and down.

Francis picked up the star and handed it to Brad. "Be very careful," she said as she lifted him up so he could reach the top of the tree.

"Mommy, turn on the lights!" Brad couldn't contain his excitement when Francis set him back on the floor.

"Okay." Francis turned the tree lights on and then went for the light switch, picking Chantel up along the way so she wouldn't get scared in the dark.

"It's so pretty!" Brad exclaimed, clapping his hands. Chantel giggled and clapped her hands too.

"Yes, it is." Francis laughed at Brad's excitement. She was thankful he was too young to realize the tree was little and scrawny and the lights didn't all work.

"Scrawny-looking tree," Mike had said last year. "I wanted to do better by you, Fran. I didn't want us to be living like this, barely scraping by."

"All I need is you and the kids," Francis had replied. "High society is not my cup of tea, Mike. You know that."

"But it's not fair to you. Things would be so much better for you if I had never appeared on the scene. Your mother's right; I'm not good enough for you."

"Don't say that. I love you. That's all that matters."

"I love you too." Mike had taken her hand and kissed her fingers.

Francis brushed her hand over her eyes. She had known at the time that Mike was troubled. She wished she'd been able to help him before everything spiraled out of control. She flicked on the lights, dispelling the memory.

There was a knock on the door, and Francis, still holding Chantel, went to answer it. She opened the door to a group of young people from church, who immediately started singing Christmas carols. Astonished and delighted, she motioned for them to come in. They filed in as they sang, filling the entrance and spilling over into the hallway. Brad came running around the corner and stopped short when he saw all the people. Francis was deeply moved. What a great Christmas surprise.

"We have something for you," the leader said when they'd finished singing.

A young man in the back of the group came forward. "Merry Christmas." He smiled at her as he set a large basket at Francis's feet.

"Thank you," Francis said, feeling overwhelmed as the group

turned and, amid exclamations of "Merry Christmas," walked out of the apartment.

"Mommy, was that Santa?" Brad asked in awe as the door closed.

Francis smiled and patted his head. "No, Brad, honey, I think those were angels."

"What's in the basket?" Brad was already trying to open the colored cellophane covering.

"Let's take it into the living room and see." Francis set Chantel down on the floor and lifted the basket. "Oh, it's heavy!"

She carried the basket into the living room. Carefully, she untied the pretty red-and-green bow. Brad jumped up and down with excitement. Chantel crawled up and started picking at the cellophane, enjoying the crinkly sounds.

"Oh my!" Francis gasped as the cellophane fell away, revealing the contents of the basket. She pulled out a small turkey, a small bag of potatoes, a can of mixed vegetables, a can of cranberry sauce, and a box of chocolates. She couldn't contain her tears when Brad pulled a small wrapped gift out of the basket.

"Can I open it, Mommy?" he asked excitedly, his eyes dancing.

"Here—let me see it." Francis wiped at her eyes before taking the small parcel and turning it over in her hands. It had Brad's name on it. She looked back in the basket and found another one for Chantel.

"Brad, this one has your name on it, and this one," she said, pointing to the other gift, "has Chantel's name on it. Do you want to put them under the tree? Tomorrow is Christmas, so we'll open them in the morning."

"Oh yes," Brad said gleefully, taking the two gifts. He carefully laid them side by side under their little tree.

Francis felt overwhelmed and thankful. Her little family would have Christmas after all, complete with gifts and Christmas dinner. For the first time in months, there was a song in her heart as she prepared the children for bed that evening.

After the children were asleep, Francis fixed herself a cup of hot chocolate and curled up on the couch. Only then did she allow her mind to rewind and relive the memories that had been nagging at the periphery of her mind during the last few weeks. She was taken back in time to last Christmas Eve, when Mike had taken their family for a drive around town to see the lights. She could still see Brad's excitement at the numerous displays. She remembered their stop at the little restaurant, the pictures with Santa, and the romantic interlude in the park with the kids sleeping in the backseat. She allowed herself to feel the strength and protection of Mike's arms around her. She recalled the loving, intimate moments they had shared and how everything had changed in a year.

CHAPTER 14

Through that unusually cold winter, Mary and David grew closer than they had ever been before. Increasingly, their social activities included both of their groups of friends. On weekends, when it was not too cold, they invited friends over to go sledding down the hill behind their house or go skating on the pond.

David still didn't enjoy school, but he put more effort into it and actually studied for exams. His marks improved noticeably. He confided in Mary that he felt God would use him in a big way someday and that he wanted to be ready for whatever God's plan was for him. He only had another year and a half of school before graduating.

Eventually, the cold days of winter gave way to longer hours of sunlight and warmer temperatures.

One thing about living through a long, cold winter is that it makes you appreciate the welcome warmth of spring, Mary thought as she raked the dry leaves together into a pile. The snow had melted, the frogs croaked, and Mary felt rejuvenated. She loved spring. The soft green of the new leaves on the trees, the newborn calves in the corral, birds singing in the trees—everything seemed to spring to life again.

"Mary, please take this coffee to Papa!" Mama called from the open doorway. "It's so warm out today. I'm sure Papa must be thirsty."

Mary leaned the rake against the side of the house and went to take the thermos from Mama. Papa was seeding the fields with his tractor and seed drill, while David had gone to town to pick up some parts Papa needed.

"Gladly," Mary said, taking the thermos. "When the weather is this nice, I'd rather be outside than anywhere else."

"But don't take too long," Mama cautioned. "I need you to hang these clothes on the clothesline."

"Yes, Mama," Mary promised.

Wash day was a busy day for Mama. The water had to be carried in, heated, and then dumped into the wringer washer. After the clothes were washed, the washer had to be drained and the dirty water carried outside. Since all the laundry was washed in the same water, Mama always washed the laundry twice, so the entire procedure had to be repeated. Then the clothes were rinsed in a tub set up beside the washer. After each wash and rinse, the clothes were fed through the wringer to remove excess water. Finally, they were hung out on the clothesline to dry.

Even though she was mindful not to dawdle, Mary still took time to relish the warm sunshine on her back, the colorful birds chirping cheerfully in the trees, and the frogs croaking at the pond. She breathed in deeply the smell of the freshly tilled fields.

She waited at the end of the field for Papa. She could see the tractor coming slowly toward her. When he reached the end of the field, Papa stopped the tractor and jumped down.

"Hi, Mary," he said.

"Hi, Papa," Mary answered, handing the thermos to him. He opened the thermos, poured some coffee into the cup, and took a sip.

"*Ach*, that tastes good," he said appreciatively, wiping the back of his hand across his perspiring brow. "I was getting thirsty already. It's pretty warm out here today. How was school?"

"Good," Mary responded. "We're finishing up the chapter on China in social studies. I have to write an essay in English class."

"Good thing you enjoy writing essays." He chuckled.

"Oh, I do," Mary responded.

An ear-splitting crash with the sound of metal scraping metal and breaking glass interrupted them. Papa dropped the thermos and sprinted toward the road with Mary right behind him.

Oh God, Mary prayed silently as she raced after Papa, adrenaline rushing through her veins. *Please let them be all right!*

She matched Papa step for step as they raced across the field and through the tree line.

"No!" Papa cried as he broke through the trees a couple of steps ahead of her.

Mary screamed as she followed close behind. At the intersection down the road, Papa's pickup truck lay on its side in the ditch. The wheels were still spinning. Together they raced as fast as their legs would carry them toward the crunched-up truck. They could see David in an unmoving heap inside. Papa pulled at the door, but it wouldn't open. Mary helped him, and they both tugged at the door with all their might until it gave way with a groan. Papa climbed in, pulled David from the wreck, and laid him on the soft spring grass.

He felt for a pulse. He put his ear close to David's mouth. He put his hands on David's unmoving chest. In mounting panic, Mary watched Papa breathe into David's mouth and then count as he pumped his chest. He did it all over again, tears streaming down his cheeks, while Mary held David's hand.

"David, open your eyes!" Mary pleaded insistently, rubbing his fingers.

An eternity later, Mary was aware of sirens piercing the air. Someone pulled her away from David while people in uniform started working on him. People were running. David was put on a stretcher and whisked into a waiting ambulance.

"Please come with me," a Royal Canadian Mounted Police officer said softly to her. "Do you know this young man?"

"David." Mary trembled. "That's David."

"Come to my car, please." The policeman gently took her by the arm and led her to his cruiser. There were many flashing lights. "Who is David?"

"My brother!" Mary cried, unaware of the river of tears coursing down her face. Her eyes searched for Papa. He was talking with another officer. "Papa!" She ran to him. The policeman let her go, sadly shaking his head.

"Listen, Mary." Papa hugged her close. "They are taking David to the hospital. This policeman will take us home to pick up Mama and Benny and then take us to the hospital. You must be brave, Mary." She could feel Papa trembling as he added urgently, "And pray!"

Mary silently slipped into the back of the police car beside Papa. The car turned around and sped the short distance to their house.

She saw everything in slow motion. Mama was hanging clothes on the line. Benny, playing in the sandbox, looked up in surprise at the police car speeding down their driveway. Mama dropped the clothes and clothespins. Papa jumped out of the car and ran toward Mama. Papa tugged at Mama's hand to come with him. He picked Benny up on his way back to the car. Mama, Papa, and Benny piled into the backseat of the car. Mama drew Mary to her as Papa put his arm around Mama and held Benny on his lap. Mama's lips were moving, her eyes were closed, and tears were streaming down her cheeks. Mary knew Mama was praying.

Lord, Mary's heart cried, *let David be okay. Please let him live!*

Sirens screamed in her ears as they sped away. All the way to the hospital, Mary prayed. Benny looked bewildered. Papa's face was pale. At the hospital, the RCMP officer led them to the emergency waiting room. He told them that someone would be with them soon and left.

A nurse came in carrying a clipboard and asked Mama and Papa questions, making notes here and there.

"Can I get you anything?" she asked kindly when she'd finished writing. "A coffee maybe? Juice or water?"

Mama and Papa both shook their heads, and Papa answered, "No, thank you," for all of them.

"The doctor is with your son right now. He will come talk to you as soon as he can," she assured them. "If you need anything—anything at all—please feel free to ask any one of the nurses." She patted Mama's shoulder and left the room.

Mary's heart raced. She wished the doctor would come tell them that David would be fine. She didn't know what to think. What did people do in these situations? She didn't know. What had happened? She realized she didn't know that either. She heard Mama and Papa talking softly, but she didn't listen to what they were saying. Her heart was pounding. She could feel it in her head. She felt weak. Benny came to her, and she pulled him onto her lap. She hugged him close. She felt nauseated.

The door opened, and the doctor came into the room. He looked tired.

"Are you David's parents?" he asked Mama and Papa. When they nodded, he continued, "I'm very sorry. We could not save your son. He died instantly. There was nothing we could do."

Mama screamed. Papa held her close as the tears poured down his weathered cheeks.

Mary sat still, holding Benny close to her. She started shaking uncontrollably. *No!* her mind screamed. *This can't be happening. Not David. Not like this. No good-byes. Nothing.*

The doctor told them that David had died on impact from a severe blow to the head. He hadn't suffered. They could take comfort in that. They would soon be able to see David's body. A nurse would come show them in. He told them he had seen Pastor and Mrs. Peters visiting patients, and asked if he should send them in. Papa nodded. The doctor left the room, and soon a nurse came in and asked them to follow her. Papa kept his arm around Mama, and Mary held Benny's hand as they followed close behind.

David was lying on a stretcher with a sheet covering his body. He looked pale, and his lips were a tinge of blue. Mama went to him. Her fingers softly touched his cheeks. She smoothed his hair back. Then she laid her head on his chest as earth-shattering sobs wracked her body. Papa held on to her and motioned to Mary and Benny to come closer.

Mary felt numb. She was still shaking. She felt as if she had run into a solid brick wall. There was no way around it, no way over it, nowhere to go, and no way back. The tightness in her chest made it difficult to breathe. She hugged Benny close. She didn't want to touch David—not here, not like this. She wanted to run out of the room. She wanted to wake up from this nightmare.

Pastor Peters and his wife entered the room and hugged each one of them. Mrs. Peters hugged Mama for a long time as they both cried. Pastor Peters reminded them that they had a living hope that David was in heaven now. He prayed with them and read comforting verses from his Bible.

Pastor Peters asked Papa if he should notify anyone.

"I suppose we should tell our parents," Papa answered. His voice sounded hollow. He turned to Mama. "Is there anyone else you want them to notify?"

"Do you mind stopping in at the Hepners?" Mama asked, wiping at her eyes. "John and David were best friends."

"We will tell them," Pastor Peters said. "We will stop by your house later."

Pastor and Mrs. Peters left the room to notify family and friends.

Soon Mr. and Mrs. Hepner and John entered the room. They stood beside David for a long time. John wept openly. Mr. Hepner put his free hand on John's shoulder.

Mary's grandparents came and hugged them all tightly, shock and disbelief written on their faces. Aunts, uncles, and cousins arrived. As more friends and church members started arriving, Mary sat down in a corner. She wanted to be alone. She could see that John wanted to say something to her, but he didn't know what to say. She understood. She didn't know what to say either. She felt as if she had a huge hole in her chest where her heart had once been.

Mr. Hepner asked Papa if they could give them a ride home. He accepted, and they all piled into the Hepners car. Soon many people came to their house, some bearing platters of food. A few ladies took over the kitchen and made coffee and snacks, while others sat in the living room with Mama, Papa, Mary, and Benny, talking quietly. They had to plan the funeral.

Mary just wanted to be alone in her room. She didn't want all these people here. She knew they meant well, but she felt stifled. She wanted to curl up in her bed until the pain in her heart went away—maybe forever.

When Lena and her family arrived, Lena immediately pulled Mary into a tight hug, and together they cried.

"I want to get out of here, please," Mary whispered in Lena's ear.

With one arm around Mary's waist, Lena led her outside and around the back of the house. John followed them, and the three of them sat on the sweet-smelling spring grass.

"I just can't believe it," Lena said softly, keeping one hand around Mary's shoulders. "Do you know what happened?"

Mary told them all she could remember about the accident, the drive to the hospital, and the doctor's pronouncement. Lena wiped tears from her eyes as she hugged Mary. John was heartbroken. He looked miserable. He was lost without his best friend.

"I can't believe it," John said, his voice breaking. "I just can't believe it."

Mary reached over and put her hand over his. John looked up at her, his anguished eyes misty.

"David was always such a careful driver," he said, "but then a truck drives right through a stop sign and …" His voice faltered, and he hung his head, unable to continue.

The police were investigating, but it looked as if the truck hadn't even slowed down. It had crashed right into the driver's side of the pickup. The driver of the truck was in the hospital with non-life-threatening injuries.

As was their custom when someone passed away, the congregation met at the church for singing that evening. Mary and her family sat in the front pew. They sang songs about heaven and about Jesus. Mary couldn't sing. The words stuck in her throat. Pastor Peters read some scripture from his Bible, although Mary could not remember what he read. After more singing, they went home.

Finally alone in her bed after everyone had left, Mary felt exhausted, but sleep wouldn't come. The scenes of the accident played over and over in her mind. She could hear Mama and Papa talking quietly in their bedroom and knew they couldn't sleep either. At times, she heard sobs come from their room. Mary's dry eyes burned from unshed tears, and her head throbbed. She had cried as she prayed for God to let David live. Now it was too late. Tears wouldn't bring him back. She felt cold and pulled her comforter up under her chin.

Eventually, she drifted off to sleep. The doctor looked at her and said, "He died instantly." Mary woke up with a start. She looked at the clock on her nightstand: 5:45. She turned over onto her other side. Accident scenes played over and over in her mind. She turned again. Her body started shaking, and she pulled her blanket tightly around her.

When she heard Mama making a fire in the cook stove, Mary got dressed and helped Mama prepare breakfast while Papa went outside to do the chores. Mama and Papa both looked as if they hadn't slept much. Even Benny stumbled into the kitchen before Papa came in with the milk.

At breakfast, Mary bit into her toast. It was tasteless. So was her oatmeal. She pushed her food aside.

"Mary, you should eat," Mama said softly.

"I can't," Mary said. "It doesn't taste good, and I'm not hungry."

"I know," Mama said, "but try to eat a little more. We need to keep our strength."

Mama poured Benny a glass of milk. Mary took another bite of oatmeal. She tried to eat for Mama's sake.

After breakfast, Uncle Henry and Aunt Sara came over. After talking with Papa outside for a while, Uncle Henry went to the field where Papa had left the tractor the day before and finished seeding. Aunt Sara came inside and got busy finishing the laundry Mama had been working on. Grandparents and more uncles, aunts, and cousins came over. Some of the women planted the garden, which was what Mama had wanted to do today, while the men were busy working outside.

Mama and Papa tried to help but soon realized they weren't much use. They mostly stood around and answered questions about where they wanted this and how they wanted that done.

Pastor and Mrs. Peters arrived. They sat down with Mama, Papa, and the grandparents to make funeral arrangements. Benny asked many questions as he tried to imagine David in heaven. He didn't want to be alone, so he followed Mama everywhere she went. Mama rocked him to sleep because he couldn't fall asleep in his bed. Their whole world had turned upside down.

Mary stayed home from school. She couldn't think of writing essays or doing math problems. She couldn't bring herself to eat more than a few bites at a time. Every time she closed her eyes, she saw David lying in a heap in the wreck.

People came and went. Mama got out photo albums, and they looked at photos of David and reminisced. People who came over shared their memories of David. They laughed at some and cried at others, and sometimes they did both.

The evening before the funeral, there was a public viewing. Mary gazed down on David's body lying still in the casket. His face bore bruises from the accident. The unruly lock of hair that usually flopped down over his forehead was neatly combed back. His lips had a blue tinge. Memories flooded over her—memories of skating, sledding, and sleigh rides at Christmas. She remembered how excited he had been about accepting Jesus as his Savior. She remembered the joy in his eyes when he'd announced that he felt God would use him in big ways.

Well, David, it seems you were wrong, Mary's tortured mind silently told him. *God didn't have great things planned for you. He didn't even give you a chance. Just took you away before you had a chance to live your life.*

Mary couldn't believe the number of people who came for the viewing. She wouldn't have come if she'd had the choice. She didn't want to remember David this way.

That evening at home, Mama sat down on the couch beside Mary.

"What are you thinking, Mary?" Mama asked gently. "You seem lost in your own world most of the time."

Mary looked up at Mama. Mama's face looked tired and worn, but there was a peace in her eyes.

"Why do people go to viewings?" Mary asked.

"Well, I imagine they want to pay their last respects," Mama answered.

"Don't they do that at the funeral?"

"Yes, of course, but at the funeral, there's not a lot of time for viewing, and maybe they want more time," Mama answered. "And they come to show the family that they care."

"I wish I hadn't had to go," Mary admitted quietly. "I don't want to remember David that way. I wish I didn't have to go to the funeral tomorrow."

"Grieving is a process," Mama said softly. "We have no choice but to go to the funeral. It's our duty as David's family to lay him to rest with dignity." Benny climbed up into Mama's lap.

Poor Benny, Mary thought. *He doesn't understand.* Benny had been subdued and clingy since the accident. Mama folded her arms around Benny.

"That's exactly right," Papa said from his chair across the room. "You want David to have a proper burial, don't you?"

"Yes, I guess," Mary answered. "I just wish David was still alive. I don't want him buried."

"The body that's in that casket is not really David," Papa said softly. "Yes, it's his body, but our body is only the house God has given us to live in while we're on earth. The real David—his soul and spirit, his inner self—is in heaven with Jesus."

"We all wish David was still with us," Mama said, wiping at the corner of her eye. "Think of him in heaven. He was so looking forward to doing God's work. Now he is right in God's presence. The Bible tells us that it's much better to be present with the Lord than to be here in the body."

"We all miss him," Papa said, "but we must remember that this is better for him. He will never experience any more pain, sorrow, or heartache ever again. Think of that. To us, it is painful, and the funeral tomorrow will be difficult, I admit. But God promises that he will be with us through the hard times. The Lord will give us grace for tomorrow."

The day of the funeral was rainy. It seemed as if even the heavens were crying. Mary thought it appropriate. It fit her mood. They drove to the church in the car that the Hepners had loaned them. The church was filled to capacity, including the foyer. Mary had never seen so many people in their church before.

When it was almost time for the service to begin, the pallbearers took their places on either side of the closed coffin and started down the aisle. Papa, Mama, Mary, and Benny walked close behind, followed by both sets of grandparents and the extended family. Once they were all seated in the section reserved for them in the front of the church, Uncle Aaron and Uncle Frederick lifted the cover off of the homemade pine casket and carried it to the back of the church before they took their seats. True to Mennonite custom, the casket would remain open for the duration of the service

From her place in the front pew with Mama, Papa, and Benny, Mary tried to concentrate on what Pastor Peters was saying. David looked peaceful.

"Matthew 11:28 tells us, 'Come unto me, all ye that labor and are heavy laden, and I will give you rest,'" Pastor Peters said to start the service. "These are Jesus's own words. When we cannot bear our burdens, he wants us to bring them to him, and he will give us rest. Jesus knew sorrow in his life. When Jesus was told that Herod had beheaded John the Baptist, who was Jesus's cousin, the Bible says in Matthew 14:13, 'When Jesus heard of it, he departed thence by ship into a desert place apart.' He wanted to be alone. But the people figured out where he was going, and they headed there on foot and got there before Jesus did. When Jesus saw the crowds of people, he 'was moved with compassion toward them, and he healed their sick.' Jesus is moved with compassion for us when we hurt. He wants to heal us. He wants to heal our broken hearts. After he spent all day healing the sick, he performed a miracle feeding five thousand men, plus women and children, before he sent them home. After everybody left, 'he went up into a mountain apart to pray: and when the evening was come, he was there alone.' Jesus feels our sorrow. He lived on this earth. He knows what we are feeling, because he felt it too. When his friend Lazarus died, the Bible tells us in John 11:35, 'Jesus wept.' He knows our sorrow."

Mary looked at Pastor Peters. *Stop!* her heart cried out silently. *Just stop. This can't be happening. Soon I will wake up, and this will just be a horrible nightmare. Please let me wake up.* She felt trapped. She let her aching head drop into her hands. She felt empty inside.

"We trust that David is with his Creator," Pastor Peters was saying. "In John 5:24, Jesus says, 'Verily, verily, I say unto you, he that heareth my word, and believeth on him that sent me, hath everlasting life, and shall not come into condemnation; but is passed from death unto life.' If David believed this, then he is not dead, but his spirit has passed into life everlasting."

Pastor Peters went on to speak about heaven. However, even the thought of heaven was no comfort to Mary. She felt lost—set afloat on a vast ocean. David was too young to die. Mary didn't know how she could go on without him. Silent tears trickled down Mama's pale cheeks, and she saw Papa wiping at his eyes. Not even Benny was fidgeting; he seemed to realize the finality of it all.

At the end of the service, Mary watched as Uncle Aaron and Uncle Frederick put the lid back on the casket. Then eight of David's closest friends and cousins took their position on either side of the casket and started their slow procession from the church to the cemetery. Mary thought about how small their family had become as they followed close behind. Her heart cried out against each step she took. She didn't want to do this walk.

At the cemetery, Pastor Peters spoke a few words of comfort, and there was more singing. The little family stood huddled together. Papa held Benny on one arm while holding Mama close to him with the other. Mama pulled Mary close in front of her. Mary watched as the casket was lowered into the ground.

No! her heart cried out within her. *You can't do that! You can't put him into the ground like that.* But she knew it was no use. She suffered her anguish in silence. Not even the tears would come. Her head ached, and her chest felt as if it would explode. There was more singing as the men took turns filling the grave with dirt. After the last of the dirt had been patted into place, they walked back to the church for the reception.

CHAPTER 15

Francis quietly pulled the blanket across Chantel's shoulders. The little girl looked peaceful in her sleep with her blonde hair curled around her cherubic face. Francis was glad she had taken advantage of the warm temperatures by taking the children to the park after supper. The children's enthusiasm as they slid down the slides and swung on the swings had warmed her heart. Chantel had recently started walking, and Francis was amazed how quickly she moved around already. She constantly had to keep her eye on the little girl to make sure she kept safe.

Francis softly closed Chantel's door and looked in on Brad, who was sleeping spread eagle across his bed. She pulled his blanket over him, gently touching his wavy brown hair. Brad had climbed up on the monkey bars and been disappointed that his arms didn't quite reach from one rung to the next to allow him to swing from them.

He needs his daddy. A frown crossed her face as the thought flitted through her mind. *A little boy needs a daddy he can look up to.* Brad had stopped asking her when Daddy was coming home, and she knew that with time, he would forget his father, but she worried that he would always carry the scar of abandonment with him.

She tried hard to be both a mother and father to her children. She was at home when they woke up in the morning and when they went to bed at night. She played with them after work and read them stories. The children were too young to realize the sacrifices she made to keep them fed and clothed. They were too young to notice that their new clothes were secondhand, bought at the local thrift shop, and that occasionally their groceries came from the food bank.

Father would help me if he knew, Francis told herself as she went into the kitchen to fix herself a cup of tea, but she was too proud to ask for help. *We'll get through this on our own..*

She struggled with the depth of loneliness that had settled in the core of her being. She hated herself for it, but time and again, her mind took her back to the years before the drinking had started, when she'd felt cherished by the man she loved. She longed for those early years.

Why did it go so wrong? The questions tortured her mind. *What could I have done differently?* She felt she was at least partly to blame. If only they hadn't gone to Cheryl's birthday party, Mike might not have started cheating on her, and maybe they could have gone for marriage counseling.

Sighing heavily, Francis took her tea into the living room and curled up on the sofa, reaching for the Bible on her coffee table. She continued attending Dale and Maggie's church. The people were friendly and genuinely cared for her and the children. She found the messages thought provoking and was thankful that Maggie and Gladys never tired of her many questions. It seemed the more she learned, the more questions she had.

Recently, she had started attending Sunday school. Brad loved his preschool class, while Chantel enjoyed playing in the nursery with her little friends. Francis was captivated by the detailed discussions their lessons evoked. She felt a spark being lit in her soul, and she was hungry to learn more.

She opened her Bible to where she had left off reading yesterday.

Grace for Tomorrow

"I'm so glad you're back," Lena said as Mary slid onto the school bus seat beside her.

"Yeah," Mary responded, aware of the sympathetic looks cast in her direction. "I'm not looking forward to it."

"It will get better," Lena said, giving her friend a hug. "One step at a time."

Mary forced herself to walk through the double glass doors into her school. The last time she'd walked through those doors, David had held the door open for her.

"I know I'm not John," he had teased, his eyes twinkling, "but will this do?" He'd gallantly bowed and swept her through with his arm. She had cuffed his ear on her way through the door, and they both had laughed.

Her heart beat erratically in her chest as she walked down the hall to her locker, glad Lena was there with her. In her mind, she saw David everywhere—laughing with his friends in that corner of the foyer, taking a drink at the fountain after a gym class.

"Hi, Mary. Hi, Lena." Sarah and Martha came up behind them as they reached their lockers.

"Mary, I'd be happy to help you catch up with the work you've missed if you want me to," Sarah said, opening her locker door.

"Thanks," Mary responded, picking up her books and closing her locker door. "I appreciate it."

Together the girls walked down the hallway to their homeroom. Mary was painfully aware of students casting sympathetic glances in her direction. In a small town where everybody knew everybody else, it was no less than Mary had expected.

"They mean well," Lena whispered.

Suddenly, John was there in front of her. Mary hadn't realize she'd kept her head down until she almost walked right into him. She saw a reflection of her own pain imbedded in his eyes.

"Hi, Mary," he said, reaching for her hand. "How are you doing?"

"It's hard," she responded. "I see him everywhere."

"I know. It will get easier," he said.

Mary allowed herself to lose herself in his eyes for a moment, knowing that he felt her pain.

"I hope so," she stammered, withdrawing her hand. "I have to get to class."

It was impossible to concentrate on her schoolwork. Memories of David kept popping into her mind.

"Mary?" Miss Wilson's soft voice interrupted Mary's thoughts. "Would you come with me, please?"

Mary turned her work facedown on her desk and followed Miss Wilson into the hallway.

The teacher closed the classroom door behind her. "I can tell you're having difficulty concentrating today."

"I'm sorry." Mary bit her lip. Miss Wilson held up her hand.

"It's perfectly understandable," Miss Wilson assured her. "It's hard to pick up the pieces after such a tragedy. I just want you to know that I'm here for you. If you need help with your schoolwork or need someone to talk to, you can come see me."

"Thank you," Mary mumbled.

"Do the best you can, and I'm sure you'll be all right," Miss Wilson said. "Things will get easier after a while." She gave Mary a hug before opening the door. Together they walked back into the classroom.

"I'm going for a walk," Mary told Mama one Saturday after they had finished cleaning up the house. The sun shone invitingly from a clear blue sky, and she needed to escape the house before it suffocated her. Skipper ran along beside her as she set out along the dusty trail across the barley field. Birds of various colors flitted back and forth between the trees that lined one side of the trail. The sun warmed her back, and she removed her sweater and flung it over her arm.

Time was passing, and the world kept on turning. The fields that Papa had sown at the time of the accident were nicely green by now, with the plants already reaching above her ankles. The trees were turning a darker shade of green, signifying the beginning of summer. Nothing had changed. Yet everything had changed.

She knew Mama and Papa were grieving, but they took comfort in knowing that David was with Jesus. Mary noticed Mama wiping tears from her eyes and Papa staring off into space. She knew they missed David too, but somehow, they went on with their lives.

Mary couldn't go on. She couldn't get past the constant pain in her heart. David had been much too young to die. He'd had his whole life ahead of him. She kicked at a stick in the path. She hoped the driver of that truck would go to jail. He should have died instead of David. The accident was his fault. Why was it that the innocent person was dead and the guilty one was alive? That wasn't fair.

David and John's cabin came into view. Mary studied the cabin as she followed the trail leading up to it. The cracks between the logs were sealed off with mud; the door was made from cut-off logs. Mary loosened the leather strap that held the door in place and stepped inside. A homemade table and chairs stood to the right. An airtight heater sat in the middle of the room. To the left were bunk beds made from wooden planks Papa had donated. David's sleeping bag and pillow lay on the bottom bed. She closed the door behind her, and her eyes fell on the pictures of fast cars that adorned the walls.

This was part of David. He'd made this place with his own hands. This was what he'd loved to do and where he'd loved to hang out. How many times had he and his friends camped out here? Mary ran her fingers over the smooth tabletop. David had spent hours rubbing it with sandpaper. This was where he'd told her about the revival meetings and accepting Jesus as his Savior. He had been so excited.

"I feel joy and peace in my heart. I can't explain it," he'd said, his eyes sparkling.

Mary felt no joy or peace. She missed David with every breath she breathed. She picked up something off the floor and turned it over in her hands. The faces of David and John smiled back at her. She sat down on the edge of David's bed and studied the picture. Tears ran down her cheeks as she focused on David's face, including the lock of cinnamon-brown hair falling over his forehead and the dimple in his left cheek.

"Why, God?" she cried, physical pain piercing her chest. "Why?"

Slowly, from deep within her, sobs bubbled up and racked her body as she clutched the picture to her chest. Heartbreaking sobs wrenched from the center of her being.

"How could you let this happen?" she asked through her sobs. "You're supposed to be a loving God. Where's the love in this?"

She looked up, but there was only silence except for her sobs and her questions.

"David committed his life to you, God!" she cried. "He would have been a preacher, a missionary—anything you wanted him to be."

She pounded her fist into David's pillow, burying her face in it.

"I don't know how to live without him," she moaned. "I don't know how to go on."

Her sides hurt from sobbing, but she couldn't stop. Eventually, she fell into an exhausted sleep, clutching David's pillow to her with one hand and his picture in the other.

Anna Hildebrandt was deeply concerned about her daughter's downward spiral into depression that summer. One morning, while Mary was still in bed and Benny was busy playing in the sandbox, Anna sought out her husband, who was building a shed close to the barn.

"How's the building going?" she asked, coming up behind him.

Jacob hammered another nail into the half-completed wall before setting his hammer down. He pulled his blue polka-dotted handkerchief from his back pocket, wiped the sweat from his forehead, and took the glass of cold water from his wife's outstretched hand.

"*Dankeshoen.*" He smiled and tipped the glass to his mouth, quenching his thirst. It was just past nine, but already the sun was beating down on him. It was going to be another hot day.

"I think the building is going well," he said.

"It looks like it is progressing nicely," Anna said, surveying his work.

"I might have to drive into town to buy some more nails. I'm running low."

"Jacob?" Anna turned her attention to her husband. "I'm concerned about Mary."

Jacob wiped his brow again with his handkerchief and sat down on an overturned five-gallon pail. Anna sat on a pile of boards.

"She is so depressed," Anna said, tears smarting her eyes. "I can't get through to her. She helps with the work, but every chance she gets, she goes into her bedroom. I don't know what she does in there, but she's spending too much time by herself."

"*Jo*, I've noticed." Jacob sighed heavily. "I wish so often that she hadn't been at the accident scene."

"I try to talk to her while we work, but she doesn't say much. She just gives short answers when I ask her questions." Anna's voice was laced with concern. "Whenever I talk about God or the Bible, she clams right up. I've tried talking to her about David, but she says she doesn't want to talk about him."

"Do you think she's angry at God for the accident?" Jacob searched Anna's misty eyes.

"I'm not sure, but I think she might be." Anna wiped at her eyes with the back of her hand. "I don't know why God took David from us, but I have assurance that David is in heaven."

Jacob stared at the ground for a while. When he lifted his eyes, he saw his own torment reflected in Anna's eyes. He got up from his pail and sat down on the boards beside her.

"The pain is so sharp in my heart." Jacob's arms encircled his wife, holding her close. "Sometimes I feel like I can't breathe." He absently rubbed Anna's shoulders. He could feel her tears soaking through his shirt. "So many times, I ask God why. Why did I send David to the store that day? Why didn't I go myself?" His voice broke.

Anna pulled back so she could look into his face. She cupped his face with both of her hands. "It's not your fault, Jacob. It was David's time to go. If you hadn't sent David to the store that day, it would have happened some other way."

"My head knows that"—Jacob blew his nose into his handkerchief—"but my heart doesn't always believe it. I wish to God I could have taken David's place that day!"

Anna hugged her husband tightly. "We can share our sorrow," she said with a sigh, "and find comfort in each other. I think Mary is trying to deal with it on her own. She won't talk about it."

Jacob dried his eyes and put his handkerchief back in his pocket. "I'll try to talk to her," he said. "You're right; she needs help dealing with this."

True to his word, when Mary helped Jacob make straw bales later that week, Jacob found an opportunity to talk to her.

"Let's take a break, Mary," Jacob said, jumping down from the tractor. He grabbed the thermos from the truck and sat down on a bale, motioning for Mary to sit on the bale next to him.

"You are a strong girl, Mary, and I'm thankful for your help," Jacob said as he poured cold water into a plastic cup and handed it to her.

"*Dankeschoen.*" Mary accepted the cup from Papa's hand. He poured a cup for himself as well.

"I couldn't do it by myself." Jacob drank the water and wiped his mouth with the back of his hand. "The day of the accident, you brought me a drink to the field," Jacob recalled. "I am sorry you saw the wreck. I should have sent you back to the house." Jacob sighed.

"It's not your fault." Mary drew a circle in the dirt with her shoe.

"Mama and I are concerned about you. How can we help you?"

Mary continued to draw a circle with her shoe. "I don't know," she admitted sadly. "I want David back. I miss him so much it hurts. I feel sad all the time. People keep telling me it will get easier, but it's not."

"I miss David very much as well, but I know in my heart that David is in heaven with Jesus. When I picture David up there in heaven, where everything is beautiful and peaceful beyond my imagination, then I'm happy for him. The Bible says we are not to grieve like those who have no hope. Someday we will see him again." Jacob hoped she would understand and that she would catch a glimpse of the joy David was experiencing in heaven.

"That could be a long time," Mary whispered.

"I know, Mary. I feel the pain of separation too. So do your mama and Benny. But we must go on. We can't stop living. God will give us the strength if we ask him," Jacob said, willing her to hold on to God.

"Why David?" Mary asked, looking up at Papa. "He was innocent. Why didn't the other guy get killed? He was the one who blew through the stop sign."

"Only God knows that." Jacob sighed.

Mary jumped up and started heaving bales onto the stack. She didn't dare voice all her thoughts to Papa, but inwardly, she fumed at the injustice of it.

Jacob sighed deeply as he got up and went back to the tractor. Anna was right. Mary needed help. She needed prayer.

That evening, in their bedroom, Jacob told Anna about his conversation with Mary. Deeply concerned, they knelt by their bed and committed their precious daughter to the Lord.

"I want to show you this job advertisement." Maggie shoved a newspaper at Francis as they sat down at the corner table for their afternoon coffee break. "And don't tell our boss I showed it to you," she added with a laugh.

Francis smiled as she took the proffered newspaper and read the advertisement Maggie pointed at.

"Secretary assistant at the elementary school." She looked up at Maggie. "I've never worked in a school."

"You graduated high school, right?" Maggie said, knowing the answer she would get.

"Yes, of course," Francis answered.

"That's all it asks for," Maggie said. "At least apply. You have nothing to lose."

Francis reread the advertisement. The posted salary was substantially more than what she made at the restaurant. "The salary would be nice. It would give me holidays and the summer off, but I don't think I'm qualified."

"Look." Maggie caught Francis's eye. "I know that you are barely making enough to get by. Dale and I have been praying for you to get a better job. Dale showed me this ad last night, and we both thought this might be it. Tell me you'll at least apply," Maggie said.

"You prayed I would get a better job?" Francis asked. A warm feeling filled her insides.

"Yes, of course."

"I don't think anyone has ever prayed for me before."

"Oh, Francis." Maggie reached across the table and covered Francis's hand with her own. "Dale and I have been praying for you and the children since before Mike left. Promise you'll apply for this job?" she asked.

Francis laughed. "Okay, I'll apply. Are you happy now?"

"Good," Maggie replied. She drank the last of her coffee and got up. "Yes, I'm happy, and now we'd better get back to work."

The next morning, Francis left home early enough so she could walk to the school and drop off her résumé before going to work.

CHAPTER 16

Francis was amazed when she received the call to come for an interview and even more amazed when she received the call that she got the job. She was ecstatic and called Maggie right away.

"Praise the Lord!" Maggie said when she heard the news. "Thank God for answered prayer!"

"Yeah, he did answer prayer, didn't he?" Francis was amazed. The thought that God actually answered prayer was a new concept to her. "I hadn't thought of that."

"Well, you're thinking of it now, so the thing to do is to thank him." Maggie laughed.

"I will," Francis promised.

Francis negotiated the change in hours with Gladys, who was also happy for her and told her she had been praying as well. Francis was overwhelmed. She hadn't known people were praying for her. More than that, it seemed that the prayers were being answered.

The more she thought of what the new job meant, the more excited she became. Then she remembered she'd need a new wardrobe. She made another trip to the thrift store and found some nice clothes and a dressy pair of shoes for herself.

Maybe someday soon, I'll be able to buy new clothes, she thought as she walked home. The sun shone warmly down on her, and her heart felt lighter than it had in a long time.

Francis started her new job that September. At first, she felt a bit overwhelmed, but the principal and staff were so welcoming and helpful that it didn't take long for her to settle in. She enjoyed the children, and the staff were wonderful. She especially hit it off with Brenda, a vivacious grade-one teacher. Brenda's energetic disposition seemed to rub off on Francis.

"Mary?" Sarah touched Mary's arm. "Did you hear me?"

"I'm sorry," Mary said, turning to Sarah. "What did you say?"

The four girls were sitting together on the grass at school, eating their lunch. Lena picked at the colorful leaves that had fallen off the trees. Mary seldom paid attention to their conversations anymore.

"Are you coming to my birthday party?" Sarah repeated.

"When is it?" Mary asked.

"You really weren't listening again, were you?" Exasperation tainted Sarah's voice.

"I'm sorry," Mary repeated.

"Friday after school," Sarah said with a sigh. "You could come to our house on the school bus."

"I'll ask Mama," Mary said, putting her half-eaten sandwich back into her lunch kit.

Lena had noticed Mary was losing weight, and she was concerned for her friend. Mary didn't take an interest in anything anymore. It was becoming awkward to be with her. Lena's thoughts went back to the last time she had been to Mary's house.

The two girls had been doing the dishes; Mary had washed, and Lena had dried. Mary had gazed out the window, the dishes forgotten in the watery suds, a faraway look on her face. Lena had looked out the window to see what had caught Mary's attention. "What are you looking at?" she had asked, not seeing anything of interest.

"Nothing," Mary had responded, her hands busy with the dishes again.

Lena sighed as she closed her lunch kit and stood. "I want to go to the library before the bell rings," she informed her friends.

"I'll come too." Mary got to her feet.

"Mary, are you ready?" Mama asked as she pulled her sweater over her shoulders. The days were getting cooler.

Mary had no choice but to go to church with her family. Papa would not allow her to stay at home. In church, she sat with her friends, but she let her mind wander. She was not interested in the sermon.

All her life, she had been taught that God was good. God was love. *David loved God and gave his life to Jesus, and what did that bring him? Death. Death at the hands of an inattentive driver. Forever gone from this world in the blink of an eye.* She mulled this over and over in her mind. She didn't want anything to do with a God like that. She had seen God in action and had come to the conclusion that he was anything but good or love.

After lunch, Mary set out down the path to David's cabin. She went there often. That was the only place where she could find some semblance of peace: the cabin that David had built with his own hands. There she felt his presence. There she talked to him as if he were right there with her.

As she walked down the dusty path, Mary noticed the ripening fields. Any day now, Papa would start combining. It didn't seem right that the seasons kept on turning. Soon David's memory would fade, and eventually, he would be forgotten by the school kids, the community, his friends, and his church—all those who had been important in his life. Even Benny would forget since he was so young.

I will never forget you, David, Mary vowed. *I will not let your memory die!* She knew that Mama and Papa would forever hold him close in their hearts as well. Of all the people David had known and loved, only three would miss him forever. The thought was unbearable.

Mary was so deep in thought that she failed to notice that the cabin door was unlatched. As she pushed the door open, she saw John down on his knees beside David's bed, his head buried in David's pillow. He must have heard her, because he lifted his face and looked at her. She could tell he'd been crying. His eyes were filled with a deep sadness that she couldn't bear to look at.

"I'm sorry," Mary stuttered, taking a step back out of the door. "I didn't mean to intrude."

How stupid of me, she thought. *This is John's cabin now.* It had never occurred to her that she might be trespassing.

"No, come on in." John waved her back inside.

Mary stepped into the room and closed the door behind her. She allowed her eyes to slowly adjust to the dimness.

"I come here when I miss David so much I can hardly bear it," John whispered brokenly, "and I pray."

"A lot of good that will do," Mary said bitterly. "What do you pray for—that he will come back to life?"

"No." John got up from his knees and sat down on the edge of the bed.

"Well, what's the use then?" Mary asked. "God doesn't care about us. If he cared for us, he wouldn't have let David die."

"Don't you see, Mary?" John asked. "That's the beauty of it. God only took David after David committed his life to him. He doesn't want us to die in our sin. David was ready to die, to meet his Creator."

"Are you saying that when we give our lives to God, we will die?" Mary asked incredulously. "All the more reason to leave God out of my life."

"God has a purpose for each one of us. A plan," John explained. "We don't always understand that plan, Mary, because God doesn't think like we do. He sees the past, the present, and the future, so he knows what is best for us. The best thing for David was for God to take him home. But through his mercy, he waited to take David home until after he received Jesus as his Savior. Isn't that beautiful?" John's eyes glowed.

Mary shook her head in exasperation. "Makes no sense to me. If God truly is a loving God, then he wouldn't take such a young person who is just starting his life. He would stick to old people who have already lived their lives."

"You asked what I prayed about," John said, changing the subject. "I've wanted to tell you for some time now, but I don't get to talk to you much. I'll be finished with all my high school courses at the end of this semester." His eyes turned thoughtful as he continued. "David and I were planning on going to Bible college after we graduated. Well, I have been praying about it, and I feel that God still wants me to go." His eyes pleaded for her to understand.

Mary stood still. John was leaving? Another part of her life was changing. Would it never stop? She felt herself withdraw deeper into herself, further away from her surroundings. She looked down at her dusty shoes. She couldn't look at John.

"Mary." John stood up, covered the few steps between them, and took her hand in his. "I feel God calling me to the mission field. David felt it too. That's what I pray about when I come here. Mary, I have cared for you for a long time. You are very special to me. Many times, I lay awake at night, planning a future with you someday." He reached up, brushed a few strands of loose hair from her cheek, and tucked them behind her ear. "Mary, I can't ask you to wait for me. You are too young for me to be asking that of you, but I do pray that God will keep you safe, and who knows …" John's voice faded. Unable to continue past the lump in his throat, he pulled her into his arms.

Mary clung to him for a few minutes as the familiar stab of pain ripped through her heart once again. She had cared for

John for a couple of years now, dreaming that they would marry someday, hoping he would wait for her—and now he was leaving her, first for Bible school and then the mission field. Mary took a deep breath to control her feelings, took a step back, and, without looking at him, turned to leave the cabin.

"Mary?" John's voice sounded strangled. "Mary, talk to me," he pleaded, taking a step toward her.

In the doorway, Mary turned to look at him. "If you want to go out into the world to serve your God," she said, her voice low and controlled, her eyes sending fiery darts at him, "then go. Just go."

Quickly, she closed the door behind her so he wouldn't see her tears and hurried down the path. The tears ran unheeded in a steady stream down her cheeks as she walked back home along the long, lonely path. All she held dear was being snatched out of her grasp. *First David. Now John.* Once again, her world was falling apart. The cloud of darkness tightened its hold on her soul. When she got home, she went straight to her room and curled up in her bed. Her heart ached, and her head throbbed.

"Hi, Gladys," Francis said to her friend when she went to pick up the children after school.

"Hi, Francis. How was your day?" Gladys asked, leading the way into her kitchen. "Would you like a cup of tea or coffee?"

"Mommy!" Chantel came up to her, and Francis stooped to pick her up.

"Hi, Mommy." Brad came around the corner and hugged Francis.

"Hi," Francis responded, putting her free arm around Brad. "No, thanks, Gladys. Pastor Bob and Dolores are coming over tonight, so I'd better go home and get our apartment cleaned up."

Church had become an essential part of Francis's life, but she still had many questions and had decided to invite Pastor Bob and his wife, Dolores, over. Maybe they could explain what was eluding her.

Brad and Chantel were excited to have company and were eager to show off their toys. Bob and Dolores played with them until Francis got them ready for bed. Dolores asked if she could read them a bedtime story, and they both climbed up onto her lap. Then Francis tucked them into bed.

On her way back, Francis stopped in the kitchen, prepared a tray of tea and cookies, and took it back into the living room with her.

"This is a nice rocking chair." Dolores smiled, taking a cookie from the tray. "It's just the right size and rocks so smoothly."

"It was a Christmas present from Mike the Christmas before last," Francis said as she poured tea into three teacups. "It's hard to believe all the changes that have happened since then."

"Dale and Maggie mentioned that your marriage was troubled and that your husband left. I understand they helped you find this apartment," said Pastor Bob. "You and Maggie are coworkers, right?"

"We were," Francis said as she offered the tray of cookies. "I just started working at the elementary school. Is that all Dale and Maggie told you?" Francis couldn't believe they had not gone into more detail. They had a close relationship with the pastor couple.

Francis sat down on the end of the couch opposite where Pastor Bob sat.

"That's all they told us." Pastor Bob took a sip of tea and smiled at her. "You have beautiful children, and it looks like they're happy."

"I think they are happy now. Gladys takes care of them when I'm at work, and they really like her. It was rough right after Mike left. Brad asked for him constantly, and I didn't know what to tell him. Mike was good with the kids, and they missed him. You see, Mike left without telling me he was leaving. He was gone when I woke up, and it was only later that I noticed his clothes were gone.

That's when I realized he planned to be gone for a while. I had no idea how long, but I haven't heard from him yet."

"What about your parents?" asked Dolores. "Are they helping you?"

"Oh no," Francis said. Somehow, she'd always thought Bob and Dolores knew about her situation. "I haven't spoken with Mother since before Mike and I were married. They are well off, and Mother did not take kindly to her daughter marrying beneath her social class. Father has come to see me when he's in town. But I haven't seen him in over a year now. I have two brothers and a sister, but they're busy with school."

Francis shared some of her good memories of Mike with them. She shared how they had met and married and their good years together. Then she shared some of the painful ones, including how he had become abusive when he was drinking. They were sympathetic listeners. Dolores cried when Francis told about her pregnancy and some of the details of the horrible night when it all had ended. Even Pastor Bob dabbed at his eyes.

"I think back to when we were first married, and I miss that Mike. We were so much in love." Francis wiped her eyes with a tissue. "When we had the children, especially after Chantel, we ran into financial difficulties. At first, he got stressed out about our finances, and then he started hanging out with the guys from work. That's when he started drinking, and when he drank, he was abusive."

"What about the children?" Dolores asked. "Did he abuse them as well?"

"No," Francis told her, "they were asleep by the time he came home. I'm thankful he never abused the children. They both loved their daddy, which made it so hard for Brad when Mike left. Chantel was so young that it didn't bother her as much."

"Praise God for that!" Dolores exclaimed. "That would have made it so much more difficult."

"Do you mind if I read to you from my Bible?" Pastor Bob asked.

"Please do," Francis told him. "I've started reading it, but I find it hard to understand. I've learned a lot in Sunday school and the church services, but it seems like the more I learn, the more questions I have."

"The Bible is God's word to us," Pastor Bob said, taking a small Bible from his suit coat pocket. "It's like a road map for our life. I know it can be difficult to understand, but the more you read it and study it, the more you will begin to love it."

He opened his Bible and read the following verse: "Come unto me, all ye that labor and are heavy laden, and I will give you rest." He told her that every person was a sinner and was living a life separated from God. He explained that separation caused a person to lean on other things, such as alcohol and drugs, when the going got tough. He explained how God sent his only son, Jesus, to be born of a virgin, live a sinless life, take all of humanity's sin on himself, and die on a cruel Roman cross.

"Francis," Pastor Bob said, moving to the edge of the couch, "Jesus died on that cross for your sin. But he didn't stay dead. He arose on the third day and later was taken up to heaven in a cloud to sit at the right hand of God. Jesus did this so you and I and every person who believes in him could have eternal life. He wants to make you whole, Francis. He wants to come live within you and give you peace. It is a gift God wants to give you, Francis." He paused, searching her eyes. "Do you want to accept that gift?"

Tears softly fell down Francis's face as she whispered, "Yes, I want to accept that gift."

The three of them knelt down right there on Francis's living room floor, and Pastor Bob prayed to God to heal Francis's heart.

"God, forgive me!" Francis cried brokenly. "Forgive me for never taking you seriously. Forgive me for all the sin in my life. Forgive me for doing things my own way and for all these years of separation from my family. Forgive me for not knowing how to help Mike. Please clean out my heart, and give me peace. I accept your gift of salvation. I want you to live in my heart and lead me and guide me. Thank you, Jesus, for dying for my sin. Amen."

Francis felt an indescribable peace wash over her as she finished praying. She knew God heard her prayer, and from this moment on, she would never be alone again.

Pastor Bob prayed again, thanking God for what he was doing in Francis's life. He prayed for wisdom for her in raising her children. He even prayed for Mike's safety and prayed that he would become a child of God as well. He thanked God for this evening and the miracle of a new life in him.

Francis's eyes shone as she got to her feet. She felt like singing.

Pastor Bob read more scripture to her, and they talked some more. Dolores told her that there was a party in heaven, because the Bible said that the angels celebrated when a soul came to know the Lord, and that Francis's baby was a part of that celebration. Francis liked that. She liked to think that her baby was being cared for by angels. She would see her baby when she got to heaven. What a joy that would be!

"I think you should go," Mama said as she folded another towel and put it on a pile. "You should get out of the house more."

"I would rather stay home," Mary responded. The weather was reasonable for late fall, so a group of friends were planning a wiener roast down by the river on Sunday—one last outing before the snow.

"You used to enjoy going out with your friends," Mama said a little wistfully. "You can't just mope around the house all the time. You need to have some fun. All your friends will be there."

"Things just aren't the same anymore." Mary sighed. She felt sad and angry all the time. She went to school, but her heart wasn't in it. She had passing marks, but she wasn't excelling, as she had in the past.

"I know it's difficult," Mama said, wondering how she could get through to her daughter, "but you need to keep on living. Spending time with friends can help ease the pain."

On Sunday morning, Mary went to church with her parents because Papa wouldn't have it any other way. She sat in the backseat of the car with Benny, who was growing up fast. He had started school last month, and so far, he loved it.

When they got to church, Lena spotted her and rushed over excitedly with Martha and Sarah in tow.

"Henry said he would pick us up this afternoon for the wiener roast," Lena said. She had a crush on Henry. She eyed Mary. "You are coming, right?"

"Yeah, I'll come," Mary answered. The truth was that if she didn't go with her friends, she was afraid Papa might drive her himself, and that would be embarrassing.

"You won't be sorry. I promise!" Lena exclaimed, eyes sparkling. The girls walked into church and sat together in their usual pew. Mary didn't bother to join in the singing, and she had gotten good at tuning out the pastor. She couldn't stand listening to all that Bible drivel. God was not a God of love, as they said; he was a God of disappointment and heartache. Mary wouldn't be the least bit surprised if God even found some pleasure in making people suffer. Maybe he was laughing at them as he looked down on their misery.

Henry is apparently giving a bunch of kids rides, Mary thought as she slid into the backseat beside Lena. The car was full of noisy teenagers, all laughing and talking at the same time. Although the weather was still unseasonably warm, there was a hint of chill in the air; it was just right for sitting around a campfire. The guys soon had a good blaze going. When more kids from school and church joined them, they played dodgeball and Frisbee. Mary didn't join in the games. She preferred to stay by the fire.

"Hi, Mary." Annie sat down beside her, her red hair pulled back into a ponytail. "I saw you sitting here by yourself. How come you're not joining in the fun?"

Mary looked up, somewhat startled. Annie was a couple of years her senior in school, so the two girls didn't know each other well.

"I don't feel like it," Mary replied.

Annie laughed and stood up as a group of girls joined her. "Well, I don't feel much like sitting around here watching that bunch either. Come on. We're going for a walk along the river."

"Okay," Mary said, surprising herself. *Why did I say I'd walk with them?* she thought as she got to her feet. Although she recognized all of the girls, some were from her class, and some—like Annie—were a couple of years older, she had never spent much time with any of them.

They slowly walked along the riverbank, kicking at the stones in their path. The girls chattered and laughed, telling funny stories about school and about the kids they hung out with. Annie pulled a package of cigarettes out of her pocket, opened it, and passed it around. When it was passed to Mary, she handed it back to Annie. Annie pulled a cigarette partway out of the pack and held it out to Mary.

"I don't smoke." Mary shook her head.

"Have you ever tried it?" Annie asked.

"No," Mary admitted.

"Try one then," Annie said.

"I don't know." Mary hesitated. She could feel all the girls looking at her.

"Oh, go on," Annie said. "You'll find it relaxing, and you look like you could use some relaxation."

Mary felt a twinge of guilt that quickly turned into an act of defiance as she took the cigarette and stuck it between her lips. Annie put a match to it, and Mary inhaled. Immediately, she started coughing uncontrollably as the smoke filled her lungs and nose. Annie thumped Mary on her back as Mary bent over with her hands on her knees, trying to gain control of her coughing.

"Okay." Annie laughed as Mary stopped coughing. "Let me show you how it's done."

Right there on the bank of the river, Mary got a lesson in smoking. She didn't like the taste, but it made her feel good. She felt grown up and as if she were in control. When they finished their cigarettes, they headed back to the group. The others had finished their games and were ready to roast some hot dogs.

"Hey, Mary," Annie said after they had finished eating and were cleaning up. "You want a ride home? We're going right past your house."

"Okay," Mary answered. She turned to Lena. "That's okay with you, right?"

Mary could see disapproval in Lena's eyes, but Lena wouldn't say anything in front of Annie and her friends.

"That's up to you," was all Lena said.

Mary waved to Lena as she fell into step with Annie. Annie's friends were already piling into the car. After sliding into the driver's seat, Annie started the engine and stepped on the gas, causing the tires to spin as they sped away. They all laughed. Annie cranked the radio up, and they sang along to popular country songs. For the first time since the accident, Mary felt herself loosen up.

"Hey, let's go to Abe's house and see who all is there," Margaret suggested.

Abe was older, in his twenties, and lived by himself in his own cabin. Mary had heard rumors of parties at his place. Of course, she'd never been to one.

"Yeah, let's!" exclaimed Tina.

Mary felt a little anxious. She knew she should ask Annie to take her home, but she didn't want to look immature in front of these girls, so she kept quiet. She knew Mama and Papa wouldn't like her going somewhere without their knowledge. She glanced at

Tina, who was in her grade, and told herself that maybe it wouldn't be so bad to go this once.

"All right." Annie laughed. "Let's party!" She gunned the car, and it shot forward.

CHAPTER 17

Loud country music and laughter greeted them as Annie swung open Abe's front door without knocking. Mary took in the unfamiliar scene. A blue haze hung over the crowd of teenagers, who were either sitting or standing around, smoking cigarettes and drinking beer. Some of them were playing a game of cards at a table. She understood why Annie hadn't knocked—because nobody would have heard them above the din.

"Hi! Come on in." Abe waved them in with a bottle of beer in his hand when he noticed the girls just inside the door. Abe was of medium build and had light brown eyes and short brown hair. He popped the caps off of some bottles and offered the girls each a beer.

Once again, Mary felt a twinge of guilt. She'd never tasted beer before, and she wasn't sure what it would do to her, but she thanked Abe as she took the bottle. Discreetly, she watched how the other girls acted and mimicked them. Mary put the bottle to her lips and sipped at the beer, careful not to make the same mistake she had with the cigarette. It didn't taste good. She waited for a moment, not knowing what to expect, but when she didn't feel anything unusual, she took another sip.

"Hey, you're cool," Annie told Mary when she dropped her off at her house later that evening.

"Yeah," Margaret agreed, "you should come again next weekend. Abe's place is always a lot of fun."

"I'll think about it," Mary said as she got out of the car. "Thanks for the ride."

Papa looked up from his reading when she came into the house.

"Who brought you home?" he asked, not having recognized the vehicle.

"Just some friends from school," Mary answered, hoping Papa wouldn't smell the cigarette smoke and beer on her. "They were at the picnic, and since they were passing by our house, I caught a ride with them." She felt a twinge of conscience at the half truth. *At least that was the original plan,* she added to herself.

Papa turned back to his reading, and Mary escaped to her bedroom.

"Be careful," Lena told Mary on the bus the next day. "You know that Annie and her group have a reputation for being on the wild side. There are rumors that her and her friends smoke and go to parties and stuff. I don't think you should hang out with them."

"I don't think you should judge them," Mary countered defensively. "They are very friendly, and I had a good time with them." She didn't dare tell Lena that she'd had a cigarette and a beer or that she'd been to one of those parties. Lena would be appalled. Mary felt guilty about that too, but she pushed the feeling to the back of her mind.

As Mary started spending more time with Annie and her crowd, her relationship with Lena became more strained. In January, Mary turned fifteen, and John left for Bible school. Mary didn't want to think about it. She pushed the accident and John's leaving to the back of her mind. She wanted to forget all the bad things, and when she was with Annie and her crowd, she was able to do that. She did her chores at home and kept up with her schoolwork, and her marks were improving.

At one of Abe's parties, Mary met Melvin, Deon's friend from the city. When Mary stepped into Abe's house that night, she noticed the new guy almost immediately. He was standing across the room, surrounded by a group of guys. He was gorgeous in his jeans and a T-shirt that accentuated his tall, lanky frame. His golden-brown hair hung loosely down over his ears, and his piercing eyes were so dark they were almost black.

"Who is that guy with Deon?" Tina asked Annie. Annie could usually be counted on to know the latest news, rumors, and gossip.

"His name is Melvin," Annie answered. "Deon brought him along to spend the weekend at Mark's house."

Just then, Melvin looked in their direction, and Mary felt a shiver of excitement run down her spine as their eyes met. She was surprised when he left the group surrounding him, grabbed a second bottle of beer, and made his way across the room to where she stood.

"Hi." He smiled at her, handing her the beer. "I'm Melvin."

"Hi. I'm Mary." Mary smiled up at him, noticing how his long, slender fingers curved around the beer bottle that he handed her.

He asked her to dance. He did the twist like no one she'd ever seen before, and she had a hard time keeping up with his moves. When he did the monster mash, she couldn't help laughing. Melvin was comical and fun, and soon everyone was on the floor, trying to mimic his moves. Mary thought he was sophisticated, and she was proud that he had singled her out. She knew she was the envy of all the girls at the party, at least the girls who didn't have boyfriends. Later, when Melvin asked if he could drive her home, she said yes.

He's just giving me a ride home, she told herself, pushing aside the guilt she felt as she sought Annie out to tell her.

"Well, you sneaky goose." Annie laughed, winking at her. "You go enjoy."

Melvin casually slung his arm around her shoulders as they left the cabin. He opened the door of his car for her. During the drive home, Melvin told her he worked with Deon in the oil fields. They both had a couple of days off, but it wasn't enough time to go back to the city. Since Deon had relatives in the area, they'd decided to come out and spend a couple of days with them.

Before she got out of the car at her house, Melvin bent over and kissed her lightly on her lips. Wishing her good night, he leaned over and opened the passenger door for her.

Mary's emotions were in turmoil. She touched her lips and could feel Melvin's kiss on them. Her first kiss. It hadn't happened the way she had dreamed it would, but it made her feel special. *Melvin must really like me to kiss me,* she thought as she quietly slipped into the house.

Mama and Papa had company, so Mary was able to avoid contact with them. She didn't want to face them tonight.

"Good morning, Francis," Brenda chirped as she came into the school staff room, where Francis was pouring herself a cup of coffee. "Isn't it a glorious spring morning?"

Francis poured a second cup of coffee with one cream and two sugars, just the way Brenda liked it, and handed it to Brenda. "Nothing like a brisk walk in the fresh spring air," she said, smiling.

"What are you doing for Easter?" Brenda asked, curling her long, slender fingers around her coffee mug.

"I'm taking my kids to see my parents in Calgary," she answered. Since she had become a Christian last fall, she'd spoken to her mom a couple of times on the phone. Maybe it was time to go for a visit. "What about you?"

"Derrick is taking me skiing." She smiled, her eyes twinkling. Derrick was Brenda's fiancé.

"Good morning," Marilyn sang out, entering the staff room.

"Good morning," Francis and Brenda chorused, moving away from the coffeepot. There was some general good-humored conversation as more staff arrived to shed their spring coats and grab quick cups of coffee before heading for their individual classrooms.

Francis entered her office and sat down in front of her typewriter. It was going to be another busy day; she had a stack of letters and reports that needed to be typed.

Bob Whitmere, the principal, stepped up to the intercom to address the school for the morning exercises.

"I'm going to be in meetings for most of the day," Bob told Francis and Linda, the other secretary, after he stepped away from the intercom. "I'll need you to hold all my calls. I'll call them back later."

"All right," Francis responded, smiling up at him. Bob was good at his job, he had a sincere love for children, and he was easy to work for.

After work, Francis hurried home to pick up the kids from Gladys and start packing. She had done all the laundry last night, and tomorrow after school, they would take a Greyhound bus to Calgary. She hoped that by next winter, she could save enough money to put a down payment on a car.

Francis was nervous about going to her parents', but she knew it was the right thing to do. Her mother had never seen her grandchildren, and it was time to go home and make amends. She hoped things would go well. She had talked her plan over with Pastor Bob and Dolores, and they were encouraging.

She hurried to Gladys's apartment and knocked on her door.

"Mommy! Mommy!" Brad and Chantel chorused as Gladys let her in with a big smile on her face.

Francis stooped down to hug her children. "Were you good for Auntie Gladys today?"

"We made cookies," Brad said, pointing at the cupboard. "Yummy chocolate chip cookies. Do you want one, Mommy?" Brad started pulling Francis into the kitchen. Francis scooped up Chantel and followed him.

"Why don't you stay for coffee and some freshly baked

cookies?" Gladys asked, leading the way into her kitchen. "We had so much fun baking them, but I told the children they couldn't eat them until you got here."

"How can I turn down an offer like that?" Francis laughed, taking a chair at the table, her children on either side of her. Gladys brought out a plate of cookies, two mugs of steaming coffee, and two plastic cups of juice for the children.

"These cookies are delicious!" Francis exclaimed after biting into one. She smacked her lips. "Mmm-mmm good."

"Yeah." Brad smiled. "We made yummy cookies."

"Chantel make cookies!" Chantel exclaimed, waving a cookie in the air.

Gladys laughed. "We sure did. You should have seen the kitchen. But we had lots of fun."

Francis turned serious. "Thank you so much for being so good with my kids."

"I enjoy every minute of it," Gladys answered. "They're a darling pair, and it helps me get through the day." Her husband had died of cancer five years ago, and recently, her daughter and son-in-law and their three little children had moved to Kelowna. "When are you leaving for Calgary?" she asked, changing the subject.

"We're taking the evening bus tomorrow," Francis responded, wiping Chantel's face with a napkin and setting her on the floor. "You two go clean up the toys, and we'll go home."

"I'm really glad you're going home," Gladys said. "I'm praying for you."

"Thank you," Francis said. "It's been so long I don't know how I feel about it. Excited, yet I'm nervous. What if it doesn't work out?"

"Trust in the Lord, and lean not on your own understanding," Gladys said, quoting from Proverbs.

"I try." Francis sighed. "I want to trust the Lord in this, but a part of me is still afraid."

"Naturally," Gladys said, "but you'll be fine."

"I want to get all the packing done today so we're ready to leave tomorrow. Dale is going to give us a ride to the bus depot." Francis started cleaning the table. The children could be messy.

"See you tomorrow!" Gladys walked them to the door and hugged the children good-bye.

In their apartment, Francis sat down on the couch and pulled both children onto her lap, as she always did when she came home from work. She asked the children about their day and told them tidbits about her day. It was a time of sharing that she had incorporated into their life to try to compensate for their being apart all day.

"We went to the store with Auntie Gladys," Brad told her.

"Chantel store," Chantel said. She had a habit of repeating what her older brother said.

"Really?" Francis smiled at them. "Auntie Gladys took you to the store?"

"Yes," Brad said, "we had to buy things to make the cookies."

"Chantel cookies," Chantel said, putting her hand up to Francis's cheek.

"Do you two know what we are going to do today?" Francis asked them.

"Go to the park?" Brad had been eagerly waiting for the snow to disappear so he could go to the park. The snow was almost gone now.

Francis laughed as she pulled both children against her in a hug. "No, we're not going to the park. We are going to pack our clothes into suitcases. Why are we packing our clothes?" she asked.

"We are going on a bus." Brad clapped his hands excitedly.

"Chantel bus." She clapped her hands as well.

"That's right." Francis hugged them again and then set them both down on the floor. "Let's go get the suitcases."

They all went to her bedroom, where Francis pulled a couple

of suitcases out of the closet. She took one into Brad's room and placed the clothes she wanted him to pack on his bed so he could place them in the suitcase himself.

"Come with me, Chantel," she said, taking her daughter's hand. She led her into Chantel's bedroom. "I'll give you your clothes, and you can put them in the suitcase."

Chantel happily agreed, and soon the children's clothes were packed, although Francis noted she would have to refold some after the children were in bed. The clothes hadn't exactly been put in neatly. Chantel put her teddy bear and blanket on top of the clothes.

After supper, Francis bathed the children, read them a Bible story, and then prayed with them before tucking them into bed. Chantel retrieved her teddy bear and blanket. Francis smiled. It was too soon to pack the essentials, but she made a mental note not to forget tomorrow. When the children were safely in bed and asleep, Francis curled up on the sofa and spent time in Bible reading and prayer.

I hope this trip goes well, she thought anxiously, and then she lifted her eyes toward heaven. *Lord, you know I'm anxious about this trip home to my parents. It's been a long time. I don't know how Mother will react to me or the children. Lord, go with us. Protect us. Help me to be a true witness for you. Help me to be a good mother to my children. And, Lord, please protect Mike. Soften his heart toward you so that he will commit his life to you. I pray this in Jesus's name. Amen.*

She still missed the Mike she had married. The dull ache in her heart never completely went away. She wondered where he was and how he was doing. Since she had become a Christian, Pastor Bob and Delores had encouraged her to pray for Mike's salvation. She prayed for him every day.

The following day turned out to be sunny and reasonably warm for a spring day. She had an extra bounce in her step as she dropped the children off and walked the couple of blocks to school. The Lord was good, and she knew she could trust him for this trip.

When she brought the children home from Gladys that afternoon and made the final preparations for their trip, she felt unsure again. She was so anxious about meeting her mom that her stomach felt a bit queasy. As she snapped the lid of the suitcase closed, there was a knock at the door.

"It's open!" she yelled down the hallway.

"Uncle Dale!" Brad and Chantel ran to give Dale big hugs. Dale laughed, bending over to hug them both.

"We're going on a bus," Brad told him, pulling on Dale's arm excitedly.

Brad had never been on a trip outside the city before, and he was excited. Chantel wasn't sure what all the fuss was about, but she caught on to Brad's enthusiasm and repeated most of what he said, with a big smile, for Uncle Dale.

Dale laughed at the children's enthusiasm.

"Does an old man good to see these children so excited," he told Francis, helping her put their jackets on. He picked up their suitcases while Francis got her bag and reached for Chantel's hand. Brad raced down the hall ahead of them.

"Brad, be careful on the steps!" Francis called after him.

Dale laughed. "He's certainly excited."

Dale deposited their suitcases in the trunk of the car while Francis opened the back door for the kids. Then she got in the front with Dale.

After he pulled out into traffic, Dale glanced at her with kind eyes. "You're doing the right thing, Francis," he said. "It's time you went to see your family. Don't worry. Just give it over to the Lord. He'll take care of everything."

Kneading the muscles in her neck, Francis sighed. "I keep telling myself that, but I'm still anxious."

"We are praying for you," he said.

"I know, and I'm grateful for that," Francis responded. "If it wasn't for you and Maggie and Pastor Bob and Dolores, I couldn't do this. You're all so encouraging."

At the bus depot, Dale watched the children while Francis bought tickets. Dale took the suitcases to the bus and hugged the children. They boarded the bus, and the children waved to Dale through the window.

Brad was so thrilled about riding the bus that he couldn't sit still. When they left the city behind, there were many new things that he pointed out and asked questions about. Chantel soon dozed off, for which Francis was thankful. It was hard enough to keep up with Brad's enthusiasm.

"Mommy, look at the cows!" Brad was jumping up and down in his seat. He had never seen real live cows before. "And there are horses." He pointed at a group of horses standing close to the fence. His little nose was squished up against the window. The only live animals he had ever seen were at the zoo.

"It's pretty exciting, isn't it?" Francis smiled at his little face all aglow.

"Do Grandma and Grandpa live here?" he asked.

"No, honey, Grandma and Grandpa live in a city just like we do, only they live in a big house," Francis replied. She wondered how much everything had changed in the years since she had last been at home. *Jesus*, she prayed silently, *keep me calm.*

She wondered if someone would pick her up or if she'd have to call a cab when she got to the station. She had called and asked if she could come for Easter. Her father had said that would be nice, but she wasn't sure how her mother would react to seeing her and the kids.

As the sun set and it started getting dark, Francis switched on the reading light and brought out picture books for Brad. He looked at them for a while on his own and then asked her to read him a story. Chantel woke up while she was reading and sat up in her lap to listen. Soon Francis could see the lights of Calgary in the distance, and again, she said a quiet prayer to still her anxiety.

Francis pointed the lights out to Brad and Chantel as they got closer, and they both got up on the seat to look out the window while she put the books back in the bag. Francis put their coats on, for the spring night would be chilly without them.

The bus slowly made its way into the depot, swaying slightly as it pulled into a space between two other buses. When the door opened, Francis slung her bag over her shoulder, picked Chantel up, and took Brad's hand, and they made their way off the bus. She led the children into the terminal, not sure how she would manage the children and luggage by herself.

Then she saw Jim and Monica. They quickly crossed the floor and hugged Francis. Francis hugged them back tightly. It was good to see them.

"I'm so glad you came," Monica told her, and Jim nodded his agreement. Chantel shyly hid her face in Francis's shoulder, and Brad stood quietly by her side.

"I'll go get your bags," Jim said. "What color are they?"

"Brown," Francis told him. "There are two, and my name and address are on both." Jim disappeared through the door.

Francis knelt down to Brad's height. "This is your auntie Monica. You don't need to be shy with her," she told the children. "Auntie Monica is Mommy's sister."

Brad looked at Monica, who also knelt to eye level with him.

"I have a puppy," Monica told him. "Do you want to play with him?"

"A real puppy?" asked Brad.

"A real puppy." Monica laughed. "Do you like puppies?"

"I love puppies," Brad answered. "Mommy won't let me have one. She says puppies shouldn't live in apartments."

"That's probably true," Monica said, "but my puppy can run around in my backyard. So you can play with him while you're here."

"Mother lets you keep a puppy?" Francis raised an eyebrow.

Monica laughed. "Oh, she doesn't care for him too much, but

as long as he stays out of her way, she tolerates him." She smiled at Chantel. "Can I have a hug?"

Chantel looked from Monica to Francis.

"Sure, honey," Francis said. "You can give Auntie Monica a hug."

Chantel looked at Monica again and then shyly reached out her arms to her. Monica held her close. "Oh, you're so darling!" she exclaimed.

Jim came back with the suitcases in tow, and they made their way to his sporty yellow Firebird.

"When did you get a car?" Francis asked, admiring its sleek design.

"I got it for my birthday." He grinned, putting the suitcases in the trunk. "You like it?"

"Yeah, it's nice." Francis felt a stab of pain shoot through her heart as she and the kids climbed into the backseat. *For my eighteenth birthday, I got kicked out of the house*, she thought, but she didn't voice her thoughts. It wasn't Jim's fault.

"What are your plans after graduation?" Francis asked Jim after they pulled out into traffic. Jim was graduating from high school that spring.

"I'll probably go to university and take political science. I have sent applications to UBC and U of A. I want to try to get into law school eventually," he answered.

"A lawyer," Francis said. "A doctor, a lawyer—what are you going to be, Monica?"

"Oh, I don't know yet." Monica laughed. "I just started high school. I don't want to think of college yet. I want to have fun first. Maybe I'll shock Mother and not go to college. My marks aren't that good, you know."

"What courses are you taking?" Francis wasn't surprised. Monica had always struggled in school. They discussed school for the rest of the drive.

They pulled into her parents' paved driveway and got out of

the car. Monica picked up Chantel, and Francis followed her into the house while Brad helped Uncle Jim with the suitcases. Francis felt her heart pounding. She had not crossed the threshold of this house in six years. How would her mother receive her? *Lord, help me*, she breathed.

"Welcome home." Her father hugged her heartily. "It's nice to have you here. Look at you." He tickled Chantel under the chin. "You're a big girl already." Chantel smiled shyly. They hung their coats up in the hall closet. Jim and Brad brought in the suitcases. Father ruffled Brad's hair and told him what a big boy he was.

"Come meet your grandma," Father said, leading the way into the living room. Mother was sitting in a leather chair—the look of perfection, as usual. Her face was carefully made up, and her dyed auburn hair was fashioned in a stylish hairdo. Not a hair was out of place.

"Mother, it's good to see you." Francis crossed the room and hugged her mother.

"So you came home," she said in a stilted tone.

"Mother, these are my children, Chantel and Brad. Come say hi to your grandma." She urged the children forward.

"Hi, Grandma," Brad said politely.

"Hi," Chantel echoed.

"Hello, children," Mother said to them. Then she turned to Monica. "Monica, please take these children to their room." She made a sweeping motion toward the door. Francis picked up Chantel and took Brad's hand as she followed Monica out of the room. She bit her lip to hold back the tears that stung her eyes. Obviously, Mother would not make this easy for her.

CHAPTER 18

Monica led them up the winding staircase to Francis's old bedroom. Memories washed over Francis as her gaze swept across the room. The big canopied bed, the bookshelf full of books, her study desk—everything had remained the same. The only change was the cot in the corner of the room.

"I thought Chantel could sleep with you, and Brad can sleep on the cot," Monica said. "Will that be all right? Or should Jim bring another cot?"

"Oh no," Francis assured her. "This will be wonderful."

"Look, I'm sorry about Mother," Monica said. "I don't know what's wrong with her."

"It's okay." Francis touched her arm. "It's not your fault."

"Do you mind if I sit here while you unpack?" Monica asked. "We don't get to see each other very often, so I hope we can get to know each other better while you're here."

"Of course you can stay." Francis crossed the room and hugged Monica. "But the children are going to be ready for a snack and a bath soon."

"Why don't I take them downstairs for a snack while you unpack, and then we can talk when the children are in bed," Monica said.

"That sounds good, if you don't mind," Francis answered. Both children willingly went with Monica since they were promised a snack.

Francis sat down on the edge of her bed and put her head in her hands. She choked back tears. She probably shouldn't have come. A knock on the door made her jump off the bed. Quickly, she dabbed at her eyes and opened a suitcase.

"May I come in?" Father poked his head around the door.

"Of course." Francis pulled the children's pajamas out of the suitcase and laid them on the bed.

Father looked around the room. "I'm sorry about your mother." He sighed, running his hand through his graying hair.

"I shouldn't have come." Francis massaged her throat, hoping her voice sounded normal despite the lump that was lodged there. She sat down on the edge of her bed, and Father sat down beside her.

"I'm glad you did." He sighed again. "Your mother can be so stubborn. I thought maybe seeing the children would soften her heart, and maybe it will yet. Who knows? I should have put my foot down a long time ago, but I was always so busy. Too busy. I've failed you miserably."

"I was a very rebellious teenager," Francis pointed out. "I had to have my own way. If I had done what Mother wanted me to do, I would be welcome in her house. I hurt her badly."

"You're still our daughter," Father said, "and your children are our grandchildren. I, for one, want you here. Ted is coming home on Saturday, so we'll all be together again. By the way, why didn't Mike come?"

Francis hung her head. "Mike left me. I haven't heard from him since he walked out a year and a half ago."

"Why didn't you tell me?" Father asked, surprised. "How are you surviving?"

"I have a job at the school now, which pays better and has better hours. A very nice Christian lady in my apartment takes care of Brad and Chantel while I'm at work."

"But I could take care of you," Father responded. "You shouldn't have to go through this alone."

"I'm not," Francis said. "I have some very good Christian friends who helped me, and I have Jesus now. I committed my life to Jesus last fall."

Father searched her eyes. "Are you still living in that apartment?"

"No, I moved to a different apartment after Mike left," Francis said. "We're comfortable, and it's close to the school where I work."

"You could move back here, and then I could take care of you and the kids. You could live in a better place and not have to go to work."

"Thanks, Father, but no thanks. I appreciate the offer. It's very sweet of you, but I am doing all right on my own." She laughed. "Although you could come visit more often."

"Tell me, Daughter." Concern clouded his gray eyes. "Did Mike ever abuse you?"

Francis inhaled sharply, the familiar pain stabbing her heart. "Sometimes. When he'd been drinking."

Father shook his head sadly. "The last time I was at your place, I figured something was wrong, but I couldn't put my finger on it. That was it, wasn't it?"

"I had some bruises on my body," Francis admitted, "but it only happened when he was drinking. He was always good to the kids; he never mistreated them."

Except that he killed your unborn baby, a little voice whispered in her head.

Father leaned over and gave her a hug. "I'll try to be there for you more from now on."

Monica brought the children into the room, and Father stood up to leave. He squatted down on the floor and hugged his grandchildren before leaving the room. After the children were bathed, Monica asked if she could read them a story. Francis got a Bible storybook from her suitcase, and Monica and the children snuggled up in bed to read while Francis finished unpacking. Then Francis prayed with the children and tucked them into bed. Monica ran down to the kitchen and came back with two steaming cups of hot chocolate. They pulled up a couple of chairs to the study desk and talked into the night.

Francis woke up to sunshine streaming into her bedroom window. She must have slept in. She checked on her sleeping children and then took her Bible off the nightstand and spent some time reading and praying before the children woke up. Today was Good Friday, but she didn't think Mother would want her to go to church with them. Francis hated missing church, but she was determined not to upset Mother more than she had to.

With a soft knock on the door, Monica peeked in.

"Oh, good. You're up," she said softly, not wanting to wake up the children. "I was wondering if you would like to come to church with me. I've started attending a little church not far from here. The people are friendly, and the messages are meaningful."

Francis stared at Monica. "Mother allows you to attend a different church?"

"She isn't enthused about it, but she allows it." Monica shrugged. "Sorry for the short notice. I should have asked you last night."

"I would love to join you," Francis said, getting out of bed. "I'll get dressed right away. I thought Mother probably wouldn't want us to go with them."

By the time Francis was ready, the children were up. Francis and Monica worked together to get them dressed and fed. Then they walked the couple of blocks to the small church. Francis and the children were welcomed by friendly people, and the pastor delivered a simple but powerful message. She was glad she had come.

On the short walk back, Francis asked the question that had been on her mind throughout the service: "Monica, have you asked Jesus into your heart?"

"Yes, I have," Monica answered. "I had friends who were Christians, and the way they talked about scripture was different.

They made it sound simple and authentic. I always thought we were Christians because we attended church. But I wasn't enthused about it like my friends were. In fact, I hardly knew what they were talking about. I realized that I didn't know the scriptures. I started attending their church, and the services spoke to me. I realized that Jesus loves me and that he made the ultimate sacrifice for me. I surrendered my life to Jesus last fall."

Francis grabbed Monica in a big hug right there on the sidewalk. "I'm so happy!" she exclaimed excitedly. "I accepted Jesus last fall as well."

Monica hugged her back. "Wow, isn't that something? I was wondering if you were a Christian when you pulled out the Bible stories last night, but I didn't have the courage to ask."

The sisters pulled apart and chattered happily as they turned into their parents' driveway.

Jim sauntered into the kitchen dressed in jeans and a T-shirt as Francis and Monica were preparing lunch.

"Did you only just get out of bed?" Francis asked.

"Yep," Jim answered, pouring himself a glass of milk. "Gotta get my beauty sleep, you know."

Francis shook her head as he went to play with the children and the puppy in the backyard.

Francis was glad that Mother didn't question her about Mike. Maybe Father had talked to her about it. They all had lunch together, and Francis was pleasantly surprised that it went well. Mother didn't say much, but at least she wasn't rude or hurtful either.

After lunch, Chantel surprised Francis by crawling up into her grandmother's lap with a children's storybook. She was even more surprised when Mother opened the book and started reading to her. By the time Mother finished reading, Chantel was nodding off. Francis thought Mother's face looked softer as she gazed down on her sleeping granddaughter. She gently took Chantel from

Mother's arms and carried her off to bed. Francis laid her on the big bed in her room and pulled a blanket over her.

When Francis came back downstairs, she found Mother sitting alone in the living room.

"Where is everyone?" she asked.

"Jim and Monica took Brad outside to play with the puppy," Mother replied. "Your Father is watching TV in the family room."

Francis sat down in the soft leather chair next to her mother. "Mother," she said. Unsure how to broach the subject, she decided to jump right in. "I want to apologize for not being a good daughter to you."

Mother's startled look was evidence that she hadn't expected an apology.

"I know you had high expectations for me," Francis said, continuing before Mother could say anything. "I was rebellious, and I apologize for that."

"You're sorry you married Mike?" Mother's look was incredulous.

"That's not what I mean." Francis hurried on. How could she make Mother understand? "I mean I should have been more patient. Maybe we should have waited longer to get married. What I'm saying, Mother, is that I should have been more sensitive to your feelings."

Mother rested her head back against her chair and closed her eyes. She was quiet for so long that Francis thought she had dozed off. Francis got up to go in search of Brad and her siblings.

"Francis?" Mother called softly just before she reached the door.

"Yes, Mother?" Francis turned around, her hand on the doorknob.

"Thank you for the apology," she said, her head still resting on the back of her chair.

Is that a tear in the corner of Mother's eye? Francis wondered.

"Thank you for letting me come home," Francis replied softly.

She turned the knob and walked out of the room. She went outside and sat on the back step, watching Brad, Jim, and Monica play with the puppy.

By the time Francis and the children got on the bus on Monday, Francis figured the weekend had gone pretty well. Not only had Mother read to the children, but also, Francis had noticed Mother standing at the window, watching Brad play with the puppy in the backyard. She smiled to herself as she thought of the soft expression on Mother's face when she'd thought no one was looking.

Yes, Francis thought peacefully, *I think Brad and Chantel wormed their way into Mother's heart.*

Whenever Mary and Melvin met at parties, they spent the evening together. Melvin made her laugh and flattered her with attention. He taught the group new games and dance steps, making the party livelier. Mary was flattered that he chose to spend his time with her. The only time she felt uncomfortable with him was when he tried to pressure her into a physical relationship.

Mama and Papa warned her about her new friends. They had heard about the parties and asked Mary if she was involved with them.

"We are very concerned about your choice of friends," Papa told her. "From what we hear, they are not the kind of people we want you to associate with."

"I don't know why you don't want me to have friends," Mary said defensively, anger rising within her. They had no right to pick her friends.

"We want you to have friends," Mama insisted. "You have many good friends that you hardly ever see anymore. You should spend more time with them."

Mary saw Annie's blue sedan drive into their yard.

"They don't understand me!" Mary called over her shoulder to her parents as she hurried out the door. She ran to Annie's car, jumped in, and slammed the door.

"Whoa," Annie said. "What's wrong?"

"Parents," Mary muttered. "They want me to spend time with the church group. They've heard rumors about parties, and they don't want me hanging out with you."

Annie laughed, turning the car around. "Don't worry about it. Here—have a cigarette." She tossed the package to Mary. "It'll help you relax."

Mary took one and lit it, dragging the smoke into her lungs as they drove off her yard.

"Do they know about Melvin?" Tina asked, rummaging in her purse for her lipstick. She always applied her makeup in the car because her parents didn't allow her to wear it.

"No," Mary said, pushing the guilt she felt into the recesses of her mind. "I'm sure they don't, or they would tie me up and not let me leave the house."

Mary was surprised to find Melvin at the party. She had only seen him a handful of times over the summer. She grabbed the beer he handed her and took a drink as he slung his arm over her shoulders. This was what she needed to unwind from her clash with Papa, she told herself. They sat side by side at the table, watching the card game in progress and nursing their beers. When someone put a record on the record player, Melvin pulled Mary into his arms. She gulped down the remainder of her beer before he whisked her onto the floor. They kicked up their heels and twirled and laughed until Mary felt exhausted. When they finally sank down into their chairs, Melvin handed her a drink. Mary downed it in a few gulps, feeling the fiery liquid wash down her throat all the way to her stomach. Melvin chuckled and fixed her another drink, which she sipped more slowly. When the card game was over and a new one started, Melvin and Mary joined in. Halfway through the game, Melvin got up and mixed them more drinks.

After the game, Melvin pulled her up out of her chair to dance again, and she was surprised to find that she was tipsy. Her head felt fuzzy, and she realized she shouldn't have downed those drinks so fast. When the music ended, Melvin kept his arm around Mary as he led her outside. A million tiny stars and a sliver of silver moon lit the otherwise black sky. The late-October night had a chill to it that made Mary shiver involuntarily.

"Are you cold?" Melvin asked, opening the car door. "Here—get in, and I'll turn the heat up." She slid in, giggling as she almost fell over.

Melvin got in after her and started the car, cranking both the heat and the volume on his eight-track player. Encircling her with his long arms, he pulled her close against him.

"You go ahead and rest," he murmured against her soft hair as she slumped against him. As the car warmed up, she relaxed against Melvin's chest, struggling to keep her heavy eyelids open.

If only my brain wasn't so foggy, she thought to herself as she sank deeper into the fog. Through the haze, she was aware of trying to push Melvin away, but she didn't have the energy. Her mumbled objections sounded garbled to her ears.

When Melvin lit a cigarette, Mary grabbed the door handle, hung her head out, and lost her supper. Melvin lit a second cigarette and handed it to her.

"It'll make you feel better," he told her. "Calm your stomach."

Mary took the cigarette and inhaled. At least it dispelled the bad taste in her mouth.

It was late when Melvin drove her home. Mary hoped her parents weren't waiting up for her. She couldn't have them see her like this. Luckily, the house was dark, although she was sure her parents weren't sleeping.

She took great care in opening the front door as quietly as she could, hoping it wouldn't creak, and remembered to turn the doorknob as she gently pulled the door closed behind her. She quietly tiptoed to her bedroom, where she undressed quickly and sank into bed. Her stomach was still a little unsettled, but her brain wasn't as fuzzy anymore. As her head sank into her soft pillow, visions of what she could remember of the evening tugged at her mind, but she couldn't sort them out now. Sleep overcame her.

When Mama woke her up the next morning for church, Mary told her she wasn't feeling well and immediately went back to sleep. She woke up with the worst pounding in her head that she'd ever experienced. The bright sunlight streaming in through her window hurt her head. She got up and downed a couple of aspirin before getting dressed. Mama had dinner cooking slowly on the back of the woodstove, so she set the table. Since she wasn't ready to face Mama and Papa and couldn't stand the thought of food, she left a note saying she had gone for a walk and then grabbed her sweater and headed to David's cabin.

I never thought it would come to this, Mary thought as she walked down the dusty dirt path. Filled with guilt and shame, she considered the depths to which she had sunk. Tears trickled down her cheeks, and her heart ached with a searing physical pain. She could never erase what had happened.

Mary let herself into the cabin and waited a few minutes for her eyes to adjust to the dim lighting. She sat down on David's bed and hugged his pillow close to her as she released her pent-up emotions.

"If only David were here, none of this would have happened!" she cried out in pain. "If only life would go back to the way it was."

But that could never be. David was gone, and her life had deteriorated to a despicable level. Smoking, drinking, partying—it was all a facade. She realized the people she was hanging out with weren't real friends. Her life had become complicated. She shuddered to think what David would say if he could see her now.

Her tears soaked David's pillow, and her head throbbed as she curled up in his bunk.

"Mary, wake up!" Mama was bending over her, shaking her slightly.

Mary looked around, confused at her surroundings, before her memory came flooding back. "Mama, what are you doing here?"

"I came looking for you." Mama stroked Mary's hair back from her tear-stained face. "I thought I might find you here."

As Mary looked into Mama's sad eyes, realization dawned on her that Mama came here to be close to David as well.

"Oh, Mama, it's so hard!" Mary cried, reaching out to Mama.

"I know." Mama wrapped her arms around Mary. "I know."

They cried together with their arms wrapped around each other, thinking their own thoughts yet communing in spirit.

"David was so proud of this little cabin that he and John built," Mama whispered, mopping up her face. "I remember the day they completed it. There was no holding those boys back from sleeping here that night." Mama reminisced, wiping the occasional tear from her eyes as she shared memories of David. Mary heard the heartache in her voice.

"How do you do it, Mama?" Mary asked. "How do you go on?"

"David is in heaven," Mama answered softly and wistfully. "God did not create us to stay on this earth. Each one of us has to die eventually." Mama's voice caught in her throat, and she took a moment to control the tremor. "God had a purpose for calling David home, and although it causes us a lot of pain, it makes it bearable to know he's in heaven waiting for us. I mourn for him, I miss him, and I always will. But I find a lot of comfort in reading the Bible. I can feel God helping me through it."

"I don't feel that," Mary said.

"That's because you've been running, Mary," Mama said softly. "Instead of turning to God, you've been turning against him. God won't help you like that. You need to ask him for help, and then he will help you. He wants you to choose him over everything else, but he won't force you. He allows each one of us to make that choice for ourselves." Mama took another tissue from her pocket and wiped her eyes.

Mary felt something stir deep inside her heart. She knew what Mama was saying was the truth. She was running. She blamed God. Because of that, she had sinned so badly that God had surely given up on her.

Mary stood up. "I'm going back to the house."

"You go ahead," Mama said, and Mary could see the pain deep in her eyes. "I'll come in a bit."

CHAPTER 19

By December, the ground was covered in snow. With the snow came flu season, and although Mary tried her best to keep up with her schoolwork, she couldn't win this fight against the flu bug. She continued to feel nauseated and tired. Even after a good night's sleep, it was hard for her to keep alert during class. She took extra vitamins, but they didn't help, so finally, Mama suggested she see a doctor.

On the afternoon of her appointment, Mary signed out of school and walked the couple of blocks to the clinic. The air was crisp, but the walk would do her good. The snow sparkled in the afternoon sunlight like a million tiny, dazzling diamonds. The nurse at the clinic ushered her into a small examining room to wait for the doctor.

"Hello, Mary," Dr. Stevens said as he entered the examining room, chart in hand. "How are you today?"

"I can't get over the flu," Mary told him.

Dr. Stevens sat down on the chair across from her and studied her with friendly gray eyes. "Tell me about it," he said. Mary told him about her continued feelings of nausea and tiredness, which were beginning to affect her schoolwork.

"You've been through a lot recently," the doctor said sympathetically. "How old are you now, Mary?" He glanced down at her chart.

"Fifteen. I'll be sixteen next month," Mary replied.

"When did these symptoms start?" he asked.

"I've had them for a couple of weeks now," Mary told him.

After more questioning, the doctor said he wanted to run some tests. He left the room, and a nurse came in, took her to the lab for testing, and then showed her back into the examining room. Soon the doctor came back into the room. He sat down in the chair opposite her. His face looked tired and serious.

"Mary, I don't know how to tell you this," Dr. Stevens said. He had been her family doctor for as long as Mary could remember. "The reason you're not feeling well is because you're pregnant."

Mary's shock registered on her face. She quickly looked down at her shoes. She felt the heat rising into her face, and her mouth felt dry.

"Mary," the doctor continued, "you'll have to tell your parents right away. They need to help you through this."

"I can't tell them." Mary looked up pleadingly. "I need to think first."

"All right, Mary," the doctor said as he started writing on a piece of paper, "but you need to tell them soon. Here." He handed the paper to her. "You can buy these prenatal vitamins at the drugstore. They will give you energy. Your hemoglobin is low, which often happens during pregnancy. You have to take good care of yourself for the baby's sake. Eat healthy, well-balanced meals; go for walks; and get lots of rest. Don't smoke or drink alcohol, as that will harm your baby. Come back to see me in a month."

Mary's knees felt wobbly as she got to her feet. Thanking the doctor, she took the paper from his hand and stumbled out of the clinic in a daze. This couldn't be happening to her.

What will I do? She crumpled up the slip of paper and stuck it in her pocket. *How do I tell Mama and Papa? They'll be devastated. How will I raise a child?* A myriad of thoughts raced through her mind, tumbling over each other.

By the time she reached the school, she had vowed not to tell anyone until she talked with Melvin, but she didn't know when she would see him again. She was glad that the school buses were already lining up outside the school. She got on her bus without bothering to go back into school.

Maybe Melvin will know what to do. Thoughts raced through Mary's mind. *We'll have to get married.* She couldn't see any other way out of this predicament.

She extracted a novel from her pocket and pretended to be reading when Lena came onto the bus. They still shared a seat.

"Hi," Lena said as she slid into the seat next to Mary.

"Hi," Mary mumbled. Lena dug around in her lunch bag for the apple she'd saved to snack on during the drive home.

I hope she starts reading so she won't want to talk. Mary stared at her book without seeing it. *How did I let myself sink this far?*

It's all your fault. You shouldn't drink until you nearly pass out, a voice in her head told her as the bus bumped down the road. She hadn't seen Melvin since that October night. She hadn't even been back to a party.

Lena touched Mary's arm. "Is something wrong?" she whispered.

"No," Mary said, casting a quick sideways glance in Lena's direction. She couldn't look Lena in the eyes.

"You're holding your book upside down," Lena whispered. Mary could hear the concern in her voice. "And you look like you've seen a ghost."

Mary looked down at her book and turned it around. She closed her eyes and leaned her head back against the seat. "I have a headache," she said, which wasn't exactly a lie. Her head was throbbing. She kept her eyes closed until they reached her stop.

"Hope you feel better soon," Lena said as Mary got up to leave.

"Thanks," Mary mumbled.

"I'll race you to the house!" Benny said as soon as she reached the driveway. He was so rambunctious that Mary didn't know how he ever got through a day in school. He started running, turning his head to look back at her. Mary jogged after him, which brought squeals of laughter from Benny. He burst through the door with Mary on his heels.

"Hi," Mama said from the kitchen. "Who won the race?" She had obviously been watching from the window.

"I did," Benny said breathlessly. "Mary can't run very fast."

Mary chucked him under the chin. "You had a head start."

"I'm hungry." Benny charged into the kitchen, leaving behind a trail of boots, jacket, and lunch kit.

"First, you clean up your stuff," Mama said. "Then you can have some milk and cookies." Mary could smell the fresh cookies. She was hungry, but she knew if she ate too much, it would make her sick. She had to be careful; she got sick if she didn't eat enough, and she got sick if she ate too much. She helped herself to a glass of cold milk and a cookie.

"No homework tonight?" Mama asked.

"Not tonight," Mary responded, biting into a freshly baked chocolate chip cookie. She hadn't thought about getting her books after school.

"How was your appointment with the doctor?" Mama asked after Benny had gone outside to find Papa.

"He said I should feel better before long," Mary said. She didn't want to lie to Mama, but she couldn't tell her everything either. "I just have to wait it out."

During lunch break the following day, Mary went to the school library to do some research on pregnancy. She wanted to know what to expect, but she couldn't ask Mama or anyone else. Sitting at a table in the far corner, she pored over the books she had pulled from the shelf, and she carefully put them back where she'd found them before leaving the library.

"Mary, wait up!" Annie called to her as she walked to her locker. Mary waited for Annie to catch up with her.

"My folks are going to be out of town this weekend," Annie told her excitedly as they walked down the hall together, "so the party's at my house Saturday night. Should I pick you up? I thought maybe I could pick you up in the afternoon. You could tell your mom we're going shopping or something."

"I can't," Mary said as she opened her locker. "I have plans for Saturday."

"Parents still giving you trouble?" Annie asked.

"Not really." Mary shrugged. Then she had an idea. "Can you do me a favor?"

"Sure, what?"

"If Melvin's at the party, can you ask him to meet me at the end of my driveway at nine?"

"I can sure do that." Annie laughed as she turned and continued down the hall.

Mary opened her locker to retrieve her books for the afternoon.

As Mary went about cleaning the house and bringing in firewood and snow for water, she fought the mounting anxiety that threatened to make her physically sick. *Will Melvin come? What will I do if he doesn't? How will I tell him if he does? How will he react?* Questions tumbled through her mind.

"Mary!"

She could hear by Mama's tone of voice that this wasn't the first time she had called her name. "What?" Mary asked, picking up a stack of plates and sinking them into the sudsy water.

"Benny is looking for his airplane. Have you seen it?"

"I think I saw it in the porch," Mary answered, scrubbing at the dishes.

Benny ran from the room to look in the porch.

"You are very preoccupied today." Mama picked up a tea towel and started drying the dishes. "Is something wrong?"

"No, I'm just tired," Mary said, careful to keep her eyes on the dishes.

"You've been very busy today," Mama said. "You'll have to relax with a good book tonight, or do you want Papa to take you to see Lena?"

"No," Mary responded. Mama was always trying to get her to go see her old friends. "Maybe I'll read a book."

Later that evening, Mary dressed in her warm coat, boots, and scarf.

"I'm going for a walk," she called to her parents, who were relaxing in the living room.

"Don't stay out too long," Mama called back.

Mary stepped through the door into the dark December night. Snowflakes floated lazily from the sky in sharp contrast to Mary's erratically beating heart as her boots crunched along the driveway.

Will Melvin come? she wondered. Part of her wanted him to, and part of her didn't ever want to see him again. She reached the end of the driveway. He wasn't there. Unexpected relief flooded over her.

She stood for a few minutes where the driveway met the road.

I might as well take advantage of the beautiful evening and go for a walk, she decided. Her step was lighter than it had been a couple of minutes ago.

As she started down the road, she thought she heard a car approaching. She looked around but couldn't see anything. Confused, she started walking again. Then, through the falling snow, she noticed a car coming toward her without its lights on. She stopped in her tracks, her heart rate speeding up.

Who would come down the road without lights? she wondered. She was keenly aware that she was all alone. What if it was someone up to no good? The car stopped beside her.

"Hey, how's it going?" Melvin asked through the rolled-down window.

Mary tried to calm her wildly beating heart. "Why are you driving without your lights on?" she asked.

"Annie said to meet you at the end of your driveway, so I figured you didn't want your folks to know I was coming, so I cut the lights. Come on. Jump in," he said.

Mary walked around to the passenger side and slid into the seat. The scent of his air freshener threatened to overpower her, so she opened the window an inch.

Melvin pulled the car off the road and then put it in park and reached for her.

"Come here," he drawled. "I'll warm you up."

"No, Melvin." She pushed him away. "We need to talk."

By the light of the dashboard, she could see him raise his eyebrows. "What's to talk about? Annie said you wanted me to meet you. Do you want to go to the party?"

"No." Mary shook her head. "I don't want to go to the party."

"That's my girl." Melvin reached out and pulled her toward him.

Mary pushed hard at his chest and managed to release herself from his hold. Sitting up in the passenger seat, she drew a deep breath and blurted, "I'm pregnant."

Melvin's arms froze in midair, and Mary bit her lip. This was not how she had rehearsed telling him.

"What?" he asked incredulously, his arms dropping like lead pipes.

"I couldn't believe it either."

"Are you sure?"

"I saw a doctor."

He pounded his fist into the steering wheel as he exploded in a few choice expletives and then turned to look at her. "What are you going to do about it?"

Mary stared down at her hands. "I don't know."

"Who all knows about this?" he asked, leaning toward her as he tried to search her eyes.

"No one," she answered. "Just me, you, and the doctor."

"Good. Keep it that way," he said, reaching for her hand. "I have an idea. I'm going home for Christmas, and I'll try to find someone who can help you. Give me a couple of weeks. I'll have it all figured out when I return from the city," he promised as Mary reached for the door handle and pushed the door open.

Melvin turned the car around and drove back the way he had come. She was glad he didn't switch on the lights until he reached the intersection. She retraced her steps, feeling relieved that she had told Melvin. At least she wasn't alone in this anymore. She didn't know what Melvin had in mind, but she felt better that he seemed confident he could work it out. She agonized over how Mama and Papa would react when she told them. It would break their hearts.

On Christmas Eve, Mary and Benny sat on the couch in the living room, looking at photo albums. Papa relaxed in his recliner, and Mama sat in her rocking chair as they reminisced about days gone by, when a car turned into their driveway.

"I wonder who that could be," Papa said, watching the approaching headlights.

"I'll find out," Mary volunteered.

After pushing the photo album into Benny's lap, she opened the door on the first knock and found herself face-to-face with John. Old familiar feelings rushed over her as she stood frozen in time.

"Merry Christmas, Mary." He grinned. "Do you mind if I come in?"

"Of course. Come on in." She gathered her wits about her and stepped aside. "I am surprised to see you."

"I can tell." John chuckled as he shrugged out of his coat. "A ghost of Christmas past?"

"Maybe," Mary said, feeling the heat rise to her face as she took his coat and hung it on a peg beside the door.

When she turned back, John was already walking to the living room to meet the rest of the family.

"Merry Christmas!" he said, greeting them cheerfully from the living room door.

"Well, what do you know?" Papa exclaimed, getting up from his chair to shake John's hand. "What a pleasant surprise."

"Came home yesterday," John said, taking Papa's outstretched hand and then giving Mama a hug. "Had to come see how you folks are making out."

"I'm so glad you came." Mama wiped a tear from the corner of her eye. "We miss seeing you. Take a seat." She pointed toward the couch, and John ruffled Benny's hair as he sat down beside him.

"Wow, you sure have grown since I saw you last!"

"I'm going to school now," Benny informed him, smiling up at John proudly.

"Good for you!" John exclaimed. "Do you enjoy it?"

Benny went into great detail about his friends at school and what he was learning.

"Are you going to show me those pictures?" John asked after a while, indicating the photo album on Benny's lap.

"Sure," Benny answered, edging the photo album closer to John. Mary sat down on the other side of Benny, trying to calm her pounding heart.

"Is that you, Mary?" John asked, holding the photo album up for a closer look. "That must be you with David. I can't remember you ever having short hair. How old were you there?"

Mary looked over Benny to see the picture he referred to. It was a picture of her and David sitting on a stack of straw bales. Her hair was cut in a short bob complete with bangs.

She laughed. "Mama wasn't very happy with me. I cut my hair, so Mama had to cut it really short because I had done such a bad job. I was probably six years old."

"Much too old to be cutting her hair." Mama laughed. "By that time, I thought she would know better."

"I got a good spanking for it," Mary said. "I never tried that again."

"Makes you look a lot different," John said, looking at Mary. "I wouldn't have recognized you, but I recognized David." He studied the picture again and then went on to the next page.

"How is Bible school?" Mama asked when they got to the end of the photo album, and Benny closed the book.

John regaled his audience with stories of his studies and his adventures in the city. Mary tried to envision John in all the situations he explained, but she found the concept of living in the city elusive.

"Do you still recite the Christmas story from memory on Christmas Eve?" John asked as the evening drew to a close.

"We haven't since David passed away," Papa said, "but if you would join us, we could certainly do it again."

"I would love to," John said, glancing at Mary. "I always loved that tradition you had."

Mary dropped her gaze to her hands lying in her lap. She had no right to feel butterflies in her stomach when John looked at her. Life had taken her down a different road, and she felt a deep sadness in the depths of her heart.

Anna Hildebrandt was hopeful that her daughter was reconsidering her rebellious ways. Mary had not gone out with her questionable friends at all over the Christmas holidays, much to Anna's relief.

"Mary seems to have changed," she whispered to Jacob one night as she lay beside him in bed. "She's been staying at home so much. I wonder if she had a falling out with her friends."

"Has she said anything to you about that?" Jacob asked.

"No," Anna said, "but she has changed. She seems less rebellious toward us. Haven't you noticed that?"

"Jo, I have," her husband answered, "but I don't want to read too much into it."

"I can't help myself," Anna replied. "I am hopeful that she'll start taking an interest in her church friends again. I sense that she has a lot on her mind, and I wonder if she is under conviction."

"I hope you're right," Jacob said thoughtfully. "Time will tell."

Shortly after school started in January, Mary noticed Annie hurrying down the hall toward her during lunch hour.

"Mary, you won't believe this." She spoke softly but with a tone of excited urgency when she reached Mary. "Melvin is waiting for you outside. He asked me to get you."

"Really?" Mary couldn't believe he would come to her school.

"He must have missed you a lot to come here in broad daylight!" Annie exclaimed.

"I'd better find out what he wants," Mary said, getting her jacket from her locker. She left Annie staring after her.

Melvin leaned over and opened the passenger door, motioning for her to get in.

"This is going to start rumors—you showing up at school like this," Mary said as she slipped into the passenger seat.

"Yeah, well, hi to you too." Melvin grinned at her. "You want to go for a drive?"

"Oh no!" Mary exclaimed. "That would be even worse."

Melvin chuckled as he patted her hand. "Always so concerned about what others will think. I came to tell you that I have a plan, just like I said I would. I found a place in the city that takes care of girls in trouble. All you have to do is go see this doctor. Here's his name, address, and phone number." He handed her a slip of paper. "He'll take care of you."

"But this address is in Edmonton," Mary said, looking down at the slip of paper in her hand. "I can't go to the city."

"Of course you can," Melvin said. "I'll take you to the bus depot, and the bus will take you to the city."

"Alone?" Mary asked, alarmed.

"Of course," Melvin replied. "It's not a big deal."

"What's so special about this doctor? How can he help me?"

"He's an abortionist." Melvin grinned. "He can get rid of your little problem in no time, and nobody ever needs to know. He'll just do a tiny little procedure. No big deal. You don't want your parents to know about this, right?"

"An abortion!" Mary recoiled, horrified. "You want me to kill our baby?"

"It's not really a baby yet," Melvin explained. "It's just some tissue that will eventually form into a baby, but it's nothing yet. Look, Mary, what would you have me do? Marry you?" He laughed. "That would be ridiculous. We're both young; we still have our lives ahead of us."

Mary turned her head and looked out the window as she fought hard against the tears that were threatening to overwhelm her. *An abortion. That never crossed my mind.*

"Look, once you get back from the city, we can pick up where we left off." He winked at her. "You pack a bag, and I'll pick you up Sunday morning while your folks are in church. Then you'll be long gone by the time they realize you're not at home."

"What will I tell them?"

"Leave them a note saying you've gone to the city with some friends for a week. You should be back by then." Melvin grinned at her confidently. "No big deal."

"I can't. I've never been to the city before. I'll never find my way around." The thought terrified her.

"Not a problem," Melvin said. "There are always cabs waiting outside the bus depot. You just give the cabbie this address, and he can take you right to the doctor's office. You'll probably need to stay in the city for a few days, so you can stay at this hotel. It's just a block from the doctor's office, so you can walk there." He took the paper from Mary; turned it over, revealing another address; and gave it back to her. "Then you can come back home on the bus."

"I don't have money for a bus ticket, hotel rooms, and food."

"I'll give you money for all that," Melvin said, brushing her concern aside. "You won't be able to tell your folks, of course, but you'll only be gone for a few days. A week tops."

"I have to go to class," Mary said abruptly, reaching for the door handle. A wave of revulsion swept over her, and she knew she had to get away from Melvin.

"Be ready Sunday morning," he called after her.

Sunday would be her sixteenth birthday. She didn't bother telling Melvin.

All day, she mulled over Melvin's plan. *I can't kill my baby,* she told herself. Then she thought of Mama and Papa. *I can't tell them. It would break their hearts.* She went back and forth in her mind all day. Ashamed and degraded, she felt as if her predicament were written all over her face, as if at any time, someone would notice she was pregnant. Mama and Papa would be ashamed. Benny would be teased. By the end of the school day, her head had started throbbing again.

CHAPTER 20

Mary stepped onto the Greyhound bus headed for Edmonton. She slumped down in a window seat in the second row and watched Melvin get into his car and speed away without a backward glance. She couldn't believe she was doing this. Over the last few days, she had mulled over her options a million times, but she couldn't see any other way out. A couple of times, she had almost broken down and told Mama she was pregnant, but she had been unable to.

I'm such a coward, Mary lamented silently. *It would break Mama's and Papa's hearts.* She had no one to turn to. If David were still alive, maybe she could have told him. He would have helped her. He always knew what to do. The bus swayed slightly as it turned onto the highway.

Mary placed one hand on her abdomen as she stared out the window at the stark, bare poplar trees as the bus left the small town behind. She was on her way to the city to kill her baby.

Baby. Melvin had said it wasn't a baby yet, but she knew better. How could it not be a baby? If it wasn't a baby yet, then when would it be? If she gave birth to it in another six or seven months, it would be a baby. But that wouldn't happen, because she was a coward, and Melvin didn't care about her or the baby. She couldn't support a baby on her own. Mary kept her face turned toward the window as hot tears flowed down her cheeks unheeded. She felt alone.

It started to snow. Mary imagined herself as one of the snowflakes drifting to an unknown destination. Many other snowflakes were around, but they didn't care about her. She was just one of many among strangers.

"This is a half-hour stop," the driver announced as he stopped in a small town a couple of hours later. "There are washrooms and a snack bar inside. Be back on the bus in half an hour."

Mary was nervous to get off the bus, but she needed a washroom break, and she didn't want to use the one at the back of the bus. She stood up. It felt good to stretch her legs. Cold wind and snow stung her face as she stepped off the bus and hurried into the depot. Warmth enveloped her as she stepped across the threshold and looked around for the washroom sign. The place was crowded, and she had to weave her way around people as she headed toward the back of the small depot.

By now, Mama and Papa will be back from church, Mary thought as she took her seat on the bus a little while later. *I wonder if they've found my note. I hope they won't worry too much.* She had told them she'd be back in a week. She didn't know what she would say to them when she got back home. All she knew was that they must never know about this pregnancy.

"May I sit here?" A pleasant male voice interrupted Mary's thoughts.

She turned to see that the bus had filled up, and a pair of clear blue eyes were smiling down at her from under a shock of the reddest hair Mary had ever seen.

"Of course." Mary shifted in her seat. She didn't want someone sharing her seat, but it looked as if most of the seats were taken.

"Thanks." The young man sat down. "I'm Patrick."

"I'm Mary," she said.

"Pleased to meet you, Mary." Patrick smiled. "Where are you headed?"

"Edmonton."

"That's where I'm headed as well. Do you live there?"

"No."

"Where are you from?"

"Up north."

Patrick grimaced. "Fair enough. I live in Edmonton, but I work in the oil fields. I'm going home to see my folks. Couldn't make it down for Christmas."

Mary opened her book and felt relieved when Patrick put his seat back and pulled his baseball cap down over his eyes. Soon Mary heard his even breathing, and she relaxed a little. She didn't want to talk to him or anyone else.

She turned her face to the window and watched the unfamiliar landscape and swirling snow as they sped by, her open book forgotten on her lap. She tried to envision what Edmonton would be like, searching her memory for what she had heard about it. John had made it sound exciting and adventurous, but to her, it was scary. Her chest felt tight with anxiety. She had never been this far away from home. She couldn't imagine what she was getting into, but she couldn't go back now. She felt her pocket for the substantial amount of money Melvin had given her.

Tears pricked the back of her eyelids as she closed her eyes in misery. She must have dozed off, because when she opened her eyes, she noticed that there was a lot more traffic, and she could see tall buildings looming up ahead.

"Looks like we're almost there." Patrick grinned at her. "Do you have someone picking you up?"

"No," Mary answered, "I'll get a cab."

"Where to?" Patrick asked. "I'm sorry," he added quickly before Mary had a chance to respond. "I tend to ask too many questions. Let me rephrase that. Are you visiting family or friends in the city?"

"No," Mary mumbled, turning to look out the window as she felt her face flush. She couldn't tell this friendly guy that she had come to the city to kill her baby. It was none of his business anyway.

"My mom was disappointed that I couldn't be home for Christmas. I'm planning to go to Bible college next fall," Patrick said, "so for now, I stay in the oil fields as much as possible to save money to go to school."

"Bible school," Mary repeated, thinking of John. "So you're a Christian?"

Patrick's eyes sparkled. "Yes, I am. Made my decision to follow Jesus when I was twelve years old. What about you?"

Mary bit her lip as she turned to look out the window. *Am I a Christian?* Her parents were. David was. John was. Melvin certainly wasn't. Was she? *"Come unto me, all ye that labor and are heavy laden, and I will give you rest."* The verse flashed through her mind.

Christians wouldn't do what I have done. What I am about to do. She sighed heavily as she tried to discreetly wipe the sudden tears from her eyes.

Patrick saw deep emotions cross the girl's face and wondered what she was struggling with. He let the question hang between them but didn't pressure her for an answer. He breathed a prayer for her and then changed the subject by pointing out various sites they were passing.

Mary felt herself become smaller and smaller as they traveled farther into the city. She looked way up to the tops of the skyscrapers. She had never seen anything that tall. What if they fell down on her? *"Then shall they begin to say to the mountains, fall on us; and to the hills, cover us."* Mary shook her head to clear her mind. Why had she thought of that verse now? It was something Jesus had said would happen in the future. She shuddered as she looked up at the tall buildings again. Would God make them fall on her because of what she had done and was about to do?

"We're here," Patrick announced as the bus ground to a stop at the terminal. He stepped into the aisle and took a step back so she could go ahead of him. Mary stepped off the bus and waited for the bus driver to get her suitcase. Once he set her suitcase on the pavement, she grabbed it and followed the other passengers through the double doors into a huge waiting area.

Mary looked around, taking in the huge room with rows of chairs in the middle. Some were empty, and some had people sitting in them, reading newspapers or books. She sat down on the nearest chair to get her bearings.

Where do I go to get a cab? she wondered as she searched the terminal. She tried to remember. *Melvin said there were always lots of cabs, but where?*

She noticed a couple of men watching her from across the room, and she shivered with a sudden surge of apprehension. *"Men pick up runaway teenage girls in bus depots, and sometimes they are never heard from again,"* she heard her social studies teacher say in her mind. For her own good, she should at least look as if she knew what she was doing. She saw Patrick talking to a pretty brunette lady who was probably a couple of years older than him. The lady turned to look at her, and their eyes made contact before she turned back to Patrick. Mary glanced back at the men on the other side of the room. One with a beaded leather coat was walking in her direction. In a panic, she rose from her seat, grabbed her small suitcase, and headed the opposite way. In her hurry, she tripped over someone's bag and felt herself fall.

"Whoa." A hand grabbed her arm. Mary lifted her panicked eyes to meet Patrick's clear blue eyes. He smiled at her. "Wouldn't want you to fall on your face, now, would we?"

"Th-thank you," Mary stammered, feeling the ever-ready tears stinging the backs of her eyes. "That was clumsy of me."

"Mary," Patrick said as the brunette lady joined him, "this is Francis. She's a good friend of the family, and she came to pick me up. She has offered to give you a ride wherever you want to go."

"Oh," said Mary, "I couldn't impose on you like that. I just need to get a cab. Do you know where I can get one?"

"Please," the lady named Francis said, "it's no trouble. We noticed those men looking at you like you were a drumstick, and

I couldn't live with myself if they made trouble for you. Where are you headed?"

"To this hotel," Mary replied, digging in her pocket for the address.

Francis raised her eyebrows and exchanged looks with Patrick, who was wearing a frown.

"Do you mind my asking why you're staying at that hotel?" Francis asked gently.

Mary looked at Francis and then at Patrick. She bit the inside of her lip. "I have a doctor's appointment close to it."

"Look," Francis said, touching Mary's arm, "that hotel is not a safe place for a young woman to stay by herself, but I have an idea. I live in an apartment with my two little children. Why don't you come home with me? I don't have much room, and you would have to sleep on the couch, but you're certainly welcome."

Mary looked from Francis to Patrick and then to the men across the room. They were still watching her, although the one man had stopped advancing. A chill ran up her spine, and she shivered involuntarily. She thought about an article she had read about young girls, especially runaways, being snatched up by pimps in the city. She didn't know Francis, but at least she seemed friendly, and Patrick was a Christian.

"Okay," she said quickly.

"Good." Francis's smile seemed to light up her face as she picked up Mary's suitcase. "Follow me."

Mary and Patrick fell into step with Francis as she headed toward the door.

During the drive, Francis told her that she had worked with Patrick's mother in a restaurant and that they had become close friends.

"Do you want to come in?" Patrick turned to Mary as Francis parked the car in front of his house.

"I have to go in and pick up my kids," Francis said, smiling at Mary. "Maggie babysat them while I went to pick up Patrick.

You're welcome to come in with us or wait in the car, whichever you prefer."

"I'll wait here," Mary responded. She was afraid to wait in the car by herself, but she didn't want to meet any more strangers today.

Francis left the car running. Patrick grabbed his bags out of the trunk and followed Francis to the door. As soon as they stepped into the house, Mary locked all the car doors. She had heard awful stories about crime in the city. Those men back at the bus station had made her jittery, and she wasn't taking any chances. It wasn't long before Francis emerged from the house with two little children in tow, bundled up against the cold winter night. Mary quickly unlocked the car doors, not wanting Francis to know how scared she was.

The front passenger door opened, and the two youngsters scrambled into the front seat with their mother. Their chatter halted when they noticed the stranger in the backseat, and they eyed Mary curiously. Francis closed the door, walked around to the driver's side, and slid behind the wheel.

"This is Mary," Francis told the children. "She's going to spend the night at our house." She turned to look at Mary. "These are my children, Brad and Chantel."

"Hi," Mary said, feeling a bit awkward.

"Hi," the children said in unison before settling down for the ride.

Mary looked out the side window at the dark night lit up by numerous streetlights. She was amazed at the amount of traffic and flashing neon signs. She felt small in this big, unfamiliar world she'd stepped into.

What was I thinking, coming to the city on my own? A sharp stab in the area of her heart reminded her of her predicament. Involuntarily, her hand went to her tummy area. Tomorrow she would go to her appointment. That was her only option. Mama and Papa must never know. She dreaded each passing minute that brought her closer to her fate.

Francis turned into the parking lot behind a large brown brick building and parked the car. The children scrambled out of the passenger door but then waited while Francis got Mary's suitcase out of the trunk. Mary took the suitcase and followed Francis and the children inside the building, up a flight of stairs, and into a long hallway. Midway down the hall, Francis stopped in front of a door, inserted a key into the lock, and pushed the door open.

Mary stepped over the threshold into a small but homey apartment. She had never been in an apartment before and was surprised that it looked like a small house complete with a kitchen, living area, and hallway, which she assumed led to the bedrooms.

Brad and Chantel removed their coats, tuques, and mittens and headed into the kitchen.

"Mommy!" Chantel called. "I'm hungry."

"You two come back here; hang up your coats; and clean up your tuques, mittens, and boots." Francis turned to Mary. "You can hang your coat in this closet. I'll get a snack for the kids and put them to bed. You can join me in the kitchen. Would you like a glass of milk?" she asked, leading the way into the kitchen.

"No, thank you," Mary replied. She pulled a well-used chrome dining room chair from the small brown chrome table and sat down.

Francis put out some fruit and milk on the table. Both children took their places at the table, and Francis prayed out loud, giving thanks for the food and asking the Lord's blessing. Mary bowed her head as Francis prayed. She had never heard anyone say grace out loud, except little children who were still learning their prayers. At home, they prayed silently before their meals. The fact that they prayed gave her great comfort.

The children chattered while they ate, telling their mother what they had done at Auntie Maggie's house.

"You two go wash up and put your pajamas on, and I'll come

listen to your prayers," Francis told the children as she started cleaning the table.

"Aw, Mommy, do we have to go to bed already?" Brad whined.

"Yes, you do," Francis responded. "It's your bedtime, and you have school tomorrow."

"Goody, school!" Brad exclaimed, running down the hall toward a door that Mary assumed was the bathroom.

"I'll put the children to bed, and then I'll make us a cup of tea," Francis said when she'd finished cleaning up the mess the children had left behind, leaving only the bowl of fruit on the table. "I won't be long," she promised as she left the room.

Mary took in her surroundings. The kitchen was small and simple, but it looked clean and homey. A row of yellow canisters, a two-slice toaster, and a yellow mug tree with six green coffee mugs sat on the kitchen cupboard in a neat row. The yellow stove had a small chip in it. A picture of Jesus holding a lamb adorned the wall behind the table. The brown and yellow linoleum on the floors looked a bit worn, especially in the higher-use areas.

"Okay, now I'll make us a cup of tea," Francis said as she came back into the kitchen. She turned to Mary. "Do you drink tea?"

"Yes, I do," Mary replied.

"Good," Francis said. "I also have some Christmas cake left over to go with it."

Mary watched as Francis set the kettle on the stove and took two cups from the mug tree. On her way to the table, she stopped by the fridge and took out a piece of Christmas cake. She set it all on the table and then went back to the cupboard for some napkins. When the kettle started whistling, she poured the hot water into a small teapot, popped in a tea bag, and put the teapot on the table between them.

"So, Mary." Francis pulled out a chair across the table from Mary, sat down, and poured them each a cup of tea. "Tell me about yourself. Where are you from?"

"Springwater," Mary responded, stirring some sugar into her tea. She took a sip of the hot liquid, appreciating the taste.

"Where is Springwater?" Francis frowned. "I've never heard of it."

"It's a little town up north," Mary responded, wrapping her fingers around her warm mug.

"So what brings you to Edmonton?" The question had been on Francis's mind ever since she'd met Mary at the bus terminal. She couldn't think of a single good reason that such a young girl would be traveling to the city on her own without a relative or friend picking her up. Who would have given her the address of that sleazy hotel? She shuddered at the thought of a young girl staying there by herself. That was a bad part of town.

Mary stared into her tea. What should she say? How much could she get by with? She hadn't expected someone to take her in. She had thought her trip to Edmonton would be completely impersonal.

"Mary?" Francis's eyes filled with compassion. "I don't mean to make you uncomfortable, but you seem to be very young to be traveling on your own. Please tell me. Are you in trouble?"

Mary didn't know what it was—the long day of traveling on the bus, the fact that she was four hundred miles from home and in a strange city, her pregnancy hormones making her weepy, or the compassion she heard in this stranger's voice—but she felt tears welling up in her eyes as a lump formed in her throat. Slowly, the tears overflowed and trickled down her cheeks. She dabbed at them quickly, hoping Francis wouldn't notice.

Francis noticed. Quickly, she came around the table and put her arms around the young girl. The show of compassion from a stranger broke the dam, and Mary was helpless to control her tears.

Francis gently rubbed the girl's back as Mary's shoulders shook with sobs. When the tears finally ebbed, Francis handed Mary a box of tissues, and she mopped up her face.

Francis sat down next to Mary, holding Mary's hand. "Do you want to tell me about it?" Francis asked gently. "Maybe I can be of some help."

Mary dabbed at her eyes as she inhaled deeply, trying to control her emotions. "I'm pregnant." She sounded resigned.

It felt good to finally be able to say it. She hadn't told anyone except Melvin, and he wasn't exactly supportive. In fact, he wanted her to …

Mary trembled involuntarily as the full consequence of what she was about to do shook her to the core. *What am I thinking? I'm pregnant. There's a baby growing inside of me.* She shuddered. *No matter what Melvin said, I know better. If I go through with the abortion, I am killing my baby.* A sharp pain seared through her heart, and she covered her face with her hands and started weeping again. Francis wrapped her arms around the young girl until the torrent of tears ebbed.

"Did your parents kick you out?" Francis asked.

"No. They don't know," Mary whispered, raising tortured eyes to Francis as the battle raged in her mind. *What will I do?* She heard herself tell Francis, "They must never know. It would kill them." Mary's mind raced for a way out of this predicament. "I can't do that to them. They already suffered so much when David got killed."

"Who is David?" Francis asked softly.

"My brother. He was killed in a car accident."

"I'm so sorry. Do you have other brothers and sisters?"

"One little brother—Benny."

"Did you run away from home?"

"No. Well, yes. I guess. Sort of." She hadn't thought of it that way. "But only for a few days."

Francis raised her eyebrows and squeezed Mary's hand. Mary sighed deeply. She might as well tell this lady everything. Maybe she could help.

"It was Melvin's idea." She sighed again.

"Who is Melvin?" Francis asked gently.

"He's the father of my baby," Mary said. "He wants me to have an abortion. He gave me money to come to the city and stay at a hotel for a few days. He gave me the address of the hotel and a doctor who would take care of it. Then, by the end of the week, I could go back home on the bus. He said it was no big deal."

Francis tried hard not to let her feelings show. *What kind of a boyfriend would do something like that?* she fumed inwardly. *He obviously doesn't care much about Mary. The pregnancy is an inconvenience to be gotten rid of. Probably took advantage of the poor young girl. Despicable.* She took a deep breath to calm herself down.

"What do you think of Melvin's plan?" Francis couldn't imagine that this girl had agreed to it. She seemed so young and innocent.

"He said it wasn't really a baby yet," Mary responded slowly. "He said this would be the easiest way out. I couldn't let myself think about it." As Mary lifted her overflowing eyes, Francis thought about how tired and vulnerable she looked. But there was a resolve in those soft brown eyes. "But I can't do it. I know that I can't go through with it." She sounded almost frantic as she clung to Francis's hand. "I don't know what to do. If I don't get an abortion, then I can't go back home."

Francis closed her eyes momentarily and prayed silently, *Dear Jesus, show me how to help this girl.* "The best thing would be for you to get back on that bus tomorrow. Go home, and tell your parents. They need to know."

"No," Mary responded emphatically, "I can't do that."

Francis said, "I think that would be the best thing. If you need a bit of time to come to grips with the situation and to think things through, you can stay here for a few days. Just promise me you won't get an abortion. There are other options."

"I promise." Mary's hand covered her abdomen protectively.

"Okay, then why don't you plan to stay here for a few days, and we'll think of something?" Francis suggested.

"If you don't mind." Mary sounded relieved. She didn't need to have an abortion. Somehow, she and the baby would make it.

"First, we'll call your parents so they know you're safe," Francis said.

"We can't do that!" Mary exclaimed. "They don't have a phone."

"They don't have a phone?" Francis repeated, incredulous.

"Our community is isolated," Mary explained. "We live on a farm. There aren't any telephone lines in the countryside. Just a couple of businesses in town have phones, and they are closed now."

"Well then," Francis replied, "we'll have to wait until tomorrow. Now we should get some sleep. I have to work tomorrow, and I take Brad to school with me. A lady from down the hall takes care of Chantel." Francis got up and pushed her chair back under the table. "I'll get you some bedding."

She left the room and quickly came back with a sleeping bag and pillow, which she put down on the couch.

"You can sleep here," she said. "Think about your options tomorrow, and we'll talk again tomorrow night."

Mary was glad to finally be able to lie down. It had been a long, emotional day, and she felt tired.

After years of looking forward to my sixteenth birthday, I never thought I would spend it like this. She sighed as she closed her eyes.

CHAPTER 21

The couch wasn't the most comfortable place, but she was so exhausted from the trip and the emotions of the day that Mary soon fell asleep and didn't wake up until she heard Francis moving around in the kitchen the next morning. She quickly got up, folded the sleeping bag, put it in a neat pile with the pillow, and then went into the bathroom to get dressed.

"Good morning, Mary." Francis greeted her cheerfully as Mary came into the kitchen. Francis handed her a glass of apple juice. "The children and I have to leave for the day, but tonight we will discuss your options."

"What will I do all day?" Mary asked, realizing she would be alone most of the day in a strange home in a strange city where she knew no one.

"You don't have to do anything if you don't want to," Francis told her as she put cereal and toast on the table, "but if you get bored and need something to do, you could wash the dishes and clean the house up a bit. There are magazines on the coffee table and a few novels on the bookshelf, if you like to read."

After Francis and the children left, Mary did the dishes and then wandered around the apartment. She picked up a picture from the mantel and studied it. Francis and the children smiled back at her, but there was also a man in the picture. Was he Francis's husband? If so, where was he? Francis hadn't mentioned him. Had he died? Did he work out of town? *I'll have to ask Francis about him,* she decided.

After a few days of discussing her options with Francis, Mary decided to have the baby and give it up for adoption. Even though Francis tried to persuade her otherwise, Mary decided she would not go home until after her baby was born and the adoption was finalized.

She would use the money Melvin had given her to live on.

"Mary," Francis said with concern in her voice, "do your parents love you?"

"Of course they do," Mary answered.

"If they love you, don't you think they would want to have you at home?"

"I cannot put them through the shame of having a pregnant teenage daughter," Mary explained. "They could never hold their heads up in the community again." *Why can't Francis understand that?* she wondered.

"Will you at least write to them? Tell them you're pregnant, and ask their advice. They might agree with your plans to stay here until the baby is born and give the child up for adoption."

"Never!" Mary exclaimed. "They've been through enough. They must never know about this baby," Mary said with finality. "I will not do that to them."

Francis sighed, her own arguments with her mother regarding Mike coming to mind. *Why do teenagers have to be so dramatic?*

"Mary, you are too obstinate for your own good," Francis said, and then she added more gently, "If you are very sure about staying in Edmonton, then how would you like to live with me and the children? You could help me with the housework and take care of Chantel while I'm at work in exchange for room and board."

"You would let me stay here?" Mary asked, astonished at Francis's offer.

"I would rather you go home," Francis answered bluntly, but her voice was kind. "But if you have your mind set against that, then I'd rather have you here with me and the kids than wandering the streets."

Mary felt a huge load fall off her shoulders. Finally, she had some definite plans for her immediate future.

Mary's voice trembled with emotion. "I would like that. I promise to help you with whatever needs to be done."

Later that evening, Mary wrote a short note to her parents. She tucked it into the envelope Francis had given her and then licked and sealed the envelope. She wrote her parents' address on the outside but omitted a return address. She wanted them to know she was all right, but she didn't want them to come looking for her. The coming months would be hard, and she hoped she had made the right decision. It would mean she couldn't go home for at least seven months. She gave the letter to Francis in the morning for mailing.

On Saturday, Mary helped Francis move Chantel's bed and dresser into Brad's bedroom so Mary could have Chantel's room. Francis had picked up a cheap but sturdy bed at the secondhand store. Mary was grateful for the privacy and a bed to sleep in.

"Mary, read me a book?" Chantel asked as she climbed onto Mary's lap after supper with a children's storybook in hand.

"Okay." Mary smiled, snuggling the child up against her. She was surprised how readily the children had accepted her. "Which book are we reading?"

"Baby Moses," Chantel answered, showing Mary her book.

Mary frowned as she opened the book. Most of the children's books in the apartment were Bible stories. They reminded her of home, when they all sat around the table in the evening reading the Bible. Holding Chantel reminded her of holding Benny when he was her age. She had dreamed of having children of her own, and now that she was going to have a baby, she was planning to give it away. She shook her head to clear the images and started reading the story.

Anna Hildebrandt's fingers trembled as she opened the envelope Jacob had brought from the post office. The handwriting looked like Mary's. She turned the envelope over, but there was no return address. She sat down and removed the single sheet of folded paper, her heart racing.

Is Mary well? Where is she? A sharp pain ripped through her chest as she stared at the paper in her hands.

After they'd found Mary's note that Sunday after church, they had questioned Mary's friends, but no one knew where she was. They were all shocked that Mary was gone. Their only clue had come when they'd asked questions at the Greyhound bus depot, where they'd been told that a girl fitting Mary's description had bought a ticket to Edmonton. They had considered going after her, but Edmonton was a big city. How would they ever find her there?

"Well," Jacob said, "are you going to read it?"

Anna unfolded the paper, her heart racing and her stomach in a knot. She quickly scanned the brief note.

Dear Mama and Papa,

Please don't worry about me. I'm fine. I had to get away for a while. Things are not the same without David, and I need to figure out how to live my life. I'm staying with a very nice lady and babysitting her children while she's at work. I am safe, so please don't try to find me. I'll come home when I can. I'll write again.

Love, Mary

Anna passed the note to Jacob, unable to read the few lines to him. Her head fell into her hands as the tears overflowed. Relief at hearing from Mary intermingled with the pain of not knowing where she was and not being able to communicate and help her.

Why won't she tell us where she is? Why didn't she include a return address so we could at least write to her? Anna's shoulders shook with sobs. *First David and now Mary. How much can one person take? Why, God, why?*

"Be still, and know that I am God." The verse popped into Anna's head. *God, it's so hard. I know you are in control, but please, Lord, bring Mary home soon.*

Anna felt Jacob's arms encircle her as he knelt on the floor by her chair.

"*Liewe Himmlische Voda*," he prayed, and then he paused as his voice broke. After a few seconds, he continued. "We come to you with broken hearts today, Lord." His voice broke again. "We don't know where Mary is, but you know where she is, and we ask, Lord, please keep her safe and bring her back to us. You know we love her, and we know that you love her even more. You created her. You died for her. Lord, we thank you for this letter. Help us through this, Lord; we can't do this on our own. Draw Mary to you, Lord, and help her wherever she is. In Jesus's name. Amen."

Anna felt a calmness settle in her heart as Jacob prayed, and she was reminded of the verses in Philippians 4:6–7: "Be careful [anxious] for nothing; but in every thing by prayer and supplication with thanksgiving let your requests be made known unto God. And the peace of God, which passeth all understanding, shall keep your hearts and minds through Christ Jesus." She wrapped her arms around her husband, and they stayed that way for a long time, their tears intermingling as they drew strength from each other and from their faith in the Lord.

"Mary," Francis said while they were doing the supper dishes one evening, "I checked into getting you set up to continue your schooling by correspondence. I found out that in your circumstances, it shouldn't be a problem for you to finish the school year that way."

Mary gaped at Francis, the dishrag forgotten in her hand. "You did that for me? Why?"

"You're living in my house and looking after my children," Francis said. "I'll do what I can to help you. Do you want to take correspondence or not?"

"Does it cost money?" Mary started washing the dishes again. Francis's thoughtfulness kept amazing her. *I don't deserve it after all I've done,* she told herself.

"You have to pay for it initially, but you get it back if you pass," Francis replied.

"I don't have money to take courses." Mary was disappointed; she wouldn't be able to continue her schooling after all.

"Didn't you say your boyfriend gave you money that you didn't use?" Francis asked, putting the dishes into the cupboard.

"Yeah, but that's not really my money," Mary responded dejectedly.

"After all he's put you through? I think you're entitled to that money. Anyway, you're getting the money back if you pass, so all you have to do is pass your courses."

"Yeah, you're right." Mary brightened. "I could use the money since I'll be getting it back. Good thinking."

After the children were in bed, Francis helped Mary complete all the required forms so Francis could drop them off the next day. Mary felt the slightest little flutter in her abdomen. Her hand quickly covered the spot, and her eyes filled with wonder as she looked up at Francis.

"What is it?" Francis asked. "Did you feel the baby?"

"I think so," Mary whispered in amazement. "It was just the tiniest little flutter."

"Well, let me tell you," Francis said with a laugh, "it won't always feel that way."

"A baby." Mary's voice was filled with awe. "A real live baby." Her eyes filled with tears as another thought struck a blow to her heart. "I almost killed a real live baby." The familiar pain stabbed her heart as she was filled with remorse at how close she had come to doing the unthinkable.

Francis reached across the table and took Mary's hand. "But you didn't," she reminded her gently. "Instead, you are going to carry that baby to term and give birth to a real live baby."

"If it wasn't for you, I would have." Mary sounded horrified.

"It wasn't me, Mary," Francis told her gently. "I didn't know anything about you when I picked you up at that bus depot. It was God. He made a way out for you. He loves you, Mary, and he loves your baby."

Mary's eyes closed at the pain those words caused. "God doesn't care about me or the baby," she muttered. She went to her room and shut the door.

Anna let her sad eyes wander from the task at hand and sweep over the freshly plowed fields to where the accident had happened. Was it two years ago?

David, her heart cried, *I miss you so much, but I know that you are with Jesus and that you are safe and happy. I know that eventually, I will see you again. But I don't know where Mary is. I don't know if she's safe or happy. I don't know if she has food to eat or a place to lay her head. She says she's safe, but is she? Is she just saying that to ease our minds?* Anna's tortured mind conjured up an image of Mary lying in a heap in a dark back alley. *Oh, Lord, have mercy on Mary!* she cried, the familiar sharp pain shooting through her chest as she crumpled to her knees. *Lord, you know where she is. You can see her. You can take care of her. Please, Lord, keep her safe. And please, Lord, bring her home. I can't bear this.*

"I will never leave thee, nor forsake thee." The voice was almost audible, and Anna felt a gentle peace flow through her. She remained motionless, her hands clasped in prayer, basking in the moment of peace.

"Thank you, Lord," she whispered. She envisioned the Lord's hand reaching down from heaven to clasp hers, and she lifted up her hand to symbolically clasp his. *Thank you for your presence, thank you for your love, and thank you that I can trust you to take care of Mary, knowing that you love her even more than I do. Keep her safe, Lord, and bring her home.*

Anna's life was broken up into moments: of desperation; of peace; of deep sorrow; of appearing normal for Benny's sake; of facing well-meaning neighbors, friends, and family; and of strength when Jacob was overwhelmed with grief. She could only face life one moment at a time, for she knew not what the next moment would hold. Life was held in a delicate balance—by a string, it seemed.

Mary wiped her hair from her damp forehead with the back of her hand. She was only making soup and sandwiches for supper, but her back ached, and her feet hurt. The hot July sun beat down day after day, and there was no escaping the heat of the apartment. The baby felt heavy within her, and she rubbed her hand over the rolling movement within her abdomen as the baby shifted.

"Any day now, you will make an appearance." She enjoyed talking to the baby growing within her. "Then we'll be separated, but remember, I will always love you, no matter what happens."

She turned off the stove and finished setting the table.

"Mary, look what we got," Brad said. He and Chantel burst through the door with Francis following close behind with a couple of bags of groceries. The children dropped their shopping bag on the floor and pulled out a long plastic contraption with a lot of string.

"A kite," Mary said, smiling at their glowing faces. "Where are you going to fly a kite?"

"At the park!" Brad exclaimed. "See, Mary? It has instructions, and Mommy said she would take us to the park after supper to fly it."

"Well then," Mary said, ruffling his hair and patting Chantel's shoulder, "good thing supper is ready. You kids go wash up while I help your mommy put away the groceries."

The children rushed off to do what they were told, and Mary turned to find Francis looking at her. "How are you feeling?" Francis asked. "You look totally beat."

"That about sums it up." Mary reached into the shopping bag. "I think it's the heat."

"Are you feeling any pain?" Francis asked, putting groceries into the cupboards.

"No, just very uncomfortable," Mary answered. "My back aches all the time, and the baby is taking up so much space that sometimes I think I'll explode. It would help if it wasn't so hot," she added.

Brad and Chantel came back into the kitchen, and they all took their places at the table. Brad volunteered to say grace, and Mary felt a pang in her heart when he thanked God for the kite as well as the food. He reminded her of Benny. She missed him terribly. She missed Mama and Papa too. Soon she would have her baby, and then she could go home.

"Are you going to fly kite with us?" Chantel broke into her thoughts. Mary looked up, realizing that the prayer was over.

"Mary might want to rest," Francis said. "She's feeling tired."

"I think it might help for me to get out of the apartment for a while," Mary said. "I might feel better if I get some fresh air. So yes, Chantel, I'll come watch you fly the kite."

"Yippee!" Brad shouted, pounding his fist into the air above his head.

It did feel better to be out in the fresh air, Mary decided as she sat on the park bench. The warm breeze made the heat more bearable and allowed the children to fly their kite moderately well. As Francis helped Brad and Chantel, Mary let her eyes wander to the children playing on the swings, slides, and monkey bars. Benny would enjoy this playground. She watched a young couple push a stroller over the lush green grass and instinctively put her hand over her abdomen as she bit back the tears that threatened. She didn't know what the future held for her, but she knew she would never marry and have children. The child she was carrying now would be the only one she would have, and there was a couple waiting for it already. Her only specification had been that the baby go to a Christian home. Even though she wanted nothing to do with God, she thought a Christian home would be more stable, and she wanted her baby to have a good, loving home.

"We're going to get some ice cream."

Mary broke out of her reverie to find Chantel crawling into her lap. Mary looked up and saw Francis and Brad standing next to her.

"Mommy said we could have soft ice cream before we go home," Brad told Mary. "Are you coming?"

Mary looked up at Francis and shook her head. "Not this time, children. You go with your mommy. I will go home." She set Chantel on the ground before getting to her feet.

"Are you all right?" Francis asked, concerned eyes resting on Mary.

"I'm fine," Mary answered. "Just tired."

"All right, we won't be long."

Back at the apartment, Mary filled the tub with water and added a little bubble bath before stepping in. The cool water felt good after such a hot day. She lay back in the tub with a sigh and let herself relax. She didn't know how long she lay there and let her mind drift until she found the energy to wash and get out of the tub. By the time Francis and the children came back, Mary was in her cotton pajamas, brushing her hair.

The children were tired, so Francis whisked them into the tub right away. After calling good night to Francis and the kids, Mary climbed into bed and fell asleep as soon as her head hit the pillow.

Sometime during the night, Mary woke up with a gasp, feeling as if a wide band were being tightened around her midsection.

Is this it? she wondered, her eyes wide open in fear as the pain in her abdomen slowly subsided. She lay on her back, staring up at the ceiling. When the pain left, she started to relax and felt herself drifting off to sleep, when she felt the tightening sensation again. She squeezed her eyes shut and concentrated on her breathing, as Francis had told her to, until the pain subsided. Then she slowly got up, donned her housecoat, and went into the kitchen in search of a glass of milk. She sat down on the couch, sipping her milk and trying hard not to panic.

Mama, I need you, her heart cried out within her as the contractions became more frequent and intense. *I'm scared. I can't do this by myself.* She wiped at the tears that spilled over onto her cheeks.

CHAPTER 22

"Honey, are you all right?" Francis put her arms around Mary's shoulders. "Have the pains started?"

Mary nodded, wiping away the traces of tears with the back of her hand.

"When did they start?" Francis's calm voice helped to soothe Mary's spirit. Francis told Mary to get dressed while she did the same. She called Gladys, who came to stay with the children while she drove Mary to the hospital.

On the way to the hospital, Francis kept up a steady stream of conversation to try to ease Mary's fears. Nonetheless, by the time Mary had dressed in a hospital gown and climbed up into the hospital bed, she was shaking uncontrollably. The pains became worse as dawn broke in the eastern sky and, later, as the sunbeams trickled into the room between the curtains. Francis sponged Mary's forehead with a wet cloth. At times, Mary heard Francis praying over her.

Is this it? Mary wondered hazily. *Am I going to die?* She had never experienced pain like this. It ripped through her abdomen and around her back. Francis held her hand and coached her to breathe through it. When the pain subsided, she closed her eyes and rested on the pillow, only to have it happen all over again in a few minutes. The nurses came in and wheeled her into another room with bright lights, and she had to scoot over onto a high, narrow bed. She had difficulty moving, but with the nurses helping her, she managed. Francis was not allowed to accompany her.

"Hi, Mary." Dr. Scott's friendly blue eyes smiled at her above a green surgical mask as he started examining her. "You're doing just fine. You'll have that baby in no time. You just do as I say." Time slipped out the window as Mary struggled to give birth. Her body was drenched in sweat when she finally heard the cry of a newborn infant.

"A healthy baby girl!" Dr. Scott exclaimed. "Congratulations, Mary. You did well."

Mary's heart welled up with love as the nurse placed the newborn in her arms. In awe, she touched her little button nose, her down-soft cheeks, her perfectly formed lips, and her fuzzy dark hair. The baby's eyes squinted open, and her dark eyes met those of her mother. As the nurse reached out to take the newborn from her, Mary hugged the baby close and whispered, "I will always love you, dear one, as long as I live." The nurse whisked the baby out of the room while a couple of other nurses prepared Mary to take her back to her hospital room.

Once she was settled in her hospital bed, Francis came in to see her. "Congratulations, Mary. You were wonderful."

"What will happen now?" Mary asked. "Can I see my baby again?"

"Did you see the baby?" Francis asked, surprised.

"Yes, I held her for a few minutes before they took her away," Mary answered. "Will I be able to hold her again?"

"I don't know," Francis answered, pulling a chair close to the bed. "I thought the social worker said you wouldn't see her at all."

"I know," Mary responded, "but I'm so glad I did. She's so adorable."

Francis's brows knit together in concern as she gazed into Mary's face. "Does that mean you want to keep her? You can change your mind, you know."

Mary turned her face to the wall, fighting back the tears

that welled up in her throat. "I really wish I could, Francis," she whispered, turning back to face her friend, her eyes brimming with tears, "but I can never go back home if I do." She swallowed hard. "And I have to go back home. I miss Mama, Papa, and Benny so much."

Francis wrapped her arms around the girl, letting her tears mingle with Mary's as she did her best to console her.

Later that day, Mrs. Baldwin, the social worker overseeing the adoption of Mary's baby girl, entered Mary's hospital room. She was middle aged, well tailored, and professional. She went over all the details of the adoption that were agreed on before the birth, and Mary signed the papers with a shaking hand.

Mary was dressed and ready when Francis came for her the day she was released from the hospital.

"Hi, Mary." Francis hugged her, and then, seeing the closed suitcase, she said, "Looks like you're all ready to go."

"Yes." Mary's heart felt heavy at the thought of leaving this place where she had given birth to her beautiful daughter. "Francis, do you know if my baby is still here?" Mary asked in a small voice.

Francis saw the torture in her eyes. "I don't know. Do you want me to find out for you?"

"Would you please?" Mary asked.

Francis left and returned a short time later with a matronly uniformed nurse in tow.

"You want to know if the baby you gave birth to is still here?" the nurse asked Mary, studying her closely.

"Yes." Mary's voice sounded small and strangled.

"She was released to her adoptive parents this morning," the nurse told her kindly. "The adoption was your decision. Am I right?"

"Yes," Mary said, straightening her shoulders. "I just wanted to know."

"All right." The nurse smiled at her. "You take good care of yourself. If you have any problems, go see your doctor right away," she advised before she left the room.

"I'm ready to go," Mary told Francis. Francis picked up Mary's bag, and together they walked out of the hospital.

Mary entered Francis's apartment with a heavy heart. It seemed ages ago that she had left in a panic in the middle of the night to go to the hospital to have a baby. Had it only been a few days? Now she was back, feeling emptier than she had ever felt before. Her darling little girl, whom she had carried for nine months, was gone, and she only had one glimpse of her to last her a lifetime.

"Mary's home," Chantel announced as she came running from where she was playing in the kitchen.

"You be careful, Chantel." Francis was right behind Mary. "Mary isn't feeling very well yet. You have to be gentle."

Chantel slowed down to a walk and looked up into Mary's face. "Can I give you a gentle hug?" she asked. Her concern made Mary smile.

"Of course." Mary reached down and hugged Chantel. "I missed you so much."

"I missed you too," Chantel responded, throwing her arms around Mary's neck. "Are you not going to be sick anymore?"

"I feel better already, just seeing you." Mary smiled, tweaking Chantel's nose.

Brad came forward for a hug as well. Taking Mary's hand, he led her to the rocking chair to have a seat.

Gladys bent down and gave Mary a hug before she left. "I'll continue to pray for you," she promised before leaving the apartment.

"Tell us about the hospital," Brad said, his eyes big. "Were you very sick?"

"Children," Francis said in admonishment. "Mary doesn't want to talk about it. You could probably get her a drink, Brad," she suggested.

Mary had never thought it would be this hard. She'd thought once the baby was born, she would be free—free to go home and pick up the pieces of her life.

You're so selfish, a voice whispered in her head. *You gave your baby away so you could go back to Mama and Papa.* She turned her face into her pillow and cried.

How would I take care of a baby? Mary asked her broken heart. *Isn't it better to give her to a good home with Christian parents who can give her everything she deserves?*

She deserves her mother, the voice whispered.

I want her so bad. Mary cried until she had no more tears. Her body was sore, and her head pounded. She had never allowed herself to think of what it would be like after the baby was born, except to look forward to going home. She had not expected to feel this sorrow that was engulfing her.

Mary lay in the hospital bed, when a nurse in a white coat took her baby girl away. She tried to cry out for the nurse to return her baby, but no sound escaped her lips. She tried to get out of bed to go after her, but her legs wouldn't move. Tears streamed down her face as she saw the nurse place her precious baby into the arms of a stranger.

"Here's your baby girl," the nurse told the strange woman with long black curls.

"No, she's my baby! Bring her back!" Mary screamed, but they didn't hear her.

The woman smiled as she held the baby close. "We have waited a long, long time for you, my dear little one," she told the baby.

"No, you can't have her! She's mine." Mary tried desperately to get out of bed, but her legs refused to move. "Don't take my baby away. She's mine!"

A tall, slim man put his arm around the woman, and slowly, they walked down the corridor, taking the baby farther and farther away.

"Come back! Come back!"

With a start, Mary woke up in a sweat, tears streaming down her face.

That was how the dreams began. In the days and weeks that followed, the dream kept recurring in some form, but always she could hear her baby crying as she tried to find her. When she finally spotted her baby crying in her crib, Mary couldn't open the door. She could only watch through the window in the door while a lady with long black hair entered the room and took the baby away, leaving Mary sobbing at the door.

"Have you decided when you want to return home?" Francis asked one evening when Mary had been back from the hospital for a couple of weeks.

"I haven't made any plans," Mary admitted.

"Don't wait too long," Francis said. "You need to get back to your family."

Guilt weighed heavily on Mary. *It was your choice,* the little voice in her head reminded her, *and you chose Mama, Papa, and Benny over your innocent baby girl. You gave your baby away so you could go home where no one would ever know.*

"I'll think about it," Mary promised, trying to drown out the voice in her head.

How can I go home and leave my daughter behind? Mary asked herself countless times. *How can I face Mama and Papa?*

August came and went, but still, Mary didn't go home.

"Mary, will you come to the park with us?" Brad asked. Francis had promised to take the children to the park after lunch.

"Not today, Brad," she answered. She couldn't bear watching parents play with their children in the park.

"You never come to the park with us anymore," Brad whined.

"Come to the park, Mary!" Chantel chimed in, pulling on Mary's hand.

"Not today, Chantel," Mary responded. "I'm tired."

"You're always tired," Brad said, pouting.

"Children, that's enough," Francis said. "Mary doesn't have to come to the park if she doesn't want to."

Mary escaped to her room, where she spent most of her time. She heard Francis and the children leave as she lay on her back on the bed, staring at the ceiling. She was still in her room when she heard Francis and the children come back a few hours later.

After Francis put the children to bed, she knocked on Mary's door.

"Come in," Mary said, pulling herself up to a sitting position.

Francis entered and sat down on the edge of Mary's bed. "Are you all right, Mary?" she asked.

"Yeah, I'm fine," Mary responded listlessly.

"You're sure you're not sick?"

"No, I'm fine."

"You're not yourself lately," Francis insisted. "I think you should see a doctor."

"What would I tell a doctor?" Mary asked. "I don't feel like going to the park?"

"That's not the only thing you don't feel like doing." Francis didn't want to upset her. "It's very normal to have postpartum depression after giving birth."

"I told you I'm fine," Mary said sharply. "I just don't feel like going to the park every time you go."

"You aren't obligated to go to the park," Francis said, trying to be patient, "but it's more than that. You spend most of your time in your room. What do you do here all the time?"

"Just whatever." Mary picked at the edge of the blanket.

"As long as you're all right, that's all I care about." Francis hugged Mary. Mary lifted her arms to lightly rest on Francis's shoulders, but her body remained stiff.

Francis left the room feeling even more concerned.

Late one fall afternoon, while the children were busy playing in their bedroom, Francis knocked on Mary's bedroom door again. She found Mary lying on her bed, staring up at the ceiling.

Francis sat down on the edge of the bed and took Mary's hand, alarmed at how thin it was.

"Mary, talk to me." Francis's voice was filled with love and concern for her young friend. "I'm here to help in any way I can."

"There's no help for me," Mary said dully. Her sunken eyes had a haunted look.

"Of course there is, Mary," Francis responded. "Jesus loves you. He understands what you're feeling."

"Would Jesus give away one of his children?" Mary's voice sounded hollow. "He wouldn't do that, would he? So how could he possibly understand?"

"Mary, can I get Pastor Bob to come talk to you? I can arrange counseling for you."

"Will that bring my baby girl back? Will that bring David back? Will that undo the terrible things I have done and allow me to see my family?"

"It will help you deal with this," Francis said. "You can't deal with this on your own. I should have realized that sooner and gotten you counseling from the beginning."

Slowly, Mary got out of bed. Her eyes looked tortured and defeated as she turned to Francis and sighed. "None of this is your fault, Francis. You have been a friend. You took me in when I had nowhere to go. You kept me from killing my baby."

"Where are you going?" Francis asked as Mary headed toward the door.

"For a walk," she responded. Francis followed her to the apartment door.

"Mary." Francis tried to keep her rising panic under control. She laid an urgent hand on Mary's arm. "Please let me help you."

Mary turned to look at Francis for a brief moment. "There's no help for me. The Bible says, 'Be sure your sin will find you out.' Well, my sin has found me out, and there's no way out for me." She stepped into the hall, closing the door abruptly behind her.

Francis felt torn. She couldn't leave her children alone in the apartment and go after Mary, but she couldn't let Mary go out alone in the mental state she was in. Anxiety hardened into a ball in the pit of her stomach. Not knowing what else to do, Francis went into her bedroom and fell on her knees beside her bed.

"Dear Lord," she prayed urgently, "you care about Mary. Lord, please protect her. Send someone into her life who can help her. I am so afraid for her. I don't know where she went or when she'll be back. You know where she is. Please, Jesus, have mercy on her, and put a hedge of protection around her. Help me to trust in you, Lord, and to remain calm." She didn't say, "Amen," because she would remain in a state of prayer even after she got up from her knees and started making supper.

Mary didn't pay attention to passersby as she walked down the street. She didn't pay attention to where she was going. She had no destination in mind. She just walked and walked. Her shattered heart felt like a ton of lead in her chest, only more painful. As the sun sank ever lower to the western horizon, she entered a park strewn with the golden, brown, and red leaves of fall. She heard the sound of children shouting in the distance as she sank down onto a hard park bench and dropped her head into her hands.

Life is over for me. I have totally messed up. I can't ever go back. Can't go back home. Can't bring David back. Can't go on without my baby. She got up from the bench and continued wandering aimlessly, the wretchedness inside her making her restless. *What will I do? I have broken Mama's and Papa's hearts, I have given my baby girl away. I am useless, vile, and contemptible. I can't ever go home. I can't go on.* On and on, her thoughts raged within her as the heavy blackness kept sucking her down farther into that bottomless pit.

Out of nowhere, a thought hit her. It hit her so hard she sank down onto the dried leaves she was walking on. There under the branches of a big old oak tree, the solution came to her. It was clear, as if someone were speaking to her: *End it. Kill yourself. You don't deserve to live.*

That's right, Mary thought. *That's the only way out. Mama and Papa will mourn for a while, but they'll get over it. My little girl is safe with her new parents; she doesn't need me.*

Her life was over. She was needed by no one and had nothing to live for. At sixteen, she had come to the end.

How can I end it? she asked herself. Her mind conjured up various ways to commit the deed. She didn't want to do it in Francis's apartment. Francis had been good to her. What if the kids found her? No, that wasn't an option.

River, the voice inside her head said.

River? Mary asked the voice. *Where can I find a river?*

She looked up and saw a bridge in the distance, arching high over the river.

It's meant to be. She felt resigned.

Do it now, the voice urged.

Mary started getting to her feet. She felt sick to her stomach.

CHAPTER 23

"Mary, is that you?"

She looked up at the man whose shadow fell across her. She knew that voice. Could it be? "John? What are you doing here?" she stammered in amazement as the tall, lanky man sat down beside her.

"I could ask you the same question," John Hepner answered, his deep chocolate eyes revealing his obvious pleasure in seeing her, "but you asked first, so here goes. This is the Bible school I attend."

Mary looked around her at the brick buildings. She had never been here before. How far had she walked? She hadn't been paying attention. John noticed the pain etched on Mary's face.

"I see you've heard. I'm so sorry." His voice was deeper than she remembered, more mature.

Her heart raced. How did he know? She looked away with shame flooding over her. How had he found out? Who had told him? *No. Wait.* Did he say she had heard something? "Heard what?" she managed in a tight voice filled with trepidation.

"About your father, of course," John answered. "Have you seen him?"

"What are you talking about?" She was confused.

"Mary, you don't know? I thought since you had obviously been crying ..." His voice faltered.

"What? John, tell me." She clutched at his arm in panic.

"Mary." John took her hands. "Your papa had a stroke. He's in the hospital right here in the city. I'm sorry. I thought you knew."

Once again, Mary's world crumbled at her feet.

"Papa!" she gasped, gaping up at John, her eyes wide. She had never once thought of her parents getting sick—or dying.

"How is he? Where is he?" Urgent questions tumbled over each other as her world spun out of control once again.

"Not good, Mary. He's in a coma." John's voice was compassionate. "I'm so sorry. They've been looking for you, and I thought they'd found you, because you were here. Sorry. I'm rambling." John stood up and offered his hand. "Come. I'll take you to the hospital. Your mama needs you."

Mary let him help her to her feet and guide her to his car. Her knees felt wobbly, so she was thankful for his firm hand on her elbow.

John closed the passenger door behind her and slid into the driver's seat of his older-model car. Mary started shaking uncontrollably. Papa was the family pillar. He was always confident.

"Here—put this on." John pulled his jacket from the backseat and gave it to Mary. "Maybe this will help."

Mary pulled the jacket across her chest. Her mind was reeling. "Where's Benny?" she asked as John merged the car into traffic.

"He's staying with your grandparents," John answered, weaving through traffic.

"When did this happen?"

"Sunday after lunch," John answered, stopping at a traffic light. "He felt tired and was going to take a nap but fell before he reached the bed. He didn't respond to your mama, so she sent Benny to the neighbors' for help."

"Today is Wednesday," Mary said, more to herself than to John.

"Yes, and your mama hasn't left his side," John answered.

They pulled into the hospital parking lot. Mary got out of

the car and looked up at the tall redbrick building with its many windows, wondering which one was Papa's room. She wondered what Mama would say when she saw her. *I've caused them so much pain.*

John took her arm, but Mary pulled back. He looked down at her quizzically. "Let's go," he said.

"I can't." Mary faltered, her voice filled with emotion, her heart pounding.

"Look, Mary." John placed his hands on both of her arms. "Your parents need you. Your mama can't do this on her own. She has no one else."

"She won't want me there," Mary said, a stab of pain shooting through her heart at the thought.

"Yes, she does, Mary," John answered softly, coaxingly. "She needs you to be here now. Trust me."

John took her elbow, and she allowed him to propel her forward. He guided her across the large parking lot, past the cars and pickup trucks, and through the big glass double doors into the lobby area. They continued right through the lobby, with its orange and yellow vinyl chairs, and past a long, narrow counter with a sign marked Information hanging over it. When they reached the elevator, John pushed the arrow to go up. The doors parted, and people poured out and scattered in different directions like leaves in the wind. His hand still firmly on her elbow, John propelled Mary into the elevator. Mary swayed slightly as the elevator jerked to life. When the doors opened, they stepped into a long, wide hallway. Walking past a nursing station, they stopped at a room that bore the name Jacob Hildebrandt on a little sign beside the half-closed wooden door.

John gently steered Mary into the room and then stayed back as Mary cautiously took a step toward the bed. *Papa.* Involuntarily, her hand covered her mouth.

Papa was hooked up to a machine that made little beeping noises and had squiggly lines running across its screen. A needle was bandaged to his left arm, which was attached to a thin tube coming out of the bottom of a clear bag of liquid hanging on a pole. The mask covering his mouth and nose had a tube attached to it that looked as if it were coming out of the wall. Another tube, also attached to a bag on the pole, went into his nose. He lay still.

In a chair pulled close to the bed sat Mama, slumped over with her forehead resting on the bed, holding one of Papa's hands in her own. Mary took another step forward, and Mama looked up. She heard Mama's sharp intake of breath as recognition mingled with joy and pain flooded her soft gray eyes.

Slowly, Mama stood up, as if her daughter were an apparition that would disappear if she moved too quickly. She took a step forward and stretched out her arms, and Mary walked into them. Only then did Mama comprehend that she was not hallucinating. She collapsed into Mary's arms, sobbing uncontrollably, clinging to her daughter, as the days and weeks and months of separation dissolved.

"I'm so sorry, Mama." Tears poured down Mary's face. "So sorry."

Mama had shrunk. She felt tiny in Mary's arms. A tidal wave of emotions swept through Mary's entire being, leaving her feeling weak. She had missed Mama so much.

"You're here now." Mama's grip tightened around her daughter. "That's all that matters."

Mama pulled back and, with a final swipe at her eyes, stood back to take a good look at Mary. She had lost weight.

"It's so good to see you," Mama told her, taking Mary's hand. She led her to the bed and placed Mary's hand over Papa's hand.

"Mary's here," she told Papa softly, her voice loaded with emotion as she held their hands together with both of her own. "Mary's here," she repeated, as if she couldn't quite believe it herself.

"Papa." Mary choked, cleared her throat, and tried again. "Papa. It's me—Mary."

There was no change in Papa, no recognition. His chest rose and fell softly, the machine with the squiggly lines kept beeping, the clear fluid kept dripping into the tube attached to his arm, and Papa kept lying still. He looked old against the stark white of the hospital bed. Mary turned to look at Mama. Her once-sparkling eyes had sunk into their sockets. A wisp of graying hair had come loose from the braids wrapped around her head. She looked thin and tired.

Mary looked away, biting her lip. She wondered how much of it was from the pain she had caused. She looked at Papa, and her heart broke within her. *Papa, was I the cause of your stroke?*

Mary's knees buckled as the burden of guilt engulfed her. She felt John's arm go around her waist, holding her up. She hadn't realized he had come up behind her.

"Here—you'd better sit down," he said, helping her to the chair he'd pulled up beside the bed. Mary hardly noticed.

I thought I was doing what was best for them. Did I really make them suffer this much? Was I thinking more of myself than them? Am I really that selfish?

Instead of sitting down, she turned and almost ran for the door. *I have to get out of here,* she told herself. *This is all my fault.*

At the door, she turned in the direction they had come and hurried down the hall. Where was the elevator? It was such a long hall. Everything looked so sterile.

A hand grabbed her arm and spun her around.

"What are you doing?" John's voice was low and urgent.

"I have to get out of here." Her voice was almost a whimper, pleading with him to understand. She started shaking again. She felt trapped. Her heart felt like a heavy brick inside her chest.

"We'll go to the cafeteria," John told her, turning her around. "You're going the wrong direction." He walked close beside her, keeping his arm around her waist. "I told your mama we would bring her some coffee."

"I can't go back there." Mary stopped and looked up at John with panic in her soft brown eyes.

"Let's get that coffee." John propelled her gently toward the elevator and pushed the down arrow.

To any onlooker, they looked like a nice young couple, albeit a worried couple, but that wasn't an unusual sight in a hospital, especially in the critical care unit. The elevator took them down to the basement, where John led Mary down another hall. They turned into a large room with many tables. They stopped at a table in the corner, where he pulled out a chair for her.

"Can I trust you to stay here while I go get us some coffee?" His deep brown eyes searched hers.

"I wouldn't know where to go," Mary said honestly.

"Okay." John smiled slightly. "Cream? Sugar?"

"Black."

"I'll be right back."

Mary watched as John walked to the coffeepot, filled a couple of cups with coffee, and paid the elderly lady behind the counter. She looked away as he turned toward her, not wanting him to catch her watching him.

John set one of the cups in front of Mary and sank into a chair across the table from her. He lifted his cup and took a drink. Mary tasted the dark liquid and shuddered slightly. It was strong.

"Do you want to tell me what happened back there?" John asked, searching her face over the rim of his cup.

Mary looked into her coffee. What could she tell him? Nothing would make sense to him unless she told him everything. She couldn't do that.

"Why did you bolt?"

Mary winced at the directness of his question. But that was John—direct and to the point. "I couldn't stay. I can't stand seeing Papa like that. And Mama—she looks so ..." Mary searched for the right word. "Old." She looked up at John pleadingly. "Don't you see? It's my fault. It's all my fault. I thought I was doing the right thing, and this is what happens. Papa looks so lifeless. Mama looks like she's carrying the world on her shoulders, and it's all my fault." She dropped her head into her hands, fighting the tears that were threatening to spill over. *Don't cry,* she told herself. She hated how weepy she had become. She took a deep breath and lifted her head, trying to discreetly dab her eyes with a corner of the napkin.

John reached across the table and gently took her hand. His gaze searched hers intently. "Stop running," he said earnestly. "Running doesn't resolve anything. You think what happened to your papa is your fault, so you want to run again? Don't you see that would just make it worse? You can't keep running away from your problems. It never works. Your mama needs you. Your papa needs you. Benny needs you."

"I don't know what to do," Mary said, her voice hinting at the anguish in her soul.

"Your mama's been here at the hospital constantly. She hasn't left his bedside. She needs a rest. I know a very nice Christian couple who would love to give her a room so she could have a good night's sleep." John's eyes never wavered from Mary's. "Here's what I think we should do. You and I should stay with your papa tonight so your mama can have a good night's sleep in a real bed. It's the right thing to do."

"I don't know anything about sick people." Mary faltered. "What would I do?"

"Just be there for him," John said. "Like your mama has been there for him. The nurses will take care of him. We just need to be there to comfort him. So he's not alone."

Mary looked into her coffee. *Can I do that? Can I try to make things right that way? Will Papa forgive me if I'm there for him now? Would he even want me there?*

"He would want you to be there for him."

Mary jerked her head up. Could John read her mind?

"Look, Mary," John said. "I don't know what made you run away from home. I don't know where you've been all this time or what you've been doing. But I do know that your mama and papa love you very much. They always have. They always will. It doesn't matter what has happened or what you've done. They are your parents. They gave birth to you. They love you unconditionally. Just like God loves us, his children," he added softly.

Mary searched John's eyes, desperately wanting to believe him, trying to grasp the concept of unconditional love. She thought of her baby. *I love her like that—unconditionally. I don't know where she is or what she is doing, and it's slowly killing me. Is Mama and Papa's love for me like that? Is God's love for me like that?*

John watched a host of emotions flicker in Mary's eyes—unbelief, desperation, anguish, hope. He silently prayed that the Lord would help her with whatever was bothering her and help her to make the right decision.

"Okay." She sighed. "You're right. Mama needs a break. I'll stay here with you."

Thank you, Jesus. John sighed. "You made the right choice, Mary."

Mary could see relief in the smile that curled his full lips. It made her heart lift just a little to see her decision meet with his approval.

"I'll get that coffee for your mama." He got up from his chair and turned to Mary. "Do you want another cup of coffee to take upstairs with you? Of course you do," he said, not waiting for her answer. "We'll each get another cup and then go tell your mama of our plan. You'll have to come help me carry the coffee." He took her hand and pulled her up out of the chair.

On the way back to Papa's room, John made a quick call from the pay phone in the lobby. Then, coffees in hand, they went back to Papa's room, where they found Mama standing at the window, gazing out over the sea of lights down below. She dabbed at her eyes and turned as they entered the room. A look of relief crossed her face.

"Here's your coffee." John sounded matter-of-fact, handing the coffee over.

"Thank you." Mama took the coffee and lifted it up to her lips, taking a sip.

"Mary and I decided that we want to stay here with your husband for the night," John told her. "You need to get some rest. Now that Mary's here, we want to give you a break."

"I don't have anywhere to go," Mama said, looking from John to Mary. "I don't know my way around the city. I wouldn't know where to go. I'll be fine staying here."

"I know a very nice Christian couple who would be happy to have you stay with them," John explained. "I took the privilege of calling them, and if you accept their hospitality, they'll come pick you up here and bring you back tomorrow morning. They don't live very far from here."

"I don't know." Mama had a worried look on her face. "I can't go to a stranger's home."

"You need to rest, Mama." Mary put an arm around Mama's shoulders. "If you don't rest, you're not going to be able to take proper care of Papa. If these people are friends of John's, then I don't think you have anything to worry about. You know John wouldn't put you in danger."

Mama searched Mary's face and then John's. She walked over to the bed and took Papa's limp hand in hers. She looked down on his face as he breathed in air through the oxygen mask. She looked at his still form lying beneath the sheet. She watched the gentle rise and fall of his chest.

Dear God, she prayed silently, *help me to know what to do. Help me to trust you.*

"I will never leave you nor forsake you." Peace filled her heart.

All right, Lord, I do want to trust you. Thank you for bringing Mary back to me. I know you have a purpose for everything. If it is your will that I go with these people, then give me the courage. She turned to look at Mary and John. Her eyes came to rest on Mary. "You will stay here with John?"

"Yes," Mary promised, "I'll stay here. You need some rest."

"All right," she said. "If you think that's what I should do, then I will do it."

"I promise you will like them, and they will treat you very well. I will call them right away." John downed the last of his coffee and threw the Styrofoam cup into the garbage on his way out of the room.

"Mama," Mary said in a soft voice as both women sat down in the chairs close to the bed, "I'm sorry for all I've put you through. I'm sorry I wasn't there when this happened to Papa. I'm sorry for so many things." The ever-present burden of guilt overwhelmed her.

"I'm just so glad to have you back." Mama reached over and hugged her daughter close. "God has brought you back to us, for which I am very thankful. We must trust that God will bring Papa back to us too."

Mary felt unworthy. Mama treated her as if she'd never been away. She didn't deserve that. She thought of what Mama had said—that God had brought her back. A few hours ago, she had been contemplating ending her life. She had no doubt she would have gone through with it if John hadn't found her. Feelings of hopelessness and despair had encompassed her.

Did God direct me to a place where John would find me? Was that God's doing? Does God really care for me after all I have done? Her head reeled with many unanswered questions.

John returned and told them his friends would be there shortly to pick Mama up. Mary helped Mama pack her bag.

A nurse came in to check on Papa. Mama told her that she would leave and that Mary and John would stay the night. "I'll be back in the morning," Mama told her.

"All right," the nurse said cheerfully. As she checked the intravenous and heart machine, she addressed Mary. "I'll be your father's nurse for the night, so if you notice anything out of the ordinary, just ring this buzzer." She pointed at the buzzer attached to the side rail of the bed. She turned to Mama. "You get a good rest. Don't worry about your husband; he is stable."

"Thank you," Mama responded, taking her place at Papa's bed again.

Mary followed the nurse into the hallway.

"What is my father's prognosis?" she asked quietly.

"You'll have to ask the doctor. I think he's still here. Come with me, and I can take you to him."

Mary followed her to the nursing station and waited while the nurse went to speak with a tall middle-aged man wearing a white lab coat. The man came over and stuck out his hand. "I'm Doctor Myers." He shook her hand. "I'm your father's doctor. The nurse said you had some questions about your father."

"Yes," Mary said. The doctor's friendly demeanor put her at ease. "What is his prognosis?"

"That's hard to say," the doctor told her. He glanced at the chart in his hands. "Right now, he is stable, so I believe he will survive if he doesn't have another stroke. To what extent he'll recover is hard to say. He could remain in a coma for the rest of his life; he could come out of the coma but be paralyzed, either partially or completely; or he could lead a relatively normal life. At this stage, we really don't know. We cannot determine the extent of damage to his brain."

Mary felt as if she'd been slapped across the face. Papa was in the hospital. Didn't people get well if they were in the hospital? How could the doctor not know?

"He'll come out of it," she said with conviction.

"It's good to stay positive." The doctor smiled. "We are doing everything we can, and the rest is out of our hands. If you're a praying person, then pray. I have seen miracles happen when patients have people praying for them."

He glanced down at his chart, bid Mary good night, and

walked down the hall. Slowly, Mary turned and started back to Papa's room. The weight of yet another burden weighed heavily on her. She pushed the door open to Papa's room and stopped dead in her tracks.

CHAPTER 24

"Mary?" Maggie Pitman exclaimed, taking a step toward her. "What are you doing here?"

Francis had called Maggie just a couple of hours ago and asked her to pray for Mary because she had left the apartment, and Francis was concerned. Maggie and Dale had spent some time supplicating the Lord on Mary's behalf.

"Do you know each other?" John looked from one to the other in surprise.

"Mary's been staying with my friend Francis for the past number of months," Maggie explained, but she stopped at the look of horror on Mary's face. "What are you doing here?" Maggie asked again more softly.

Mary looked skittish. Her eyes darted from Maggie to the lady beside the bed to Dale to John and back to Maggie. Maggie cautiously walked toward Mary, speaking softly. "Why are you here? Is something wrong?"

"You know John?" Mary's throat felt parched. *What are the Pitmans doing here? How do they know John? Why would they come see Papa?*

"Yes, we do." Maggie was surprised at the mention of John's name. "You know him too?" Slowly, realization dawned on Maggie's face. "Mary, are these your parents?"

Mary nodded, feeling faint. The impossible had happened. Her two worlds had collided.

"John asked if we would take your mother to our place for the night," Maggie said, standing in front of her at the doorway.

"He called you?" Mary croaked. Her heart pounded, choking off the words in her throat. "Can I talk to you?"

"Of course." Maggie turned to John. "We'll be back soon."

Maggie took Mary's arm, and together they left the room and walked down the hallway to a small waiting room. Soft yellow and orange chairs lined the walls, but otherwise, the room was empty. Maggie sat down and patted the chair next to her. Mary sat on the edge of the chair.

"You know John?" Maggie asked.

"He's from my hometown," Mary said, her mind racing. "He was my brother's best friend. I ran into him when I went for a walk today. He told me what happened to my father and brought me here."

"Thank you, Jesus," Maggie breathed softly.

"Pardon me?"

"Never mind. You wanted to talk to me?"

Mary swallowed hard. She didn't know how to say this. "My family—they don't know ..." Her voice trailed off. She fidgeted and wrung her hands.

Again, realization dawned in Maggie's mind. Mary was terrified her parents would find out about the baby. Being a close friend to Francis, Maggie was privy to details of Mary's situation. Mary herself had been to their house numerous times before the baby was born.

"My dear child." Maggie took Mary's hand. "Your secret is safe with us. Please believe me. Neither Dale nor I would discuss your situation with anyone. It is your story to tell or not to tell. Oh, my dear." Maggie put her arms around Mary, giving her a motherly hug. "You've been through so much."

Relief swept over Mary as she hugged Maggie back. Maggie promised to call Francis and explain the situation when she got home. She hugged Mary close again. *Thank you, Jesus, for keeping*

Mary safe. Maggie sent up a silent prayer. Francis had been beside herself with concern for the girl, and now Maggie had found her in a hospital room. *Lord, you do work in mysterious ways.*

"I don't want to rush you, dear," Maggie told Mama when they got back to Papa's room. "Dale and I can wait for you in the waiting room down the hall. Take your time. Come get us whenever you're ready."

"Oh no," Mama responded, "I'm ready." She leaned over, kissed Papa's cheek, and then softly stroked the hair back from his forehead. "*Gudnacht*, Jacob. I'll be back in the morning. Mary and John will take good care of you till then." She turned to Mary and John. "Thank you so much for staying with Papa." She hugged Mary. "I hope you have a peaceful night."

"*Shloop gesunt*, Mama." Mary hugged her back. "Sleep well, and don't worry. We'll take good care of Papa."

"I know you will," Mama responded. Holding Mary at arm's length, she smiled into her eyes. "I'm so glad John found you."

After they left, Mary bent over Papa as she adjusted his blankets and pillows, trying to make him as comfortable as possible. Then she sat on a chair next to the bed, the one Mama had been occupying.

The last time I saw you, Papa, you were headed to church, and I was all packed to leave as soon as you left. I never once thought anything would happen to you. You're the strong one in the family—always working, so full of wisdom. And now this—completely immobile, totally dependent on others. Oh, Papa, how you must hate it. What have I done? Can you ever forgive me?

She felt a touch on her shoulder as John handed her a tissue. Only then did Mary become aware of the tears trickling down her cheeks. She took the tissue and dabbed at her face. She could feel John's hand resting comfortingly on her shoulder. Fighting to regain control of her emotions, Mary stood up and walked over to the window. Darkness had fallen, and the lights of the city spread out below her for as far as she could see.

"See that long building over there?" John stood beside her, pointing off into the distance.

"The one that's set back from the street?" Mary asked, trying to locate the building John was pointing at.

"That's it," John said. "That's my school. See those buildings to the left of it?"

"Yes."

"That's the students' residence. It's where I live."

"Do you enjoy living here? In the city, I mean."

"Guess it's not too bad," John said. "I prefer the country, but for the time being, I guess it's all right."

"I don't like the city," Mary said firmly.

"Then why are you here?" John saw the pained look cross Mary's face. "I'm sorry, Mary. That's none of my business."

"I don't know what to do anymore," Mary said.

"Well, for now, I would say you'll have to see how things work out with your papa. You can decide after he gets better."

"How do you know the Pitmans?" Mary asked, deflecting the subject away from herself.

"Patrick started attending my college this fall." John smiled. "We met in the cafeteria and hit it off right away. I've been invited to their house for Sunday dinner a couple of times, and I started attending their church."

"Really? You go to church here?" Mary didn't know why she was surprised. "I went to their church when I first came here. It's not like our church back home."

John laughed softly. "No, it's not," he agreed, "but they have very good services, and the people are friendly. I like it. If I heard Maggie correctly, she said that you are staying with Francis. What's her last name?"

"Webber." Realization dawned in Mary's eyes. "You probably know her. She goes to the same church and is a good friend of the Pitmans."

"I have met her at church a couple of times." John laughed

softly again. "I'd say it's a small world. What do you know? You and I in this big city, and we've never run into each other until now, but we know the same people. Isn't God wonderful?"

Mary felt queasy. She had gone to church with Francis on occasion when she was still able to conceal her pregnancy. She hadn't gone back after the baby was born. What if she had run into John at the church? What if the Pitmans had invited them over for Sunday dinner at the same time John was there? Mary's knees felt weak as she turned from the window and sat down beside Papa again. *Best not to think about what ifs.*

The night went by surprisingly quickly. The nurse said there was a possibility that Papa could hear even though he was in a coma and couldn't respond physically. After the nurse left the room, John picked up Papa's Bible from his nightstand and read to Papa from the book of Psalms. He prayed out loud over Papa. Mary listened as John read and prayed. *He talks to God like he's talking to a friend.* She remembered when she used to pray like that, before David died. Everything had changed after the accident.

CHAPTER 25

Mama looked more rested when she entered Papa's room the next morning. Mary was glad about that, but she protested when John suggested he take her back to Francis's place so she could get some rest.

"I'll stay here with Mama."

"I think you should go get some sleep and then come back," Mama said. "We need to get rest, or we'll burn out. We have no idea how long it will be until Papa comes out of this coma, and even then, he'll still need us."

"That makes a lot of sense," John said.

"All right." Mary agreed reluctantly. "I suppose I should talk to Francis about my babysitting duties."

John and Mary left Mama at Papa's bedside and headed for Francis's apartment. When they got in the car, Mary gave John the address, and he reversed the car out of the parking stall.

"Can I ask how you met Francis?" John asked as he pulled out of the parking lot and into the flow of traffic.

"I happened to run into her first thing when I arrived in the city, and she needed a babysitter, so I took the job," Mary answered, gazing out the passenger window. "I've stayed with her ever since."

"What time do you want to go back to the hospital?" John changed the subject, although he was almost exploding from all the unanswered questions he had.

"It's still early enough that I can talk to Francis before she goes to school. I'm sure she will have arranged for Gladys to look after Chantel today. Brad is in first grade now, so Francis takes him to school with her. I could sleep till noon and then go back."

"I don't have a class this morning, but I have a class from noon to one thirty. What if I pick you up after my class and take you to the hospital?"

"Oh, you don't need to do that," Mary said. "I can get a cab." She didn't tell him that she'd never taken a cab before.

"You may have to do that some days," John said, "when I have class. But today I can take you. Tomorrow I have class in the morning, so I probably won't be able to stay all night. Are you going to be all right to stay there alone for the night?"

"Yes, I think so. You've already done so much. Thanks for staying last night." She thought about how he had matured since the day at the cabin when he'd announced he was going to Bible school.

"It was my pleasure." He smiled the crooked smile she remembered well as he parked the car on the street in front of Francis's apartment and turned to look into her soft brown eyes. "You're not going to run away again, are you?"

"No, I won't." Mary bit her lip. "I promise. Mama and Papa need me, and this time, I'll be there for them."

She saw relief spread over his face as he reached for her hand and squeezed it gently.

"I'm glad to hear it." He smiled. She noticed how his eyes changed when he smiled like that, as if he were smiling with his eyes.

Mary bade him good-bye as she opened the car door and climbed out.

Francis was making lunches in the kitchen when Mary let herself in the front door. She wiped her hands on a dishrag and gave Mary a hug.

"Oh, you poor dear!" she exclaimed, hugging Mary tightly.

"Maggie called me last night and explained about your father. How awful for you."

Mary was overwhelmed by the genuine feeling of compassion exuding from Francis, and before she could stop them, the tears that had been stinging the backs of her eyelids all night were released on Francis's shoulder. Francis let her weep, patting Mary's back as her own tears slid down her cheeks.

Francis's tears were tears of joy and thanksgiving to her heavenly Father. As she held Mary tight, she lifted her thoughts in prayer. *Your ways are truly unsearchable, Lord. I thank you again for intervening in Mary's life and bringing her family to her. Lord, help her to see her need of you. Lead her, guide her, and help her to deal with all the pain and heartache in her life. Lord, thank you for answering my prayers last night.*

When Mary's tears subsided, Francis grabbed a tissue and handed it to her, and Mary sat down at the table.

"You need to go to bed, and sleep as long as you want to," Francis told Mary. She went back to the cupboard and quickly put the lunches in their lunch boxes. "Gladys is happy to take care of Chantel, so you are free to take care of your father."

Francis set two cups of steaming hot tea on the table, one for herself and one for Mary.

Over tea and toast, without too much detail, Mary explained the events of last night and how she had ended up at the hospital. She omitted the part where she had come close to ending her life.

"I spoke with the doctor, but he doesn't know how long Papa will be in a coma or how far he will recover," Mary said, wrapping her fingers around the hot cup of tea. "I have to be there for them, but I don't want to leave you stranded without a babysitter."

"Don't worry about that," Francis said. "Family comes first. With Gladys offering to look after Chantel and with Brad coming to school with me, I am officially releasing you of your duties. You can still keep your room here as long as you need it."

Brad and Chantel came running into the kitchen, and Francis

got up to get their breakfast of cereal and toast. The children gave Mary a hug before sitting down to their breakfast, chattering as usual.

After the three of them left for the day, Mary went to her room and prepared for bed. She set her alarm for noon, which would give her time to shower and eat before John came to pick her up. Sitting on the edge of the bed, she picked up her Bible from the nightstand. It had been a long time since she had read in it.

"*They are your parents. They gave birth to you. They love you unconditionally. Just like God loves us, his children.*" John's words from last night flitted through her mind. She turned the Bible over in her hands. *Is that really true? Does God really love me unconditionally? Just like I love my little girl?* She opened the Bible randomly and started flipping through it. "Lo, I am with you always, even unto the end of the world." Mary reread that portion of Matthew 28:20 a couple of times. The words were in red, indicating they were spoken by Jesus himself.

But she had done so many bad things. She read a couple of verses before that and realized Jesus was speaking to his disciples as he sent them to evangelize the world. She laid the Bible back on the nightstand. She was pretty sure the disciples wouldn't have given their children away or considered killing them.

No, that verse is not meant for me. Guilt weighed heavily on her as she pulled back the blanket and got into bed. Exhaustion overtook her as she laid her head on the soft pillow and pulled the blanket up under her chin, and she was asleep in minutes.

Francis couldn't get Mary's family situation out of her mind as she went about her work that day. She knew God answered prayer, but the way he had answered last night was incredible. Her heart felt as if it would burst with joy at the thought. She had prayed "without ceasing," as the Bible said, for God to intervene in Mary's life, and he had. She felt overwhelmed and humbled.

Yes, God answers prayer. She believed that, but she realized now that she had believed it with her head but not with her heart. Last night, God had answered in a tangible way. The answer had unfolded right before her eyes.

What if... A clear vision of Mike's face came into focus, his blond curls forming a frame for his handsome face, his eyes as blue as a clear summer sky. Francis brushed the back of her hand over her eyes as she took the papers off the photocopier.

What is wrong with me? After all Mike did to me, why do I still miss him? She shook her head as she left the workroom and went back to the office.

Anna set her Bible back on Jacob's nightstand after reading at length in the book of Psalms to him. She took Jacob's right hand in her own. This man whom she had lived with and loved for so many years was still. Her mind wandered back over their life together. They'd had good times and hard times, but always they had been there for each other—until now.

"Jacob." Anna talked to him when they were alone together. "I don't know if you can understand, but our Mary is back. John found her and brought her here. Mary and John stayed with you all night. Wasn't that good of them? They are coming back this afternoon. Isn't that wonderful? God has answered our prayers, and we have been reunited. All those times we prayed for Mary's return, we never thought that you would have to get so sick to bring us back together. But God's ways are not our ways, and I know you would willingly go through all this just to have Mary back. So, Jacob, please get well. Maybe then we can be a family again." Anna paused. "I know what you would say. You would say, 'Let's pray about it.' And you're right. Let's pray."

Anna took both of Jacob's hands in her own and prayed out loud and at length to her heavenly Father. She thanked the Lord again for bringing Mary back to them. She prayed for Jacob's healing and asked the Lord to take care of Benny. She poured her heart out to the Lord, sometimes with tears rolling down her cheeks. She talked to her heavenly Father as if he were sitting across the bed from her, and she felt at peace in her heart. *"I will never leave thee, nor forsake thee."* The words from Hebrews 13:5 resonated in her mind. *Thank you for that promise, Lord. I know you are with me. Your plans are higher than my plans, and your ways are higher than my ways. Already good has come from this, and I am trusting that you will continue to uphold all of us.*

When Mary and John arrived at the hospital that afternoon, they found Mama asleep with her head resting on her arms on Papa's bed, holding Papa's hand. They paused at the door, not wanting to disturb her. John motioned to Mary that they would wait outside, but just then, Anna stirred and lifted her head.

"Sorry we woke you up." Mary was quick to apologize, giving Mama a quick sideways hug.

"Oh, don't be," Mama said. "I didn't realize I had fallen asleep. I had such a good night at the Pitmans'. I don't know why I'm sleepy now."

"That's probably why you are still sleepy," John said. "Your body has been sleep deprived for too long, not to mention the stress. Here—we brought you a coffee." He handed the paper cup to Mama.

"How's Papa doing?" Mary asked, bending over Papa and smoothing back his hair. She noticed he was graying at the temples. She had never seen that before.

"He seems the same to me," Mama responded, "but the doctor

said that he's not in as deep of a coma anymore, so maybe he'll come out of it soon."

"Papa, can you hear me?" Mary asked, watching him closely. There was no change. The IV needle was still stuck in his arm, dripping methodically. The oxygen tubes were still gently emitting oxygen into his airways. The heart monitor was still beeping as it magically drew its jagged line across the screen. Papa lay still, his eyes closed, the only movement being the gentle rise and fall of his chest.

Please, God, heal Papa. Mary choked back the lump that rose in her throat.

"Well, that's good news!" John exclaimed. "Maybe he will wake up soon."

"The doctor sounded more optimistic today," Mama said, her voice hopeful.

Mary touched Papa's arm. She couldn't see any improvement. Maybe the doctor just wanted to give Mama hope. All Mary saw was the nearly lifeless form of Papa, and her heart felt heavy in her chest. She sighed as she lifted her eyes to search Mama's face and noticed again the dark circles lingering around Mama's sunken eyes.

"John is right," she said. "You need more rest. Francis has arranged for her little girl to stay with a neighbor, so I'm free to spend all my time here with Papa. You should go back to the Pitmans' and rest."

"Oh no," Mama said, "I had a good night's sleep, and I very much appreciate you and John staying with Papa last night. But now I'll stay here with him again. You can come whenever you want to or even stay here with me when you have time, but it's not your responsibility. I don't want this to interfere with your job."

"I have an idea," John said as he pulled up a chair close to Mama's. "I know you both want to stay here with Mr. Hildebrandt, but we don't know how long this will take, and you need to be careful not to get burned out. When Mr. Hildebrandt comes out of this coma, he's going to need both of you. I suggest that you split the day into shifts and each take a shift. If we split it into three shifts a day, then we could each take an eight-hour shift and still get the rest we need."

"What do you mean 'we'?" Mama asked. "You have school and homework. I cannot ask you to sit with my husband as well. It's good of you to come see him when you can, but I will not impose on you this way."

"Mrs. Hildebrandt, believe me—this is not an imposition," John said, gently taking Anna's hand as he gazed deeply and seriously into her eyes. "Mr. Hildebrandt is my best friend's father. I have known him most of my life. I want to help for David's sake. I'll take his place in caring for his father."

Anna's eyes were misty as she raised her hand to touch John's cheek. "I am deeply touched, John. If that is how you feel, I will not take that from you. But how will you be able to do that and not fall behind in your studies?"

"My latest class goes to six, but most days, my classes end at three thirty," John responded. "If I come at four o'clock and stay till midnight, I could bring my homework with me and do it here and still keep an eye on Mr. Hildebrandt. If Mary is willing to take the midnight-till-eight shift, then you could be here all day and still get your rest at night. The only thing would be that on those days when my classes go to six, you would have to stay a couple of hours longer."

"Are you sure you want to do this?" Anna asked as she searched John's face.

"I have never been surer of anything in my life." John grinned his lopsided grin. "I want to help."

Mary was amazed at this interchange. She realized sheepishly that her mouth hung slightly open and quickly closed it before attention turned to her. She turned away as she swiped the back of her hand over her misty eyes. John's devotion to David and to her family took her breath away.

I have been so selfish, she realized. *I just thought about myself when David passed away. I didn't consider how Mama and Papa felt or how John felt. I rebelled and made it even worse for them.*

Mary mumbled something to the effect that she would be right back as she hurried from the room. She kept her head down as she almost ran down the corridor and sought privacy in a washroom stall, where she could contain her tears no longer. Her body shook with sobs at the mess she had made of her life.

So many people are suffering as a result of me, she thought, berating herself. *My darling little girl is growing up with strangers. Papa is hanging in the balance between life and death. Mama looks like she's been through the wringer and must be missing little Benny something awful, and Benny will be missing Mama and Papa. Even John is suffering, and why wouldn't he? He and David were always so close.*

Guilt and remorse weighed heavily on her heart as the pain seared through her chest like a sharp knife. *I can't bear it, God,* she told the God she had turned her back on. How foolish and selfish she had been for the last two and a half years; she had made many bad decisions.

"*Lo, I am with you always, even unto the end of the world.*" The verse she'd read last night flitted through her mind and gave her a semblance of peace.

She realized if she didn't go back soon, they would come looking for her, and she didn't want them to find her like this. Mary struggled hard to gain control of her emotions. After giving her eyes a final wipe, she blew her nose and washed her face with cold water at the white oval sink. She couldn't completely hide all traces of her tears, and she hoped Mama and John wouldn't comment.

"There you are," Mama said as Mary walked into the room. "John was just saying that he will take you back, so you can get some rest if you're going to spend the night here, and he wants to get his homework. Are you all right?" she added, looking up at Mary's face. "You look exhausted."

"I'm fine," Mary responded. "That's a good idea, John. It will give me a chance to tell Francis our plan."

Mary was quiet on their way back to Francis's apartment. John sneaked a few peeks at her while he was driving. He didn't know what had made her leave home and come to the city, but he was relieved he had found her yesterday. *Was it only yesterday?* Somehow, he thought Mary looked much older and more mature than her years, as if she were carrying the world on her shoulders. *But of course, first David and now her papa.* He could understand that was a lot to bear. When they pulled up to the apartment building, John reached over and covered Mary's hand with his.

"It will be all right," he assured her.

Mary looked up into those chocolate eyes filled with concern and nodded. Then she reached for the door handle and climbed out of the car. She didn't dare speak, for fear she would start crying again. She turned and waved to him as he pulled into the street.

Francis and the children were not at home, so Mary went straight to her bedroom and lay down. She was tired. Sleep overtook her as soon as her head hit the pillow, and when she woke up, the light was fading in her room. She couldn't believe she had slept that long. She lay there for a moment, trying to get her bearings. She knew Francis was trying to keep the children quiet, because all she heard was the sound of the TV coming from the other room. Francis didn't usually allow the children to watch TV after school. Everyone was thoughtful and good to her.

Slowly, she lifted herself up and swung her feet over the edge of the bed. She sat there for a minute, rubbing the sleep from her eyes, before she got up and went in search of the others.

CHAPTER 26

"Good morning." Francis smiled cheerfully as Mary entered the kitchen. "Glad you got some sleep. Maggie called and told me about your plans to stay with your dad. I think that's a wonderful way of splitting up the responsibilities so everyone can get their rest. Here's a cup of hot chocolate for you." Francis placed a steaming cup on the counter.

"Thank you." Mary took the cup and sat down at the table. "It was nice of John to offer to stay with Papa too. Everyone is so kind." She took a sip from the steaming cup and felt the hot liquid run down her throat.

"Hey, we want to do what we can to make it easier for you and your family." Francis joined her at the table with a cup of hot chocolate in her hand as well.

Mary bowed her head and watched the chocolate swirls go round and round in her cup as she stirred. "I am such an awful daughter." She lifted pain-filled eyes to meet Francis's sympathetic ones. "If I hadn't rebelled, gotten pregnant, and run away from home, this might not have happened. I feel like it's all my fault. Oh, not that David died. I didn't have anything to do with that, but I made life very hard for everyone after that. I was so selfish." She wiped at the tears that trickled down her cheeks. "I can't bear this. I have lost a brother, a daughter, and now maybe a father."

Francis came around the table and held Mary in a close embrace as Mary's emotions found release. After Mary's sobs subsided, Francis sat on the chair next to her, gently rubbing Mary's shoulder.

Mary wiped at her tears. "It seems that all I can do these days is cry."

"I want you to listen carefully to me." Francis looked earnestly into Mary's eyes. "When I was your age, I was very rebellious as well." Francis told Mary about how she had gone against her mother's wishes and married at a young age without her parents' blessing. She told of the months of abuse and the details of her husband leaving. She told of the times she was unable to feed her children and the trips to the food bank. Then she told about how Jesus had come into her life when she'd accepted him as her personal Savior and the peace he had given her.

"I had no idea!" Mary exclaimed, astonished.

"Everybody has their own story, Mary," Francis said. "We all make mistakes. We all have regrets. But through God's great love, he sent his only Son to die for us so we could be restored into a loving relationship with him. Listen to me, Mary. You don't have to bear all this alone. Jesus died for your sin. He wants to help you. He says, 'Come unto me, all ye that labor and are heavy laden, and I will give you rest.' Ask his forgiveness, and he will help you deal with all this."

"I don't know." Mary sighed heavily. "I have messed up so bad. How can Jesus forgive me? I know he died that we might live, but I gave up my daughter! I have lied to my parents and forsaken them in their greatest time of need. What kind of a daughter and mother am I?"

"Oh, Mary." Francis's heart broke for her young friend. "Jesus knows all that. He's waiting for you to come to him. He's waiting to take that burden from you. Satan has put you in bondage of guilt, but Jesus wants to release you from that."

Francis sighed as she watched Mary's face reveal the battles raging within. She stood up and hugged Mary again as the children came into the kitchen, asking for supper.

Mary hugged the children as they came to her, and she asked them how their day was. They chattered away while Mary helped Francis put supper on the table.

Francis insisted that she drop Mary off at the hospital later that evening. Gladys agreed to come watch the children for the fifteen minutes it would take to drive there and back. The Pitmans would take her home when they brought Mama to the hospital in the morning. Mary argued that she could take a cab but was inwardly relieved that she wouldn't have to do that. She didn't trust cabs.

Francis pulled up to the emergency entrance. Since it was after hours, that was the only entrance still open. Mary climbed out of the car, thanked Francis, and hurried toward the glass doors. The city still scared her, especially after dark. She pushed through the doors and was immediately stopped by a middle-aged man in a blue uniform who was wearing a name tag with a picture identifying him as hospital security.

"Where are you headed, miss?" The man smiled, the wrinkles at the corners of his eyes deepening. Mary told him she had come to spend the night with her father. After asking her name, her father's name, and his unit number, the man picked up the phone and spoke into it. When he put the phone down, he motioned to Mary that she was free to go.

"All the best to your father, and have a good night." He smiled again.

"Thanks and good night," Mary murmured, and she went in search of an elevator.

John looked up from his books as she entered Papa's room.

"Hi there," he said, looking at his watch. "You're early."

"I know." Mary set her bag on an empty chair. "Francis insisted on driving me, so I thought it would be better to come a bit early. Gladys stayed with the children. How's Papa?" Mary stepped over to the bed.

"The nurse says she thinks he's coming out of the coma, but I haven't seen any signs of him waking up." John closed his books.

"He doesn't look any different to me," Mary said, bending over Papa and taking his hand. "Papa, this is Mary. Can you hear me? How are you doing?" She watched closely but couldn't see any movement.

"The staff seem optimistic, so that's good." John gathered his books. "I guess I might as well go home then."

"Did you get your homework done?"

"Not done, but it's not due yet either. I did quite a bit, though." John grinned down at her. "Kept me from getting bored. Hope you have a good night."

"Thanks. You too," Mary said. John headed to the door, where he turned and gave her a quick wave before disappearing into the hall.

Mary pulled her chair close to Papa's bed and studied his face. He had lines around his mouth and across his forehead that she didn't remember. He lay still—too still.

"Papa, I'm so sorry," she murmured. "So sorry for all I put you and Mama through. I was selfish. I know that now. I didn't intend to stay away so long. But I couldn't bring myself to go back after what I'd done. I couldn't face you and Mama and my friends. What would I say? What would I tell you? Most of all, I couldn't bring myself to leave the place where I gave birth to my daughter. Oh, Papa, I need you. Please wake up so I can tell you how truly sorry I am."

The only responses were the gentle rise and fall of Papa's chest and the continuous beeping of the heart monitor.

A sound at the door made Mary look up.

"I figured it might be a long night and you'd need a snack." John grinned as he offered her a coffee and a muffin.

"Thanks," Mary said, quickly searching his face, especially his eyes. How long had he been standing there? What had he heard, if anything? "That's very kind of you." She tried desperately to make her voice sound normal as she accepted the items he was extending toward her.

"You're welcome." John grinned again. "Good night again," he said, turning back the way he had come.

"Good night," Mary said to his retreating back.

Her hands shook as she placed the coffee and muffin on the nightstand. Sinking back into her chair, she placed a hand on her chest. Her heart was pounding.

I have to be more careful, she thought. *What if John heard me?*

She took a deep breath and removed the lid from her cup of coffee. She could sure use some now.

After she drained the last of her coffee, Mary got out her books. If John could do his studies here, maybe she could as well. She hadn't been keeping on top of her studies lately, and she needed to get to it.

The nurses came in around midnight to tend to Papa and take his vitals. They needed to reposition him every couple of hours to keep him from getting bed sores, they told her. They were cheerful and talkative, and when Mary asked, they confirmed that they thought Papa was not in as deep a coma as he had been. There wasn't much they could do for him except keep him comfortable and make sure all the equipment was doing what it was intended to do. Mostly, they needed to wait for his body to heal itself.

"That is where the uncertainty is," one nurse told Mary. "Every case is unique, and it is impossible to tell how much he will recuperate. However, at this point, his life is not in danger anymore."

"Really?" Mary exclaimed. For the first time since John had broken the news to her, she felt a real surge of hope course through her body.

"Really." The nurse smiled at her. She spoke as she worked, checking the feeding tube and hanging up a new IV bag. "Just remember that we can't know what he'll be like when he does wake up. He might not be able to remember things, he may be paralyzed, or he may not be able to speak. There's a lot of things that can still go wrong. So keep praying. Besides being here for him, that's the only thing you can do for him at this point. There you go, Jacob." She patted Papa's hand. "You have a good rest now, and I will see you later."

Mary had a lot to mull over after the nurses left her alone with Papa and her thoughts. She was relieved that Papa would survive.

Forgetting her studies, she took Papa's motionless hand in hers and searched his face again. What would he be like? Would he remember her? Would he remember the pain she had caused him? She remembered how strong Papa had always been, physically as well as spiritually. Theirs had been a happy home. Mama had sung as she worked in the kitchen or in the garden. Mary had enjoyed working alongside Mama and talking with her as they worked. Papa and David had spent long hours tending to the various duties that came with running a farm. A smile curved Mary's lips as she remembered Benny running around with his arms stuck out beside him, pretending to be an airplane. In her mind, she could see David tackling him and wrestling him to the ground. Yes, those had been happy days. She remembered how excited and sincere David had been after the revival meetings he'd attended with John. She thought about their discussion at the cabin that fall. Then the accident had happened, and their lives had gotten all messed up.

Mary was lying in the hospital bed. She looked around the sterile white room as an eerie sense of foreboding enveloped her. From her bed, she watched as a nurse came through the door. Her heart swelled with love as the nurse placed a newborn baby in her arms. She pulled back the pink blanket, but before she was able to see its tiny face, the nurse snatched the baby from her and left the room.

She could hear the baby crying. She climbed out of the hospital bed. She had to find the baby before it was too late. She searched with an increasing sense of urgency. She ran down the hallway, flinging doors open. Finally, through the window of a door, she spotted the crying baby alone in a room. She tried to open the door. It wouldn't budge. She pounded on the glass. She screamed for someone to open the door.

A nurse in a white coat came into the room through a second door. The nurse calmly walked to the crib, picked up the baby, and handed it to a beautiful woman with long black curls.

"Here's your baby," the nurse told the woman.

"No, it's my baby! Bring my baby back!" Mary screamed, but they couldn't hear her.

The woman smiled as she held the baby close. "We have waited a long, long time for you, my dear little one."

"No. That's my baby!" Desperately, she pounded on the glass window, but no one heard. "Don't take my baby away! Please."

A tall, slim man put his arm around the woman as they slowly walked out of the room and down the corridor, taking the baby farther and farther away.

"Come back!" she screamed as the tears of a thousand rivers flowed down her face.

With a start, Mary woke up in a sweat. Tears were streaming down her face.

Weeping uncontrollably, Mary laid her head on Papa's bed, her shoulders shaking. The dream had seemed so real. It always did. It increased the empty void and incredible loneliness in her heart.

"Oh God!" she cried out in desperation. "I have sinned! I have tried to cover up my sin, and now I am paying the consequences. Dear God, how I want my little girl back. If only I could do it over again, Lord, I would do it differently. I was selfish and thoughtless and have hurt so many people. I've hurt you, Mama and Papa, and my beautiful baby girl. Oh Lord, please forgive me if you can. Help me to live my life. I cannot go on by myself anymore. God, I am so sorry for being angry with you for taking David. Please forgive me."

As Mary poured her heart out to God in desperation and submission, she felt a peace come over her that she'd never felt before. Her racing heart calmed, and sometime in the wee morning hours, she dozed off again.

Mary didn't know how long she had slept, when she awoke to a movement in her hand. Confused, she sat up. What had awakened her? Was it another dream? Then she realized she was still holding Papa's hand. Had he moved his fingers? She moved her hand gently over his and felt his fingers tighten around hers. She looked into his face and straight into his dark brown eyes.

"Papa!" she exclaimed. "You're awake!"

"Mmm," Papa mumbled, clearly trying to say something.

"Yes, Papa," Mary said. "I'm here, and I'm here to stay."

An incredible joy filled her heart. Papa had come out of his coma. Mary reached for the buzzer and summoned the nurse.

When the nurse came into the room, she immediately noticed Papa's conscious state. "Good morning, Jacob," she said to him cheerfully. "So you decided to wake up."

Papa looked confused and closed his eyes. The nurse checked his vitals and then turned to Mary and said, "I will call the doctor right away." With that, she turned and left the room.

Papa opened his eyes and looked into Mary's face.

"Papa!" Mary hugged him. "I'm so glad you woke up."

Papa looked confused. "Mmm." His mouth moved as if he were trying to say something.

"What is it, Papa?" Mary asked, brushing the hair back from his forehead with her hand. "Do you want me to call Mama? Are you asking for Mama? Mama went to a friend's place to rest. She will be here later."

Papa closed his eyes, as if whatever he was trying to communicate was making him tired.

Just then, a young intern entered the room with the nurse in tow.

"Good morning, Jacob," He bent over Papa's bed. "The nurse tells me you have decided to wake up. That is excellent." Papa opened his eyes and looked at the young doctor. "I know you're confused, Jacob. You had a stroke and are in the hospital. Your daughter is right here with you. You don't need to be afraid; we're taking good care of you. I just want to examine you briefly so we know what we're dealing with." He worked as he talked, and Mary slipped out to find a pay phone.

With shaking fingers, she dialed the Pitmans' number.

"Hello?" A sleepy voice greeted her.

Mary glanced at the clock on the wall. It was five o'clock in the morning. "Hello. This is Mary," she said. "I'm sorry to wake you. I didn't realize it was still so early. Papa woke up, and I wanted to tell Mama."

"That's great!" Dale Pitman was wide awake now. "I'll get Maggie to wake up your mama, and we'll take her to the hospital right away." Mary could hear the excitement in his voice.

"Thanks," Mary responded. "I thought she would want to know."

"Absolutely," Dale said. "We'll be there as soon as we can."

After she hung up, Mary realized that her knees felt weak, and her hands were shaking. She hurried back to Papa's room. She felt excited and anxious about this new turn of events. What would happen now? What would Papa be like?

The intern and nurse were just leaving as Mary entered the room.

"How is he?" Mary asked anxiously.

"It is too early to determine," the intern responded. "We will let him relax for now and maybe do some more tests later on today. Right now, I'm happy he's come out of the coma." He had a peculiar way of smiling with his eyes. "He's still confused and can't talk because of the feeding tube down his throat. I'll see about removing that later today. He seems to have feeling in his arms and legs, so that is good news. Mostly, we will have to wait and see how far he recovers."

Papa was sleeping, so Mary sat down in the chair by his bed and picked up the Bible lying on his nightstand. She opened it randomly, and her eyes were drawn to part of a verse that had been underlined: "I will never leave thee, nor forsake thee." Had God ever left her? Mary reread that portion of the verse: "I will never leave thee, nor forsake thee." Growing up, she had been taught about God. She had never doubted the reality of God. David had believed in God, and God had taken him home.

That's it! Mary's epiphany caused excitement to swell up in her heart. *God took David home. God didn't leave me. His purpose wasn't to take David away from us; it was to take him home. Oh, Lord.* Tears slid down Mary's face—tears of joy mixed with sorrow and excitement. *I'm so sorry. You took David to a better place, and all I thought of was my pain, not David's gain.*

It was hard to explain, this joy in her heart. It was as if a veil had been lifted, and she knew David was in heaven with Jesus. Then she thought of how badly she had messed up. It was all her fault. Jesus had never left her, but she had left him, making a bunch of stupid choices, and now she was left with the consequences. She had a daughter whom she would never see. Right there and then, Mary bowed her head and committed her daughter into God's care. She finally found peace, knowing that God would take care of her baby girl.

CHAPTER 27

Papa kept improving, and two weeks later, he was released from the hospital. He was unable to speak intelligibly, but he could usually convey what he needed. Papa's brother Henry came to Edmonton with his car to take them home. The Pitmans offered Uncle Henry a room to spend the night, and Mama went back there as well. Papa would spend this last night in the hospital, and they would pick him up in the morning.

John asked Mary to join him for supper. He picked her up from Francis's apartment, and they went to a cozy restaurant a few blocks from his college, where they were seated at a semiprivate table.

"Mary." John searched her face after they had ordered their food. "I have enjoyed spending time with you these last few weeks. I didn't realize how much I missed you. I wish I had known sooner that you were right here in my backyard."

Mary dropped her eyes and looked into her coffee. There had been a time when she would have given anything for John to come back into her life. But her life had changed. She shuddered involuntarily as she thought about how different this conversation would be if he knew the truth.

She looked up and met his chocolate-brown eyes head-on. "Thank you for all you have done for my family. You did more than you had to, and I appreciate that. I know that you did it for David's sake—"

"No," he interrupted, taking her hand across the table, "you don't understand."

"I understand." This time, it was Mary who interrupted. "I appreciate your friendship, and I'll always cherish the memories of our time together. But some things are not meant to be." She gently released his fingers from her hand. "Now, let's enjoy this meal," she said as the waiter put the plates of food in front of them.

John looked at her quizzically with a hurt expression in his eyes, but not one to push the agenda, he followed her lead, and they bowed their heads to say grace. Mary steered the conversation to lighter subjects and was glad when John responded. They had a good time, often referring back to the old days and the good memories they shared of David. Mary was glad she was finally able to remember David as he would have wanted her to remember him—as the fun-loving, humorous guy he was.

When John walked her to the door of her apartment, he wrapped his arms around her in a brief hug and planted a quick kiss on her forehead. Mary hugged him back and thanked him once again for being a friend. John opened the door, and Mary slipped into the apartment.

Later that evening, Francis's eyes were moist as she shared a cup of tea with Mary at her kitchen table. "I'm going to miss you so much, but I'm happy for you that you can go home. You have very good parents, Mary. I don't want to tell you what to do, but I think they might understand if you told them your story." A concerned look spread across her face. "You'll need their support."

Mary's grip tightened around her teacup as she swirled the brown liquid around and around. "I've been thinking about that," she said, "but I don't know. Maybe when the time is right. They've been hurt so badly already. I don't want to hurt them more. At this point, I don't know if Papa could comprehend it. It would devastate them to know they have a granddaughter they will never see." Mary choked on the words and fell silent for a while as she gathered her emotions. "I've given that all over to the Lord now, so I will trust him to show me if and when I should tell my parents."

Francis jumped off her chair and hugged Mary. "Oh, I'm so glad to hear that!" she exclaimed. "I knew there was something different about you lately. Did you commit your life to the Lord?"

Mary laughed as she hugged Francis back. "Yes, I did. The night Papa came out of his coma." She hadn't told anyone of her experience with the Lord that night.

"Tell me," Francis said excitedly, resuming her seat.

Bit by bit, Mary told Francis about her spiral down into the pit of despair. She told her that she had not been able to cope anymore and had determined to end her life, when John had appeared in the park at that crucial moment.

"I knew it!" Francis said excitedly. "I prayed for you and called Maggie and Dale to pray for you. I was so very concerned, but I couldn't leave the children to follow you."

"Really?" Mary raised her eyes in surprise to Francis's excited face. "Then God answered your prayers?"

"He sure did." Francis beamed. "Tell me the rest."

Mary continued her narrative, and by the end of the evening, the two women were sharing tears of joy mixed with sorrow, as they saw how the Lord had moved in their lives. It was past midnight before they bade each other good night and retreated to their separate bedrooms.

Mary sat down on the edge of her bed and lifted her Bible from the nightstand. Thoughtfully, she turned to Psalm 27:1: "The Lord is my light and my salvation; whom shall I fear? The Lord is the strength of my life; of whom shall I be afraid?"

It seemed to Mary that she was standing on the precipice of her changing life. Today one chapter was closing. Tomorrow another chapter would begin. Tomorrow she would leave the city and her baby daughter behind. Tomorrow she would face her friends and family back home. She reread the verse: "The Lord is my light and my salvation; whom shall I fear? The Lord is the strength of my life; of whom shall I be afraid?"

With this verse in her mind, she knelt beside her bed and once again put her future and her daughter's future in the Lord's hands. God would grant them grace for tomorrow.

ACKNOWLEDGEMENTS

First and foremost I want to thank the Lord Jesus Christ for his finished work on the cross, that "whosoever shall call upon the name of the Lord shall be saved" Romans 10:13. What a promise!

A big thank you to my husband, who loves me even when I mess up; to my children, who are my inspiration; and to my grandchildren, who make me feel young. I love you all. May the Lord bless you!

I thank my parents, who have both passed on to their heavenly home, for teaching me about Jesus, and for instilling in me a love for writing. I look forward to seeing you again.

Thank you to everyone who reads this book. Without you, there would be no point in writing. I pray that you are encouraged.

Lastly, a big thank you to each Westbow Press staff member, who diligently guided me through the publishing process. You helped me bring a life-long dream to fruition.

FROM THE AUTHOR

Grace for Tomorrow touches on a number of serious topics: depression, death, suicide, and abuse. I realize that some readers may be dealing with one or more of these issues. If you are in a situation that you feel you cannot cope with, I encourage you to get help. Talk to your doctor, counselor, police, pastor, or someone else you can trust. If you are in a crisis situation, find out if there is a crisis line in your area that you can call. Please get help. You are worth it! Jesus loves you!

"For I know the thoughts that I think toward
you, saith the Lord, thoughts of peace,
and not of evil, to give you an expected end." Jeremiah 29:11

CPSIA information can be obtained
at www.ICGtesting.com
Printed in the USA
LVOW12s1200260816
501719LV00001B/1/P